lingered

PUBLIC FACES
PRIVATE SECRETS . . .

Rae—Beautiful and dedicated, she is trapped emotionally and physically—until she decides to risk all that is safe and secure. . . .

Daniel—Gorgeous, giving, honorable, he is everything Rae admires, needs—and can't have. . . .

Carl—His money, Harvard MBA, and gallantry mask a ruthless quest for power. . . .

Wilbur Stanley—A shrewd businessman and community leader, his public persona hides deadly perversions. . . .

Lynn Stanley—She's an ambitious attorney, consummate snob, and daddy's little girl. . . .

Vincent Terrell—Investigator for the D.A., he's determined to get to the decadent truth behind a bizarre crime. . .

ARMS OF THE MAGNOLIA

Amanda Wheeler

FAWCETT GOLD MEDAL • NEW YORK

A Fawcett Gold Medal Book
Published by Ballantine Books
Copyright © 1994 by Amanda Wheeler

All rights reserved under International and Pan-American Copyright Conventions. Published in the United States of America by Ballantine Books, a division of Random House, Inc., New York, and simultaneously in Canada by Random House of Canada Limited, Toronto.

Library of Congress Catalog Card Number: 94-94199

ISBN 0-449-14889-0

Manufactured in the United States of America

First Edition: August 1994

10   9   8   7   6   5   4   3   2   1

To my mother, Velma,
whose strength is the source of my inspiration.

My sincere appreciation goes out to Barbara Dicks, my editor, and to Adele Leone, my agent, for their insight and assistance.

To my dear friends Regina Tholmer-Ford, Violet Rabaya, and Hilda Vest I extend deepest gratitude for your support and encouragement.

Marion and Nigel, thanks for hanging in there when I had nothing but a dream.

Chapter One

PRECIOUS MOMENTS HAD passed since the bartender signaled "last call" to the nearly empty room of dreamers. She lingered in the tavern long after hope had turned to gloom. The waitress glanced sympathetically at the proud, dispirited lady languishing in a shadowy corner. The door would soon close on her secret rendezvous.

They had not spoken of him specifically, but the waitress knew him well from the many hours the woman had waited for him to come and cool the fever that engulfed her. She longed for him in a way that left her open to abject emptiness. She could not recognize herself, sitting and waiting interminably for the man who had stirred the sleeping sensuality within her soul.

The million excuses imagined for his absence did not alleviate her misery. "You know there is less than ten feet of visibility in this heavy fog tonight," a compassionate patron reassured her. With drooping eyes she nodded "yes," but she did not speak. They sensed her sadness and quietly hoped for a happy ending to the long vigil. Their eyes followed with anticipation the headlights that occasionally appeared on the sleepy road beside the tavern.

The concierge at the inn had warned Rae that the fog rolling in was extremely hazardous, particularly on the narrow, winding road leading to the Tavern By The

Shore. The danger was inconsequential, as she had committed herself to a far more dangerous adventure when she agreed to meet Daniel.

Rae had known him for months, but kept him at a distance until their kiss, a friendly kiss, turned to passion. They had avoided each other's eyes, refusing to acknowledge their mutual attraction. To look would have caused them to commit an indiscretion in their hearts, if not in their lives.

Her plan was to depart swiftly, assuredly, to indulge no more in the sea of pity. Two captain's chairs in her path barred her exit, intensifying her sense of humiliation. The waitress asked if she needed a taxi, but they knew no taxi would come to claim her in the fog. Rae bid them farewell and stumbled to the gravel-covered parking lot, which was almost completely deserted. She wished that the fog would consume her and save her from the reality of having acted as a fool. But the fog was like angel hair on a Christmas tree, surrounding, adhering, then floating away.

The room at the inn was close and warm as Rae plummeted into an uneasy sleep. She spiraled into a world of paradoxical dreams. Running through thick fog, she tried to anticipate the invisible water's edge. An unevenly shaped boulder loomed out of the darkness. She opened her mouth to scream, but terror muffled the sound into a hollow echo. Rae struggled to awaken from the nightmare, but the fog compelled her, like ropes, to remain against her will. An undecided knock at the door released her.

His apologies for being late and his explanation of how the waitress told him where to find her were lost in the joy she felt now that Daniel had come to be with her.

Without asking, he slipped the velvet nightdress from

her shoulders and held her, very still, against his body. Tears filled her eyes as she rationalized that this was right. His kiss alone filled her up, shook her foundation, and caused her to shudder uncontrollably. Thinking that she was chilled by the air, he picked her up and carried her to bed.

Daniel undressed in silence, unbuttoning his shirt to reveal a well-toned chest speckled with soft, curly hair. The pants and underwear were removed at once, but his back was to her. She studied the definition of his smooth, tight behind before he turned to unveil the crescendo of his desire.

Wanting to feel the full length of his body, Rae slipped from beneath the covers and stood to embrace him. His tongue found her mouth, sensitive hands cupped her bottom. Daniel positioned her against the wall and secured her long legs around his waist as they unleashed months of repressed passion.

Sounds of ecstasy made them laugh between deep kisses. He came quickly, but she did not mind because he belonged to her completely, if only for the moment.

The wine and spirits consumed before their union betrayed love's unspent passion, and so they slept, coiled together, holding on to the intimacy that would be relinquished just after dawn.

As sunlight filtered through the fabric of the curtain, solitude enveloped Rae like a shroud. Perhaps the dread of this aloneness had caused her to sleep longer than was customary. Surely she felt him slip from her embrace, heard him shower before leaving. He had kissed her neck, her back, and gazed upon her delicately sculpted body. His kiss was not one of good-bye, but a reminder of moments to come. They knew it was not over.

Still feeling the imprint of his body, she lay there

smelling his scent, pulsating at the thought of Daniel, knowing she had surrendered far more than was prudent. He was betrothed and could not avoid his commitment without loss of honor. His sense of honor drew her to him.

Chapter Two

RAE REMEMBERED CLEARLY the first time she met Daniel. She had volunteered to do *pro bono* legal work through the African-American Bar Association, which assigned her to work with Daniel's job training program. Within minutes of their first meeting, Rae agreed to help Daniel fine-tune a proposal he had been working on for months. The vibes between them were instant and unsettling. Daniel's refreshing idealism melted her ingrained cynicism; Rae's attention to detail gave structure to his innovative but cluttered schemes.

During the weeks that followed, Daniel called Rae frequently to discuss minor details of the proposal. She suspected, and hoped, that his interest was not limited to business. Her cool, professional demeanor withered each time she politely pushed pages between them while discussing changes to the proposal. They moved gently in each other's presence, channeling the brewing sexual tension into their work. When their joint efforts culminated in a grant of city funds, they celebrated the victory with participants in the job training program. The celebration ended as soon as the cheap wine and beer ran out.

In his usual gentlemanly fashion, Daniel escorted her home to make sure she would be safe. "I want to thank you again, for all your help. We couldn't have done it

5

without you." Daniel reached for her hand and held on to it.

"Yes, you could have. I just fine-tuned an already excellent idea." He bent forward and kissed her on the cheek, then sensing no resistance, stepped closer and kissed her the way they both wanted. She leaned against the door and tasted his full, sweet lips. Reluctantly she pulled away. "I think we'd better call it a night. I'll talk to you tomorrow."

"Is that a promise?" he asked.

Rae winked and hurried inside while she still had the presence of mind to send him home. She was in a heavenly daze, already anticipating the next time she would see him. The following day they talked on the phone for an hour, dropping all pretense of pursuing business as usual. She promised to stop by the center later that evening, never suspecting that the euphoria was about to end.

Daniel was startled to see his fiancée, Latonya Johnson, enter his office just minutes before Rae was expected. "Hi, hon," Latonya greeted Daniel, who strained to look pleased with her unexpected visit. "I thought I'd stop by to see if you wanted to grab a bite to eat."

"That was thoughtful of you, but Gerald volunteered to help me finish some paperwork. We may be here for a few hours." Daniel avoided telling her that he was expecting a guest at any moment.

"Oh . . . hello, Gerald." Latonya turned to acknowledge Daniel's assistant, Gerald Austin, whom she usually ignored. "Why don't I run out for some goodies? Then I can help you with the typing."

"Latonya, you really don't have to do that. Why don't you go home and get some rest," said Daniel, intent on discouraging her from staying.

"But I'm not tired. You always complain that I never take an interest in your work. Now I'm taking an interest. It'll only take a second to pick up the food."

"I guess we should eat before it gets too late," he responded, eager to be gone. "I'll get the food. Is Chinese okay with everybody? Be back in a minute."

The silence after Daniel left was palpable. Gerald was ignoring Latonya, his head buried in a magazine to avoid dealing with her. After a long pause, Latonya launched into the subject uppermost on her mind.

"You don't like me very much, Gerald. Why is that?" Latonya asked point-blank.

"What I think of you doesn't matter. Just leave me out of your business."

"I wish it were that simple. I know Daniel confides in you. I regret whatever caused this rift between us, but we can't resolve it unless you talk to me. It would be nice to have you in my corner rather than sniping at my back. Think about that."

Gerald continued reading the magazine without responding. Frustrated in her efforts to win Gerald's support, Latonya concluded, "Think I'll visit the ladies' room before Daniel gets back with the food. Maybe we can continue this conversation later." Gerald was thankful for the five minute reprieve before Latonya reentered the office.

Rae stood motionless at the entrance to the center, her hand glued to the doorknob as she studied the silhouettes of a man and woman engaged in conversation. He sat with his back to the window. She stood over him. Her outline was distinctive—slender and erect to the point of stiffness. Rae's first impulse was to leave, but she decided to go inside and check it out. Her instincts warned, "Brace yourself." She walked into the office and faced the man she had assumed was Daniel.

-entering scene

The woman glanced at her, then quickly turned her attention elsewhere.

"Hi, Gerald. Is Daniel around? I have an appointment to deliver these documents to him." Rae clutched the papers to her chest, thankful she had not arrived empty-handed.

"Come on in. Have a seat. Daniel is expecting you. He should be back in a minute. He ran out to pick up food."

"Latonya, this is Rae Montgomery, the lawyer who is working with us."

"How sweet." Latonya forced a smile and shook Rae's hand firmly. "I'm Latonya Johnson, Daniel's fiancée." She emphasized the fiancée part.

"Glad to meet you. You must be very proud of Daniel's work." Rae managed to appear friendly while trying to avoid passing out. The glow was gone from her face.

Daniel walked in before Latonya could respond. "Hey, Rae. I hope you didn't have to wait too long."

"No. I just got here. Perfect timing."

"Do you have a minute to go over the documents?" Daniel asked nervously.

"Not really. I have another stop to make before I go home. Everything is pretty much self-explanatory. Give me a call at work if you have any questions. It was nice meeting you, Latonya." Rae rushed out before she could feel any dumber than she already did. She would have kicked herself while driving, had it been physically possible.

When Daniel called the next day, Rae made a point of being businesslike and brief. She was about to hang up when he said, "I owe you an apology."

"You certainly do. Why didn't you tell me you were engaged?"

"I was going to."

"When?"

"As soon as we had a chance to talk."

"Maybe you should find another lawyer."

"I don't want another lawyer. I want you." He could tell by her silence that she was annoyed by the double entendre. "Now I've really messed up. Listen, I wasn't trying to offend you. The center is the most important thing. Forget everything that's happened. Stay with the center, please. We really need you," Daniel begged.

"Well . . . let's see how it goes."

For the next few weeks they played hide-and-seek—seeking every opportunity to be with each other, then hiding from the attraction weighing heavily on their minds. She wanted to prove that she could control her feelings; he was compelled to respect her wishes. Afraid that she could no longer trust herself, Rae began skipping meetings and refused to take his phone calls at work. Each time he called her house, he was greeted by a machine. Rae managed to keep him out of sight, but her emotions were tuned to one channel and he was the feature film. She knew she was hooked when Daniel's gentle voice on the answering machine made her want to forget about principles. Principles made sense in the abstract, but left her edgy and alone.

While Rae was talking on the phone one evening, the operator interrupted with an emergency phone call from Daniel LeMond. Imagining some major problem with the center, she allowed the operator to put the call through.

"What's the emergency?" she asked without saying hello.

"I need to see you immediately."

"Is there a real emergency?" Rae asked.

"Yes. Can I come over?"

"No."

"Well, if I can't come to your house, I'll have to come to your office. . . . Rae, stop being cruel. I just want to talk to you and explain my situation. I'm not the horrible person you're making me out to be. Everything is depressing and dull without you."

"I can't see you because I'm on my way out of town."

"Where are you going?"

"To a conference."

"Where's the conference?"

"Don't even try it, mister."

"I won't interrupt the conference, but you must have some free time."

"We're working all weekend."

"Rae, please. Let me meet you someplace close to your conference. We can talk this out instead of pretending that nothing is happening between us."

"Is something happening between us?"

"Quit trying to be so tough. You know exactly what I'm talking about. I didn't say anything about the engagement because I knew you would react like this. I was having second thoughts about Latonya before I met you. I've been struggling to deal with the situation for some time. I admit that I'm still confused, but I can't stand not seeing you. Please, please tell me where to meet you." Daniel could hear her thinking on the other end of the phone.

"Meet me at nine at night on Saturday at the Tavern By The Shore." Rae held on to the receiver long after the conversation ended, trying to convince herself that she could handle seeing him.

Sitting through the conference had been like counting sand pebbles on a beach that stretched for miles. Rae thought of nothing except Daniel, until the long, torturous wait for him had ended. The speech she had rehearsed (doing the right thing, keeping their relationship in proper perspective) was promptly discarded as pride yielded to passion. When he entered her room at the inn, she had taken the first step down a path too compelling to turn away from. The road was littered with conflicting signs: savoring what she was doing, hating the deceptive way she was doing it, yet loving the man she was doing it with.

"How was the conference? Did you meet anyone interesting?" Sonya probed.

"The conference was fine," Rae responded, shifting the phone to a comfortable position, "but the only men there were misfits from the office who have no redeeming social qualities." Both women laughed heartily at the inside joke, which had become a standard refrain between them. Rae was itching to confide to her longtime friend that the real scoop was what had happened after the conference. Her thoughts drifted momentarily to Daniel. Before Daniel, Rae had experienced a prolonged drought in her social life. Saturday night entertainment had consisted primarily of watching videos with girlfriends and munching popcorn until the taste became obnoxious.

"What are you wearing to the party tonight?" Sonya asked for the second time. "Girl, are you with me, or is your mind someplace up on cloud nine?"

"Oh, I'm sorry, I was thinking about all the work I have to do. I may skip the party and try to get a jump on next week."

"Don't even try it! You were the one who convinced me to go to this soiree. You know I can't stand the hostess, Lynn Stanley. Lynn gets on my last nerve with all that hoity-toity shit. It'll probably be the same old crowd—Lynn's stiff law partners and all the wanna-be politicos preening for attention. And of course Lynn's shadow, Latonya Johnson, will be there pretending to be upper crust. Latonya is about as upper crust as I am. We both grew up in the Hightower projects, a fact Latonya has conveniently forgotten. The only reason they invite me to their parties is to have somebody to talk about. And I plan to give 'em something to talk about tonight. You should see the dress I'm wearing. It is too tough!"

"Tell me, Sonya, why did Lynn invite me?" Rae asked.

"Anybody with letters behind their name, be it M.D., J.D., Ph.D., or MC, as in MC Hammer, is acceptable."

Rae was laughing so hard that it took a minute to catch her breath. "Girl, you oughtta quit it."

"But seriously," Sonya continued, "the food should be good and you really need to get out more and meet new people. Get my drift? Besides, you told Carl you'd go with him. It will break that poor man's heart if you cancel on him again."

Rae wanted desperately to say that she had already met the man she wanted in her life, but she knew Sonya was the last person on earth to entrust with a secret. She would never understand why Rae had broken the vow they made to only date men who held promise of a serious relationship.

"Yeah, you're right. I can't do it to him again. I swear this is the last time that I'm going out with someone I really don't want to be with. I am too tired and too old for this."

As she ended the conversation with Sonya, Rae thought about the real reason she was reluctant to go to the party. "If Latonya is there, Daniel might be there, and more importantly, he might be there with Latonya.

But I can't start altering my life to avoid them. I have to meet this head-on," she reasoned out loud.

Carl and Rae arrived more than an hour late to the party. Sonya immediately descended on them in the vestibule of the magnificent mansion. The owner of the house, Lynn Stanley, was a partner in a prestigious downtown law firm and was financially secure for life, thanks to her father, Wilbur Stanley, who had amassed his fortune in real estate. Wilbur Stanley arranged an associate's position for Lynn with the firm after Lynn's law school graduation. Lynn's meteoric rise through the ranks of the firm was attributable as much to the substantial legal fees paid to the firm by Stanley Enterprises, Inc., as to Lynn's legal acumen and facility in attracting significant clients.

"Isn't this place something? And look at that spread!" Sonya gushed as they stepped out onto the opulent lawn. Rae gazed at the brightly striped canopies covering the bounty of food and drinks provided for the two hundred invited guests. There was enough food to feed the city's homeless for a year. The ravenous crowd devoured giant prawns, brimming over the edge of crystal serving platters, as quickly as servants could place them on the tables. Ice statues in the shape of gargoyles emitted a billowing mist that floated upward toward the enormous yellow moon hovering over the river. The jazz trio playing in the gazebo drew her into their mellow groove. Rae's determination to hate the party melted as she surrendered to the lush surroundings.

"You look spectacular, baby." Rae trembled at the sound of Daniel's voice.

"You scared me." Catching her breath, Rae glanced around furtively to see if they were being watched. "Where's the warden?" Rae asked sarcastically before spotting Latonya engaged in conversation at the far end of the lawn.

"We need to talk." He led Rae by the arm to the only quiet area on the grounds. "This isn't easy for me. You know how I feel about you, but Latonya and I have been engaged for a long time. She trusts me."

"I know it's not easy, but it's killing me to see you with her," Rae answered. "You know me as the cool, aloof lady tied to her work and needing no one to get by. All of that changed for me when I met you. It's better to be up-front with Latonya than sneak around behind her back. She wouldn't want a man who's involved with someone else and neither do I."

They were so wrapped up in pouring out their souls that they never heard Lynn Stanley approach.

"Rae, I'm so glad you could make it. I see that Daniel is keeping you entertained. How's things at your office? Did you get promoted to senior counsel? It's too bad those idiots haven't come to their senses and given you the job. You're clearly the most qualified lawyer they have."

"Well, Lynn, you know that it's not always a matter of qualifications. There are a lot of political considerations that don't speak in my favor. Besides, I'm not sure that I want the responsibility. My freedom is fairly important to me now and I get a good deal of satisfaction from my work outside the office. This is a great party, by the way."

"I'm glad you're enjoying it. Excuse me for a second while I have a chat with the caterer. Daniel, get Rae another drink."

Lynn's intrusion into their intimate conversation was a stark reminder of the impossibility of the situation. Rae's pained expression conveyed to Daniel her feelings of frustration. His soulful brown eyes sought understanding and forgiveness, but Rae felt she was the transgressor, the one who should turn away.

"Let's take a walk down by the river and finish our conversation," he said.

Conversation was not what he wanted. As soon as they escaped from the view of the party-goers, he pulled her to him, holding her so close that she could hardly breathe. Daniel's insistent fingers slipped the black beaded dress from her shoulders, exposing her French lace bra. She began to protest when he bunched the dress around her waist; he smothered her words with kisses. Rae wanted him badly, but common sense ultimately prevailed. She squirmed away to find breathing space.

"I can't do this," she insisted, rearranging her clothing. Rae dug into her purse for tissues and wiped beads of perspiration from her face. "Look, this isn't the time or place for lovemaking. I thought you wanted to talk."

"I do want to talk. I just got carried away. I'm sorry."

"I think we should get back to the party before they miss us. Let me head back first. I'm sure my date is searching frantically for me by now."

"Don't let that turkey touch you. I'll break his neck."

"I won't, if you promise not to touch Latonya."

Her comment shamed him into silence.

Returning sheepishly to the party, she spotted Carl leaning against the gazebo, looking like a lost puppy. "Where were you? You missed Kim Barnes, the jazz singer. She was fantastic. Are you okay? You look a little out of it."

"Oh, I'm fine. I took a walk to neutralize the effects of the champagne. If you don't mind, I'd like to cut out early. I'm working on a very complex transaction at work and need to put in a few hours in the morning to make Monday manageable."

"Sure, babe, I'll get your wrap."

Rae was silent during the drive home. Carl did his best to draw her into conversation, but her mind was back at the river. Was this just lust she was experiencing, she thought, or had this man become a major part of her life? She had had plenty of good sex before, but it had never thrown her into a complete tailspin.

Carl rambled on about his recent promotion and how his increased responsibility and higher pay had made him more serious about life. Rae hoped he wasn't trying to get serious about her. He was really a sweetheart, but talk about lack of chemistry. On an objective level he was a great catch. There were a million women who would die to get next to this intelligent, Harvard-educated brother. And he looked quite good, well-built and fairly well-dressed. He could give up those loafers, she thought wryly, but nobody is perfect. Carl certainly fits the bill of the available, success-oriented fellow that Rae claimed to be waiting for. Under different circumstances she would have jumped all over him.

She watched his lips form words that she failed to focus on. Carl had cute, proper lips that begged to be kissed by the right woman. I must be nuts not to capitalize on what could be the best thing that has happened to me in ages, Rae thought. As he pulled up to the curb in front of her town house, she placed her hand on his to keep him from removing the keys from the ignition. "I'd love to invite you up, but I need to turn in early."

"I understand." He leaned forward to kiss her and she instinctively offered her cheek. "Uh-uh," he moaned as he took her chin in hand and kissed her full mouth. He didn't try the old tongue-in-mouth trick, but he did allow his lips to travel to her neck for a quick nibble. Hmm, she thought. Carl has a little more pizzazz than I expected. She gracefully managed to free her body from his embrace, which was becoming more intimate by the second. "Can I call you?" he asked as she pushed open the car door.

"Of course you can. I had a great time. Let's do it again." His eyes penetrated her back as she walked self-consciously up the steps, throwing him a Miss America wave before closing the door. Inside, she dropped her purse and shawl in the hallway, which was totally uncharacteristic, considering her penchant for neatness, but a lot had happened in the last forty-eight hours and a little messiness was the least of her transgressions. She went straight to the refrigerator for the wine that she desperately craved despite the fact that she had felt high an hour earlier. Her mind raced and her body begged to be brought down to a level of calmness. As she raised the slender glass shakily to her mouth, the shrill ringing of the phone startled her, and the drink crashed against the ceramic tile floor. She rushed to the phone, oblivious of the shards of glass scattered on the floor.

"Hello."

"Rae, you said that I could call you."

"Carl, you just left. Where are you calling from?"

"The car phone. You, you in that dress, the sweetness of your perfume, were so heavy on my mind that I had to call you. You sure you don't want company? I promise to be good."

"Yeah, I bet. Don't try to keep me from getting my work done, you rascal. Listen, I'm a little beat tonight, but call me tomorrow afternoon. Maybe we can get together for a late afternoon snack. How does that sound?"

"I'll take whatever I can get. I can't wait until tomorrow. Think about me. Good night."

She decided to forgo the drink and go straight to bed.

The mess in the kitchen could wait until morning. This love thing was turning her into a slob. In the comfort of her cotton nightshirt, she curled into her usual position in the left corner of the bed near a slightly opened window. The freshness of the air created the perfect mood for rambling thoughts. Carl seemed to be making his move rather quickly, maybe too quickly. It was probably good to balance out her fixation on the unavailable Daniel LeMond. She should have showered, but was too beat. Her dreams were vivid and not altogether pleasant.

She was awakened, sweaty and confused, by the sound of the answering machine. She hadn't heard the phone ring and it took a moment for her to gather her senses before the machine clicked on. "Hi, Rae. It's Sonya. Wasn't that a marvelous party last night? Call me. I have to tell you about this fabulous man I met. Girl, this is the one. . . ." While half listening to Sonya's monologue, she glanced at the clock that registered eleven forty-five A.M. How could she sleep this late, especially feeling this grungy? She moved to get out of bed, but an imaginary rubber band pulled her back to the soft pillow. Sonya's voice continued to whine on the answering machine. Sonya was the only person Rae knew who was not the least bit intimidated by an answering machine. She would continue her conversation whether or not a real person answered. Poor thing, Rae thought, she's desperate to tell me this long, drawn-out story about her latest catch and I'm too hung over and too tired to listen. The tape must have run out, because she finally shut up. Rae tried getting up again, this time a little more slowly. That's it, Rae, stay low to the ground and pretend that your head is not attached to your shoulders. Easy, easy now. Don't look too quickly in the mirror, because you might not like what you see.

Now, crawl into the bathroom and fill up the tub. A shower will not suffice this morning. She propped her head against the door and brushed her teeth while running the bathwater. *I have to get a grip on myself*, she thought. *This self-abuse must end.*

She eased into a hot, hot tub of water that threatened to take her skin off. One thing she learned was that the second you add too much cold water, you can never get the bath hot enough again. She opened her knees real wide to allow water to flow into the inner crevices. Oh, yes, this was what she needed to feel refreshed. Shoulders submerged under steaming suds, relaxing the tension and allowing the funk to roll away.

Was that the phone again? *Sonya never gives up.*

"Rae, we need to talk. Call me as soon as you get in," she heard Daniel's voice chime in before she could drag her dripping, waterlogged body to the phone. She turned to get a towel when the phone rang again. The ring had not ended before she grabbed the receiver.

"Hello . . . oh, hi, Carl. I was just about to call you. I finished up a little earlier than expected. . . . Sure, one o'clock would be fine. I'll meet you outside."

For someone who has spent an eternity with no love life, things are sure popping around here, she thought to herself. *I'd better get a cup of coffee before returning Daniel's call, which is destined to be a heavy-duty conversation. Where in the heck is the measuring spoon? "Ouch! Oh, shit, I cut myself." That's what I get for leaving broken glass everywhere.*

Coffee in hand, she moved toward the couch to settle in. Rae was determined to glance at the Sunday headlines and sip her coffee like a civilized person. The thought crossed her mind that she should put on a decent robe to retrieve the paper, but she decided that the frayed, faded chenille was all that could be managed this morning. Besides, if the newspaper was placed as she had meticulously instructed the paperboy, only the tiniest portion of her arm would be subjected to public view. Much to her dismay, the newspaper wasn't visible as she cracked the door, requiring her to take a full step outside to determine its location. Straightening from an inelegantly bent position, her eyes focused on a man's shoe attached to a trousered leg ascending her steps. With great trepidation, she gazed up at Daniel.

"What are you doing here?" she asked, closing the door behind them.

"I called earlier, but got no answer."

"I was in the tub and was planning to call you back as soon as I had a cup of coffee and read the paper. Would you like some? Pardon my outfit, but I wasn't expecting company this morning."

"I was afraid you might still have company from last night."

"That isn't fair. You have no right to comment on my private life in view of your situation."

"That may be true, but it doesn't keep me from feeling the way that I feel and being afraid that you might let another man into your bed. I don't know what's right anymore."

"Neither do I, but I know that I can't stop living while you resolve your situation with Latonya. Don't worry, I'm not sleeping with anyone else. I couldn't if I wanted to. I don't know how long I can keep up this charade."

They held on to each other for a long time without saying anything. No words could change the situation. He untied the belt of her tattered robe, pushing it away from her shoulders, caressing her back. His head dropped to take her nipple into his mouth, knowing her weakness.

"Danny, no. I want to take some time to think and not just respond to you physically. Anyway, I have an appointment this afternoon, which I will never make if I keep fooling around with you."

She grabbed her robe, dashed into the bedroom, and then yelled through the door, "Finish your coffee and I'll be out in a second."

When she finally emerged, fully dressed, he was gone. A note left on the table read:

Rae,

You unleashed feelings in me that I didn't know existed. I hate myself for being selfish, but I don't want to share you with anyone. Please give me some time to work things out. I can't stand the thought of being without you. I will try my best to respect your privacy, but I can't promise anything.

Daniel

Fortunately, she had a few minutes to gather her senses before Carl arrived. Rae ran out to meet him to avoid an amorous confrontation. At her suggestion they ate at a nice, crowded restaurant. Her intent was to eliminate the risk of intimate conversation. Why she continued to see Carl was a mystery, except for her need to have that safe harbor to run to. Up to this point in her life, she had been in control. Her job was safe, although not challenging. She ate right, exercised, and did everything necessary to be a sane, healthy person.

"You seem a little distant, Rae, do you feel okay?"

"Oh, sure, I think I'm a little hung over from last night."

"I don't mean to bore you, but I thought you would be interested in hearing about the deal I'm working on with Wilbur Stanley, Lynn's father. He's quite an interesting fellow, really shrewd and still quite a ladies' man. He's a little worried about Lynn, you know, being so dedicated to her work and still unmarried. He tried to set me up with Lynn, but she wouldn't hear of it."

"You were interested in going out with Lynn?"

"Well, I was new in town and hadn't met any women. She's not bad looking, but we didn't click. Not feminine enough for me, nothing like you. Do I detect a little jealousy?"

"Don't flatter yourself, buddy, and pass the French fries."

They decided to take a walk down by the river to work off the humongous meal they devoured. The river was entrancing, choppy from the storm hovering on the horizon. Wind ruffled the waves and made sounds like muted horns in the distance. They walked close to the edge and toyed with the ebbing tide as the sun stretched out to say its final good-bye. The weather was threatening, but inviting, lightly warm, yet cool on the face. Rae held the hand of a stranger who wanted to enter her world, a world confused and uncertain. Was it the wind that made her shiver or the fear within her heart? She felt unworthy to be with a wonderful man who was making a gallant effort to woo her. Carl epitomized everything she had wished for during years of aimless dating. Rae wondered why God would let someone so nice want her at a time when she was unable to desire him in the same way.

"Getting chilly, sweetheart? Ready to go back?"

"I probably should. I've got a big day at work tomorrow."

When they arrived at Rae's place, she felt she had to invite him inside. She made tea and they talked about their families, their work, and a little bit about themselves. Rae was touched; she rarely shared private thoughts with anyone. The conversation was interrupted by a call from Sonya, chomping at the bit to continue the conversation she had started on the answering machine.

"Sonya, I can't talk right now. I've got company."

"Oh, my god," she chirped in a black valley-girl accent. "Call me the second he leaves. Carl must have more going for him than you let on."

Rae hung up quickly without risking a reply that could lead to a twenty-minute conversation. Walking back to the living room, Rae noticed that Carl had left his place in front of the fireplace and was standing near the table. The thought raced through her head that she had left the note from Daniel on the table in plain view. She tried to sound calm.

"That was Sonya with another of her elaborate tales."

Carl stared at Rae with vacant eyes. She suspected that he had uncovered her secret. He leaned toward her, kissed her on the cheek, and said that he should be going. She had no reason to feel guilty or ashamed, but could not drive out these emotions. Rae walked him to the door and felt compelled to say something, but the proper words escaped her. She reached up and kissed him good-bye, which he responded to by drawing her closer in a lingering embrace. As he turned and walked away, she studied him in earnest for the first time since they met. His shoulders were squared and he moved with dignity toward the car. Closing the door, she wondered if she should see him again, unsure that she deserved to.

Chapter Three

TO WARD OFF the Monday morning blues, Rae rolled out of bed at five A.M. for a slow run in the park, slow being the only speed she could tolerate. Her eyes refused to cooperate with this early-to-rise plan, and so she blundered outside, half-blinded with sleep, despite the ten minute stretch in which she dutifully engaged.

The first breath of fresh air was invigorating. Her skin tingled and she was pleased at having gone forward with her plan for an early beginning. She ran with her arms down, shaking them gently to ease the shoulder tenseness that frequently ruined a run. Her headset was not tuned to the right station; she needed something stimulating, but easy on the nerves for this presunrise cruise through the park. She fell in step with the soothing voice of Luther Vandross. Her heart rate slowed, no longer pounding erratically.

She relaxed her stiff knees and her feet touched down easily. When her arms swung effortlessly to Prince wailing "When Doves Cry," she knew she had it goin' on. Rae's unabashed passion for Prince amused her friends who could not understand why a woman who hated large concerts would brave gigantic arenas packed with screaming teens to see a short, skinny man gyrate his hips. Rae could not explain it, but she was fascinated with Prince, even as a "nasty boy," wearing garter

24

belts and too much makeup. Something about his music rang her bell.

Her corporate office had become a prison to which she was confined for many hours of the day. Rae found little comfort among co-workers who she had known and endured for five years since law school graduation. She worked in their midst, but was apart from them—a foreigner in their world, speaking the same, but a different language. They experienced life from similar economic perspectives, but from radically divergent social viewpoints. Each night they headed home to the suburbs, while she returned to the familiarity of the city.

Rae's search for role models within the company was disheartening. The one or two African-Americans who had reached the upper rungs of the corporate ladder were anxious to distance themselves from nonwhites, as if they feared contamination. They struggled unsuccessfully to blend into the corporate walls, but their blackness would not mix smoothly with the stark white environment.

Ever mindful of eyes watching as they passed her open door, she tried to appear busy to avoid the intrusion of bored associates ritualistically visiting the coffee station. Rae worked at exchanging pleasantries, but inevitably landed in uncomfortable territory when the conversation ventured from the inane. To express an honest opinion among company robots was a sure form of political suicide, which she committed on many occasions. She could not remain silent while misinformed co-workers made racist or sexist remarks, and so she become a pariah among her peers.

She would sit alone in the lounge and read during lunch hour to avoid the inevitable indigestion she'd experience following lunch with co-workers. She could not stomach another conversation about football, basketball, or golf. Unable to monitor what she was thinking, her boss falsely accused her of being antisocial. He warned that fraternizing with the clerical help would not improve her standing within the corporation. Rae naively reserved the option of socializing with whomever she chose.

Each time she became disgusted with her job situation, she remembered being hired as a double token—the only African-American and the only woman on the legal staff of Landis Motor Company. Rae had thought she could change things, but the only thing changing was her. Her cynicism grew each day and began spilling over into other areas of her life. Within two years three other women joined the legal staff, but they tried to look and act as much like the boys as possible, perfect corporate clones. They wore boxy, conservative suits with ribbons tied under their collars to simulate the male bow tie. Their presence was a minor relief, but no solution to Rae's problem of being the odd woman out. Privately they shared their own frustrations, but were too intimidated to rock the boat.

Determined not to ruin her day by dwelling on the negative, she attacked her work and summoned false enthusiasm to make the minutes pass. Focusing on the clock would only make matters worse, she figured. It had taken five years to accept reality; she was not the "chosen one" destined to break through the glass ceiling inhibiting ambition and destroying dreams. She knew that she would never receive accolades, never obtain the rewards that would easily flow to one of the "team players." Her politics were too "liberal" and she refused to become an opinionless, soulless being just to gain conditional acceptance. Rae had to escape the dullness before it infected her, invaded her spirit and caused her to join the ranks of the walking dead. The solution lay beyond the walls of Landis Motor Company.

When five o'clock came Rae was released from her chamber of horrors. A fresh blanket of snow had fallen, requiring homebound employees to remove fluffy white powder from their windshields while warming up their cars. Unlike most days, Rae was not annoyed by this task since it gave her the chance to unwind and breathe fresh air into her lungs. She needed to discard the staleness of the office and to stretch her muscles that were tense, not from exertion, but from introspection.

Rae applied makeup in the car before going to meet Carl for happy hour at Ruby's, a slick new soul food restaurant. Upon entering Ruby's, Rae collided with Lynn Stanley, standing near the door, arguing with a flustered coat-check girl who was feebly defending the restaurant's policy of nonliability for fur coats.

"What kind of place is this? If you can't handle patrons of my caliber, you won't be in business very long," Lynn threatened.

Fortunately the owner, a pleasant-looking woman, arrived in time to rescue the coat-check girl from Lynn's fury. She placed her arm very gently on Lynn's shoulder and whispered words of apology, assuring her that the coat would be secure. Placated, Lynn sashayed into the main dining room without noticing Rae. Lynn had a way of excluding from view everyone and everything that was nonessential to her.

Rae watched as Lynn joined a group that included Latonya Johnson, Daniel's fiancée. Oh, hell, here we go again, she thought. Surveying the room, Rae focused her attention on a man's familiar posterior. It was Daniel talking to an older, distinguished-looking gentleman. She was amazed at how the sight of Daniel caused her to forget everything else around her. She locked onto him, as if her mind were a homing device implanted with his signal. His body mesmerized her. Well-defined, long muscles gave him an appearance of thinness, but underneath the clothing he was solid and powerful. Her fingers loved the nappy texture of his hair. She envied the baby-soft smoothness of his toffee-colored skin. No man should have eyelashes so thick and naturally curly, no man should have a smile so bright, she thought. He was model-perfect, but unlike many handsome men, not the least bit aware of it. She had generally shied away from his type, preferring a man more rugged in appearance, less beautiful.

The spell was broken when Rae noticed Carl approaching the two men. She was tempted to run out the door, but her feet were planted on the carpet. Had Carl made the connection between the note in her apartment and Daniel? No, she thought, there must be a thousand men named Daniel in this city and Carl has no way of knowing the truth. Rae gathered her courage as the men shook hands. She decided to join them rather than stand by idly and assume the worst.

"Rae, sweetheart, have you met Daniel?" Carl asked.

"Yes, I've met Daniel," Rae answered while looking around. "I thought I saw your fiancée with Lynn Stanley when I came in."

"Yes, you did. They're at a table over there," Daniel said, pointing in their direction. "Lynn invited us out for happy hour to celebrate a deal she just closed. Ruby's must be the hottest spot in town."

"It's pretty hot tonight. Looks like the gang's all here." Rae glared at Daniel to make sure he understood her meaning, then thought to herself, Obviously he hasn't spoken to Latonya. This scene is getting old real fast.

Carl filled the lull in the conversation. "Rae, I want

you to meet Wilbur Stanley. Mr. Stanley and I have been doing business together for some time now."

Rae realized she hadn't met Stanley at Lynn's party. She certainly would have remembered him if she had. "Meeting you, my dear lady, has been the highlight of my day," he said smoothly. "I don't know how they managed to keep someone as lovely as you out of my sight. I understand that you're also an attorney. Beauty and brains in one fantastic package." Wilbur Stanley took Rae's hand and held it a few seconds too long.

"You are really too kind, Mr. Stanley." This old buzzard certainly deserves his reputation as a womanizer, Rae thought. His penetrating eyes burned holes through her fuzzy sweater dress. She felt like a slave standing nude on the auction block, undergoing inspection.

"If you'll excuse us for a moment, Daniel, I have something I need to discuss with Wilbur and Rae," Carl interjected.

"No problem. Check you folks out later."

The trio moved to a booth reserved for their meeting and Carl ordered champagne.

"As you both know, I have been working with the same company for several years in anticipation of eventually starting my own firm. The timing now appears to be right for me to make that move. Wilbur, I hope that you will see fit to move your accounts to my consulting firm, New Hope. But I will understand if you decide not to make the move. My firm is, after all, the new kid on the block."

"Nonsense, Carl. You are the best and the brightest young businessman I have encountered in many years. You're the only one I would trust to handle my accounts. You remind me a lot of myself when I was a young man. I would be honored to continue to do business with you. I need not remind you to handle the transition smoothly. Avoid any legal entanglements with your current employer," Wilbur Stanley cautioned.

"That brings me to your role in this new venture, Rae. I want you to be my general counsel."

She was speechless. Rae heard the words, but could not imagine that he was directing them at her.

"We can discuss the specifics later, but I have to warn you that I intend to make you an offer you can't refuse."

The champagne arrived just in time to save her from having to respond to the overwhelming news.

"Carl, I'm so happy for you. You have certainly worked hard for this."

"Be happy for us. I want you to share in my excitement. I know you're one of the most competent lawyers in the city. I checked you out professionally before I decided to make the offer. I didn't want my personal feelings to lead me to a bad decision. I need you by my side to make this work."

"Let's drink a toast to New Hope," Stanley chimed in, and they raised their glasses.

After the toast Stanley excused himself to go to join his daughter. Carl arranged to meet with him on Monday to go over the details. "Young lady, I expect to see a lot more of you in the near future. Take care of this young man, will you?" With that, Stanley left.

"I feel like celebrating. Let's go downstairs and listen to some music before we go," Carl suggested to Rae.

Unavoidably they passed Lynn's table where she held court before Latonya, Daniel, and her other subjects. Lynn was loud and inebriated, arguing with one of the men at the table who was withholding the keys to her car. Lynn slurred in Rae's direction, "Rae, make this bastard give me my car keys. I'm not drunk, he's the one who's drunk. Don't leave, we're just starting to party."

Without breaking her step, Rae responded over her shoulder that she was not leaving. Daniel was staring into space, fidgeting with his drink. His jaws were tight.

The downstairs room was a relief from the frenetic energy of the dining room. In contrast to the loud, boisterous jabber of the group upstairs, the mood downstairs was relaxed, refined. Maybe it was the difference in the decor. They say that loud and vibrant colors impact on the behavior of people. The focal point of the music lounge was a grand piano attended by a young woman with a voice reminiscent of Sarah Vaughn. The face did not match the voice, she was almost too beautiful to sing with such power and expression. The singer reminded Rae of the first time she saw Whitney Houston at a small club in New York City, pre-fame and in concert with her mother, Cissy Houston. Rae had sat spellbound while Whitney belted out solos with a strong, clear voice that seemed at odds with her petite body.

There were large squares of black-and-white tile on the floor surrounded by minimally decorated white walls. Red carnations adorned small tables, which were strategically placed to maximize privacy. Polite waiters and waitresses outfitted in black tuxedo pants and crisp white shirts took their order. Carl led Rae to the dance floor just in time for the hypnotic singer's rendition of "Anyone Who Had a Heart." Talk about pressure. He held one hand at the base of her back and the other at the nape of her neck and spoke softly into her ear. "Rae, I didn't mean to put you on the spot by asking you to work with me in front of Stanley. The timing just seemed right. I want you to know that there are no strings attached to the offer. You know very well how I feel about you, but if you decide to take the job and to pass on me, I'll understand. I'd be disappointed, but I want to have you in my life in some capacity. I know how frustrated you are with your job and I promise that I will never let you down. I intend to go to the top with this one and I want to take you with me."

For some reason she didn't believe the part about "no strings." From what she knew about Carl, everything he did was calculated to bring about a certain result and his results so far had all been positive, she mused. So why worry?

"There was nothing wrong with your timing. This is the kind of break that I've been looking for, praying for. When it finally came I was so stunned that I couldn't respond. I do need to think carefully about the offer. I'm not so sure that I would be able to separate the business and the personal aspects as easily as you say you can. I've never worked in a situation where there were romantic entanglements."

"I'm glad you see the possibility for romantic entanglement, because I've been trying like crazy to get entangled with you without much success," Carl said with a laugh.

"But seriously, I've heard a lot of horror stories about romance on the job, and it's something to be considered."

"I'm just kidding you, Rae. I won't pressure you, but I need to know by the end of the month when I tender my resignation. I want the general counsel involved in the planning stages as much as possible."

As he kissed her on the forehead, she closed her eyes and surrendered to the comfort of his arms while she silently contemplated, Why can't I give in to the logic of all of this? Psychotherapy has never been a science in which I placed much faith, but it seems that I need analysis now. It seemed too quick, too neat to be real. The eternal pessimist lurked within, reminding her of the risk of happiness, the risk that it would go away and leave her alone with her old self. Perhaps she was afraid to trust anyone. Maybe she didn't know how.

Carl understood when she said she needed to be alone, after they left the restaurant. She had a lot to think about. Once home she absentmindedly proceeded with the ritual of preparing for bed, removing makeup, washing her face, and brushing her teeth. While patting her face with a towel, it suddenly hit home that she had been offered the job as general counsel of New Hope. She let out a scream, a tiny scream, consistent with her normally controlled nature. Rae visualized walking into the offices of Landis Motor Company, submitting her resignation, and directing that bunch of deadheads to take a hike. Her heart raced, her scrubbed face beamed, and she thanked God for giving her a wonderful opportunity.

When reason crept in, she questioned the morality of entering into a business relationship with Carl without resolving the situation with Daniel. Common sense said that Daniel should not be a factor. Neither she nor Daniel had defined what was expected from their relationship. All Rae knew was that when she saw him, she wanted him. When she didn't see him, she wanted him. The greatest mystery of all was why he was so attached to Latonya, aside from the fact that they had been together for a long time. Daniel had said that he was reevaluating his relationship with Latonya before he met Rae. Rae wondered if she had fallen for the oldest line in history. Latonya seemed pleasant enough, but did not have a spectacular personality. Daniel did not bristle with electricity when he was with Latonya as he did with Rae. Daniel and Latonya's relationship appeared to be one of inbred familiarity. How could he choose comfort and familiarity over passionate love? Rae wondered. There were many kinds of love, and although it hurt Rae to think it, she believed that Daniel loved Latonya in a way that she would never understand. As much as she loved Daniel, Rae could not accept the role of the "other woman."

Rae's state of deep contemplation was broken as she responded to the gentle knock at the door. She assumed it was Carl, returning for one last kiss or to press her for an answer to his offer. It was not Carl, but Daniel who stepped into the room. His strong arms directed her to the bedroom where they stayed until morning, oblivious to the world, the world oblivious to them, except for the man in the steel-gray Mercedes parked around the corner.

Chapter Four

RAE'S STRUGGLE TO get out of bed the next morning was abnormally fierce. The good-bye mumbled to Daniel as he dutifully departed for his job at the training center was barely audible. Daniel's dedication to his job and clients, predominantly young, black men who had been written off by many within the community, impressed Rae. As director of the program, he recruited staff, raised funds, and was involved in every level of operation. She often teased Daniel that he should watch out for the young women who, despite the rules, hung out at the center, allegedly looking for their boyfriends, but who were actually checking out Daniel. One word of acknowledgment from Daniel would make their day.

No matter how late he stayed up the night before, no matter how much partying he had done, Daniel was always there bright and early to receive the first troubled soul who showed up in need of counseling, a place to stay, or food to eat. Rae worried that he might be over-extending himself. More than once he had been burned by unscrupulous schemers: the teenage father who headed straight for the crack house after borrowing money allegedly to buy milk for his baby, the street hustler who begged for a job recommendation and then spirited away his employer's cash receipts. But as long as the successes outnumbered the failures, Daniel's enthusiasm remained intact.

Slowly contemplating getting out of bed, Rae thought back on their lovemaking the night before. It was passionate, but tinged with anger. They did not talk until the sexual sea had calmed inside of them. Daniel's appetite could not be satisfied. He thrust into her as if to drive out any desire for another man, to satiate her need for physical contact. Rae had proclaimed herself free of any interest in Carl, except as a business associate, but Daniel knew that a subtle change had taken place. He sensed that she no longer viewed Carl as a mere companion or escort, that she saw the potential for a relationship with Carl.

Eyes of suspicion peered down as he arched above her, beads of salty sweat dripped cold onto Rae's breasts. His look contained the unasked questions. Daniel's kiss was deeper, his hold tighter than before. They knew, without saying it, that a change was near. Even after he achieved his physical, if not mental, release, he lay on top of her, their bodies slippery with sweat, still joined.

Daniel had said, "I've decided to talk to Latonya tonight. The wedding is scheduled for August, but I can't go through with it, not with the way things are between us. I don't expect her to react very well. Latonya's family has gone all out for this wedding. They did a lot of planning and spent tons of money. I feel really low about this. We've been together since college and if we break up, it's going to cause bad feelings, but it would be wrong to go through with the wedding feeling the way I do about you. I haven't been able to sleep for days. No matter what I do, somebody gets hurt."

"Daniel, you're not doing this because of Carl, are you?"

"No, but the fact that the son of a bitch is trying to move in on me doesn't help. Let's just say he is my motivator."

Her alarm rang a second time, reminding her that she had less than one hour to clear out the cobwebs and get to work. She did allow one final thought of how stupid it would be to continue to go to a job which she dreaded so much when she had a perfectly lovely offer to work with Carl at New Hope. Of course, the deepening developments with Daniel were not making it any easier to come to a decision. Rae knew that she could not work with Carl, if Daniel made a commitment to her.

Daniel had found out about Carl's new venture by listening to conversations between Lynn and Wilbur Stanley at the restaurant. When Stanley mentioned that Rae was offered the position of general counsel, Daniel was incensed and fell into a quiet, foul mood. In bed that night he accused Rae of being interested in Carl because of his money and Harvard M.B.A. Rae bitchily retorted that at least she could define her reason for involvement with Carl, which was more than she could say for his involvement with Latonya. He apologized quickly, saying that he did not want to waste their time together arguing about people who would soon become insignificant in their lives. Rae accepted the apology, but tactfully avoided apologizing for her remarks about Latonya, which she meant.

Rae recalled Sonya's comments about Latonya's background. Latonya seemed to be working hard to disavow her past. Rae pondered how Daniel could be engaged to a woman who aspired to everything that he claimed to hate and then accuse Rae of being after Carl's money. What the hell was he after?

* * *

Rae folded the newspaper under her arm on the way out the door since it was too late to read the headlines or grab a cup of coffee. Another beautiful day, she thought. The temperature had dipped below thirty degrees, but there was no new snow on the ground and the sun was shining. She didn't mind the cold, but slippery streets gave her the blues. She tuned the car radio to her favorite morning station. The announcer, who called himself Breezy, invited listeners to sit back, relax, and enjoy the cruise into the office. Rae was starting to relax until he mentioned the office. For the hundredth time she asked herself, "What am I going to do about this job situation?" She wished she could separate her personal and business life as Carl had suggested, but she knew that wouldn't work for her.

"This report just in from the Channel 2 newsroom. Police report that a local woman was badly beaten and left bleeding on a street of an upscale downtown neighborhood. The woman has been identified as Latonya Johnson, an employee of the Department of Social Services. Miss Johnson had apparently left the home of a friend, attorney Lynn Stanley, when she was attacked outside Miss Stanley's home located in the exclusive Waverly Glen subdivision. Details are sketchy at this point because police have been unable to question Miss Johnson, who remains unconscious and in extremely critical condition at a local hospital. According to Miss Stanley, the victim left her home at approximately one A.M. A family spokesman indicated that Miss Stanley has been placed under a doctor's care due to shock from hearing of the attack on Miss Johnson. The spokesman indicated that Miss Stanley would be meeting with police later today to give a more detailed statement. At this time police are holding no suspects and are asking the public to provide any information that might aid in the investigation."

Reflexively Rae swerved the car to the side of the road, ran over the curb, and made a U-turn toward the center. "Oh, my God, I wonder if Daniel has heard about this?" Desperate thoughts bombarded her brain. How could this happen when everything was starting to go right? She tore open the newspaper while steering the car with one hand and driving at a dangerous speed. There was no mention of the incident in the paper. Tires squealed as she rounded the corner. The nerve-grating sound made her realize that she should slow down before the police pulled her over. The final blocks to the center felt like the longest mile. The center was surrounded by policemen when she pulled up. Rae dashed from the car, barely stopping long enough to turn off the ignition and place the car in park. Myriad distressing thoughts raced through her mind as she pushed her way through the crowd, randomly asking, "What's happening, what's happening?" Her heart pounded as she elbowed her way closer to the front door, which was blocked by edgy police officers. She didn't see Daniel anywhere among the throng of hostile spectators, which included several of Daniel's clients. A burly, no-nonsense policeman halted her advance with his nightstick when Rae attempted to march past him.

"Hold on. Where do you think you're going?"

"I have business to conduct with the program director of this center and I would appreciate it if you would let me pass." Rae unsuccessfully tried the bold approach.

"I don't care what your business is, ours takes priority. Now be a nice lady and move along."

Rae's determination seemed to bolster the aggressiveness of the swelling crowd, which edged closer to the door as they hurled insults at the officers. "Y'all ain't got nothin' better to do than fuck wit' somebody tryin' to do somethin'," a snaggle-toothed woman yelled from the rear.

"Tell me what's going on here. What is going on?" Rae's persistence intensified along with her fear. The agitated officer glared down at her and took a deep breath to calm his growing impatience.

Just as she was contemplating her next, possibly foolish move, Gerald grabbed Rae by the arm and pulled her aside.

"Gerald, I've got to find Daniel. Is he inside?"

"Rae, Danny found out about Latonya right before the cops showed up. He asked me, no, he ordered me, to keep you away from this. He said that he would talk to you later and to let him handle it."

"What are you talking about? What are the police doing here?"

"They're taking Danny in for questioning. They think he had something to do with Latonya's beating."

"That's absurd! Let me talk to them."

"I can't let you do that." Gerald's grip tightened around Rae's arm. "I've had a lot of unwanted experience with this type of situation. The last thing you want to do is start talking to the cops, especially when you're upset. Chill out for a minute."

How was she supposed to "chill out" with her brain in overdrive, feet standing still, and time rapidly wasting? she wondered.

By the time the police led Daniel, handcuffed, out to the squad car, she was frantic. She wanted to run to him, but Gerald laid on a body block. Just before they pushed his head down into the back of the police car, Daniel glanced quickly in Rae's direction and shook his head to discourage her from approaching. The police drove away followed by the angry taunts of neighbors and young men from the training program. They all loved him. Rae loved him, and all she could do was stand there in the street, feeling useless, unable to think. Fortunately Gerald was there to think for her. They walked back to Rae's car and Gerald drove her home.

"How do you know where I live?"

"I dropped Daniel off one night when he was having car trouble. Look, it's none of my business what you two have going on. I figured he was into something different a couple of weeks ago when I noticed a definite change in his attitude. You know, he had the look of a man in love. I knew it wasn't Latonya that had him all tuned up. That broad, excuse the expression, has been with him forever and whenever she comes to the center she acts all uppity and shit. You know, like she's better than us."

"Can you come up for a minute? Right now I'm scared to death and I need to figure out how to help him."

Once inside Gerald complimented her on her town house and said, "Daniel is a very lucky brother to have such a classy lady."

"I should go down to the police station to see if I can do anything."

"He doesn't want you to do that. They'll probably let him go after they question him."

"I don't understand why they took him downtown. He was with me last night, as you probably already guessed. Why don't they go after the real criminals? Daniel couldn't hurt anyone, especially someone he loves." Her pain intensified as she heard her own admission that Daniel loved Latonya.

"It may be a mistake to call what Daniel feels for Latonya love. She's like a bad rash that won't go away." Gerald tried to soften the blow.

"I don't understand why they suspect Daniel. That's not the kind of thing he would do."

"Of course not. It's not his nature. I know you're upset right now, but you have to understand that you could make it worse for him, if they find out about you. The police are under a lot of pressure to solve any violent crime in the city because it's election year. They'll try to blame my man Dan or you even, if they think they can make it stick. Right now, nobody knows about you, except me. I owe that brother my life, so my lips are sealed. Let me go downtown and snoop around to try and find out what's happening. I'll check back with you as soon as I know something. Meanwhile, just hang tight."

Easier said than done. It was tough to hang tight while Daniel was in police custody, being interrogated like a common criminal. She had never practiced in the criminal justice system, but knew all too well how the police operated. They would do everything to break him down, to make him feel vulnerable in order to substantiate whatever theory they seized upon to solve the crime.

Rae decided against taking a Valium to calm her nerves, wanting to be alert in the event Daniel needed her. Minutes felt like hours as she awaited word of what was happening. News from the television and radio brought no comfort as announcers rehashed the same statement from earlier that morning. By five o'clock she was resigned to receiving no new information from the media when a local anchorman announced that they had previously unseen footage from the incident that would be broadcast after the station break. Riveted to the television screen, she stared in disbelief as a gurney was wheeled into an ambulance, carrying a badly beaten person. She could not recognize Latonya's face as she squinted to focus on the telecast.

The newsman continued, "Earlier today prominent attorney Lynn Stanley provided a statement to police concerning the incident. Apparently Miss Stanley and a group of friends, which included Miss Johnson, dined together at a local restaurant. Miss Johnson visited briefly at the home of Miss Stanley before proceeding home alone." The camera flashed on a distraught Lynn Stanley, wearing oversize sunglasses that failed to conceal dark circles underneath her eyes. She sobbed almost unintelligibly into the microphone, "I can't understand how someone could do this to Latonya. She's such a sweet person. My family and I will do everything that we can to make sure she gets the best possible medical treatment and that the assailant is brought to justice." The announcer concluded with the statement that the victim remained unconscious at a local medical facility while police were continuing their investigation into this bizarre crime. No mention was made of Daniel.

Rae must have held her breath for the entire two minutes that the story ran. Her head pounded and she felt warm, although the temperature in the house was quite cool. There was nothing worse than being in the midst of a crisis and unable to talk to anyone. "What's happening downtown and why haven't I heard anything from Gerald?" she wondered out loud. As if by magic, the phone rang.

"Hi, Rae, it's me, Sonya. Why weren't you at work today?" Without waiting for an answer, Sonya continued, "I know by now you've heard the awful story about Latonya Johnson. I tried calling you at work, but they said you weren't in. What's the matter? I hope you don't have that awful virus that's been going around. Anyway, I hear that they picked up that ultrafine boyfriend of hers for questioning. Can you imagine that he would do something like this to her? She must have really gotten under his skin. It's not safe to be in this city. I'm going to get me a gun because you don't know who to trust anymore. Is that your phone clicking?"

"Yes, it is. I really have to hang up now, Sonya, I'm expecting an important call. I'll call you at work in the morning."

Click. "Hello, Rae, it's Gerald. The police let Danny go for now. He said he would call you tonight at eight and explain everything. After they released him he headed over to the hospital to check on Latonya. Do you need anything?"

"No, thanks, Gerald."

Of course he had to go see about Latonya. She was, after all, the victim.

Rae dragged through the evening like a lone husky pulling a sled. The stress became so overwhelming that she gave in to the earlier impulse to take a Valium. She hated that drugged feeling, the lack of control. She wanted to remain lucid, but craved a moment of peace from the anxiety. Settling into her chair, she realized that she still had on her work clothes from the morning, complete with heels and stockings. Work. She completely forgot to call work. Too late. She would handle it in the morning. Maybe a little music will soothe me, she thought. Searching through a rack of compact discs, she found a compilation of ballads by one of her favorite artists whose melancholic yet soothing music captured the essence of her mood. She reverted to an old habit acquired during college of playing the same song over and over again. The compact disc player emitted the bluesy arrangement smoothly and clearly.

Rae mused, how did the artist know what I would be feeling when she wrote this song with its prophetic talk of momentary splendor, of flowers with colors too intense to endure more than one season? She realized that she was indulging in self-pity, but gave in completely. Rae hoped, for everyone's sake, that Latonya would recover. Infirmity and weakness were unexpected demons against which Rae had no defense. She wanted to get the man, but not this way.

The appointed hour came and went without a call. Rae lapsed into artificially induced tranquility. The strain eased like a wave flowing from the outer extremities inward, relaxing her feet, hands, arms, shoulders, and finally, her face.

Rae intentionally avoided the morning news, not wanting to experience the sting of being outside an event so much inside of her. She informed her secretary that she would be taking a few days off due to illness in the family. Breaking office protocol by not seeking prior approval from her superior was considered a major infraction. The secretary probed for additional information; Rae avoided giving specifics. She knew that her abrupt action would be the main topic of conversation in the legal department of Landis Motor Company, but she was totally focused on regaining control of her life, at any cost.

Rae had to exit the paralysis enveloping her for the last twenty-four hours. She was numb, but forced herself to begin packing without being sure where she was going. She wondered if the warmth of the tropical sun would raise her spirits. Maybe she should venture to the icy mountains to freeze out the pain in her heart. But then she knew where it was she needed to go, and where she would be welcome—home. Her need for distance and solitude got her through the mechanics of departure.

The taxi lurched to a stop in front of the hospital. Rae instructed the driver to wait. He cautioned her to hurry if she wanted to make the flight. She walked directly to the intensive care unit without stopping at the front desk for a pass. Instinctively she found Latonya's room. Daniel was sitting with his back to the door, his head in his hands. Peering through the tiny window, she saw tubes protruding from Latonya's nostrils, needles probing her veins. A triad of machines simultaneously pumped air into her lungs and monitored her heart rate and breathing. As reality set in that Latonya's life was balanced on a fragile beam, Rae was flooded with guilt for every unkind, selfish thought.

The sight of Latonya lying helpless in the bed confirmed the correctness of her decision to leave. As Rae was turning to go, Daniel saw her reflection in the window.

Daniel rose wearily and joined Rae in the hallway. His shoulders slumped. He was drained by the ordeal. Rae led him by the arm to the lounge, resisting the urge to comfort him in her arms.

"I'm sorry I forgot to call you, but I'm not thinking too clearly. I knew that she was hurt, but I never expected her to look like this, to be hooked up to life support."

"I feel terrible that I can't do anything to help. How is she?" Rae asked.

"It's touch and go. We won't know anything for certain until the test results come back."

"Why didn't you use me as an alibi with the police?"

"It's not that simple. Lynn Stanley gave a very damaging statement to the police. She blew out of proportion the argument that I had with Latonya before leaving her house that night. Lynn had been drinking too much and was being more obnoxious than usual. I couldn't stand being around her while she was in her 'nobody loves me' mood. I told Latonya that I was ready to leave and she insisted on staying. As always, Lynn butted into our conversation, insisting that we stay for just one more drink. Lynn has this incredible ability to manipulate people. Latonya and I exchanged some pretty harsh words, all to the delight of Miss Stanley. The police think that I was so angry that I waited for Latonya to leave and beat her up. Rae, you know that I could never hurt Latonya like that. I came directly to your place after I left Lynn's. The police have no real evidence against me and I see no reason to drag you into this mess."

"In case you've forgotten, I'm already in this mess. I would rather tell the truth than see them charge you with a crime you didn't commit." Rae quietly wondered if Daniel's real motivation was to protect her or to avoid revealing the truth about their relationship. Whatever the motivation, now was not the time to question it.

"Don't worry about me. If they had enough evidence to charge me, I wouldn't be standing here talking to you. Even before we got involved, I had started to question whether I could live my life entrapped in Lynn Stanley's circle of phony friends. Latonya seems to glory in it, but I always hated it. I never had enough material ambition to please Latonya. Although she would never admit it, she has no respect for my work at the training center. Rae, you were a lifeline thrown out to me, giving me a chance to save myself from a commitment that I would inevitably regret."

"Is that all I was? A way out?"

"No, no. You are the most sensitive, down-to-earth woman I have ever known. So far, I've caused you nothing but misery. You have to stay away from me until this is over. If the police find out about you, they'll use it against me. Before this happened I had found the courage to walk away from Latonya, but I can't in good conscience leave her in this condition. She's in a coma, she may not make it. I couldn't live with myself if I didn't see her through this."

"I know. I couldn't live with you either. You're right. We should cool out for awhile. I really didn't want to disturb you here, but I wanted to let you know that I'm leaving town for a while."

"Where are you going? For how long?"

"I'm going down south for a little while. I need to relax. Latonya has to be your first priority. We'll have to put our relationship on hold until this gets resolved. I agree with you that it's not a good idea for us to be together right now. . . . Don't forget to take care of yourself. You can't be much help to Latonya if you allow yourself to get run down. I hope she'll be all right. I really mean that. I'll miss you."

"Call me when you get back, okay?"

She smiled and touched her lips to Daniel's forehead, which was all that seemed appropriate under the circumstances. Rae walked away briskly, knowing that their lives would never be the same again.

Chapter Five

THE FLIGHT TO Atlanta was uneventful, except for the noise of the infant seated in front of Rae on the Dallas to Atlanta leg. His shrill cries could not compete with the noise inside her head, the clash of competing thoughts, the uncertainty and fear. Rae broke a rule established a few years ago, which was to avoid drinking on flights. Two glasses of wine were not only desirable, but necessary to dam the tears welling in her eyes.

A call to Aunt Mary Alice from the Atlanta airport was greeted with whoops of excitement. Aunt Mary Alice, who was actually her great-aunt, was Rae's oldest living relative in Duncan, Georgia. She insisted that Rae stay with her and wouldn't hear of Rae's plan to stay in a motel. The solitude of a motel actually appealed to Rae, but she knew that it would break her aunt's heart if she refused her hospitality. She resigned herself to tolerating Aunt Mary Alice's cluttered little house and the unending attempts to "put some meat on your bones." She looked forward to smothered steak in the morning, fish fried outdoors in a deep metal pot, and cakes and pies too tempting to resist. She needed to forsake, at least temporarily, the inhibitions of city life, the constant striving for fitness, the continuous reminders to think thin, and the ever-present guilt each time she indulged in a forbidden dessert.

The drive across the level Georgia countryside was therapeutic, rather than exhausting, as she had anticipated. There were no reminders of the turmoil she left behind. Rae drove away from the stress into a simpler way of life, uncomplicated by the need to produce results every moment and to keep busy even in her free time. It was comforting to find much of the scenery unchanged from the time she left Georgia more than fifteen years ago.

Rae was born and raised in Atlanta, where she lived until the age of thirteen. Duncan was her mother's birthplace, and the place where Rae, her brother, and her sister spent practically every summer of their lives until her family moved north. She never returned to Duncan, keeping in touch by phone and occasionally entertaining relatives from Duncan when they vacationed in the northern states. Business had brought her back home to Atlanta on several occasions, but never long enough to venture beyond city limits. Strangely enough, it would only take one phone call or one hour back on Georgia soil before she found herself speaking with the accent and using expressions indigenous to her native land.

Her feet sank into red Georgia soil as she exited the rental car in front of Aunt Mary Alice's house. Sagging steps creaked underneath her, sounding her arrival on the front porch. The next-door neighbors, in a not-so-subtle fashion, stopped shelling peas to stare at the stranger on Aunt Mary Alice's porch. Rae waved hello to them and smiled. They would inevitably be introduced in this small town where there was no such thing as a secret or a stranger. Eighty-seven-year-old eyes lit up as Aunt Mary Alice peeked through dusty curtains. With the help of her cane she pushed up from the well-worn couch, which was covered by a wildly flowered bedspread. Her arthritic hands struggled to unlatch the screen, Aunt Mary Alice all the while exclaiming how happy she was to see Rae and thanking the Lord for bringing her niece to her.

"Babygirl, this is the best thing that coulda happened. Come on in, come on in and let me look at you. You is prettier than ever. Need a little meat on your bones, but Aunt Mary Alice take care of that. I been sittin' here thinkin' 'bout what to cook since you called. I know you still love crowder peas and I got some fresh ones in the icebox. Made a pound cake, too. Go on in there and have a slice. Need some help with the bags?" Before Rae could answer, she pushed the screen door open with her cane and yelled out to the boy next door, "Junior, bring my niece's bags in from the car. Pearl, this here is my niece from up north come down to visit. She's a big-time lawyer, you know. We'll be over to visit a little later, after she gets settled in."

Aunt Mary Alice had an insatiable desire for information about the family. Rae endured the inevitable questioning that began with, "Why is it that a beautiful and smart girl like you is still single?" The question reminded her that she should call Carl and let him know that she was all right. In the haste of getting out of town, Rae had forgotten to tell him she was leaving.

"You may still look eighteen, Babygirl, but you ain't. Don't be like your grandmother and wait to have a baby too late in life. I don't care what these doctors say, it's best to have babies when you young."

"I hear you, Auntie." Tiredness from her journey had begun to set in, and despite her attempts to stifle her yawns, fatigue was evident in her face.

"You go lie down whenever you ready. This old lady will keep you up yakking all night. Don't get much company anymore and I gotta get in all my talkin' when they do come. Most of my friends have gone on to live with the Lord, but I'm too stubborn and too nosy to rest just yet."

"Oh, I love listening to you. Those flights took a lot out of me. Aunt Mary Alice, when did they cut down the magnolia tree up on my grandparents' property? I knew that the house was razed years ago, but I expected to see the tree when I rounded Slawson Circle."

"The city cut it down about two years ago when they paved the road. That tree had been there as long as I could remember. It was so big that the branches hung out over the road and I guess they didn't want to keep trimmin' it. Let me show you the bed I made up for you."

An imposing four-poster bed dominated the elaborately appointed room. The frame stood high off the floor, requiring some effort to climb aboard the seasoned quilt, which Aunt Mary Alice had sewn by hand. The room, chock-full of antiques, stood apart from the rest of the house in its careful detail and tidiness. Delicate lace on the curtains matched doilies resting on the back and arms of the wing chair. In the corner of the room a stately chifforobe stood at attention. Obviously Aunt Mary Alice had enshrined in this room her best furniture and most prized possessions. Rae was honored to be deemed worthy to sleep among such treasures.

Old family photographs decorated the walls. Her attention was drawn to a picture of Aunt Mary Alice as a woman of about twenty, decked out in her Sunday best and wearing a straw hat cocked to the side to show her irrepressible haughtiness. Mary Alice Buford had been a fireball from the time she was a child. Close scrutiny revealed that the woman next to her was Rae's grandmother, by far the most attractive of the sisters. She had a thin waist and big, shapely legs, a favorite of many southern black men. Rae recalled that after her grandmother grew older and much fuller, young men still flirted and complimented her pretty legs. Unfortunately, pretty legs were not a genetic quality passed on to succeeding generations. Rae's mother possessed rather skinny ankles that were passed on to Rae.

As Rae sank into the pressed sheets and feather pillows, she troubled over the absence of the magnolia tree that had been an anchor in her life and a source of memories that would stay with her forever.

From high atop the magnolia tree, Rae watched the flow of life in Duncan. Perched in the uppermost branches of the magnolia, she could see the entire circular path that spiraled from the crest of the hill. The leaves of the tree sheltered her from sweltering summer heat that bronzed her skin. Exotic white flowers blossomed in early spring, emitting a rare, clean fragrance, less sweet than honeysuckle, fresher and more pungent than the orchid flower. Waves of heat rippled through the air, creating the sensation of slow movement in outer space. Many hours of observation made her a master at detecting who was at the top of the hill and calculating how long it would take them to descend to the bottom. Pointy rocks in the rich, red clay created an obstacle course for the uninitiated.

Mrs. Pinkey, who lived over the hill and around the bend, would make her daily journey down the hill, for no certain purpose, except to visit whoever might be working in the yard or making a cool pitcher of lemonade. Her conversations usually concerned how it was hotter than she could ever remember, and she remembered everything, or how the hens were not laying because of space exploration. Mrs. Pinkey had lived more than nine decades within fifty miles of Duncan. Her parents had been slaves and she prided herself on having acquired property at a time when Negroes were not

expected, and usually not allowed, to own anything.
She loved to tell stories of segregation and lynchings,
not because she enjoyed those topics, but because she
wanted young children to know her history, which was
also their history. Mrs. Pinkey was related in some degree to every Duncan inhabitant, black or white, although the whites would never admit it. She, too, took
no pride in the "other half" of her heritage.

Mrs. Pinkey's sojourn down the hill took her an aver-
age of half an hour on her good days. Rae could tell
when her rheumatism was acting up because her hands
would quiver on the wood-carved cane that she used to
maneuver about or to gently swat an unruly juvenile.
Often during the course of her walk she encountered
neighbors who stopped to exchange pleasantries or inquire about the price of eggs. They rarely slowed to
walk alongside her because they knew that she kept her
own deliberate pace. "I ain't in no hurry," she would
say to anyone who tried to rush her or to the occasional
automobile driver honking his horn to get her out of the
middle of the road. She had traveled this road long before it was navigable by automobiles and had no intention of yielding the right of way.

The slow, leisurely pace of Mrs. Pinkey was out of
sync with the frenzied athleticism of Jesse Chaney, who
purposefully whizzed by her doing wheelies on his bicycle. Mrs. Pinkey had become accustomed to his reckless riding and attributed his antics to "bad upbringing."
On one occasion Jesse came barreling down the road
just as Mrs. Pinkey reached the midpoint of her trip. In-
tending to razz her a bit, he peddled with total abandon,
making sounds with his mouth and throat that mimicked
a hot engine. She would not be moved nor would she
acknowledge his presence. Attempting to swerve to the
left as he screeched within a foot of her, he hit a jagged

rock in the road, propelling Jesse and his red bicycle into a high acrobatic tumble that ended with Jesse sliding, face first, down the road. Mrs. Pinkey never missed a step.

Rae scrambled down the branches of the magnolia tree and performed her usual somersault to the ground and then rushed to see if Jesse was hurt. In his usual coarse fashion, he pushed her away, screaming, "Git away from me, girl; I don't need no help."

"Okay, fool, but you look like hell to me."

Jesse was one big bloody scrape. There were cuts all over his face, arms, and part of his stomach. He limped as he tried to stand. Rae was startled by the swat on her behind inflicted by her grandmother who warned, "Don't want to hear that kinda language from you, Babygirl."

"Yes, ma'am," Rae replied meekly as her grandmother took Jesse by the arm and escorted him, reluctantly, inside the house. Big Mama, the name her grandchildren called her, made Jesse lie down on a cot and went to work concocting a salve for his wounds. It was all black and gooey when she finished mixing it. The only ingredients Rae could identify were leaves from various plants and soot and ashes from the fireplace. Once Big Mama had covered the bloody areas with the poultice, Jesse looked like the victim of a tar-and-feather party. Rae laughed in his face; Jesse retaliated by calling Rae a big old tomboy.

For as long as Rae could remember, summers were spent in the country with her grandparents. Oftentimes boredom would set in, but she relished the change from city life. Being in the country allowed her to appreciate natural things: running barefoot through fields of towering cornstalks and hiding beneath their wings; capturing lightning bugs in mason jars to study the source of their glow; picking sweet, succulent blackberries growing wild in untamed fields; cramming more berries into her belly than she saved for cobblers and preserves. Best of all, food was always plentiful in the country where meals consisted of vegetables from the garden and meat from animals raised on the farm. Big Mama would warn, "Don't get too familiar with the animals, because you'll feel bad when we have to kill them," but Rae always ignored the advice. When her uncle marched out to ring the neck of Charlie The Chicken, Rae begged and pleaded for Charlie's life, swearing that she would never, ever taste the flesh of Charlie. After smelling the aroma of Charlie deep-frying in hot oil and catching the scent of fluffy, homemade biscuits and buttery corn, her loyalty to Charlie evaporated. The following day there would be a new Charlie pecking for food around the back doorstep. By the end of the summer, Rae would begin to miss her friends in Atlanta, but she never missed the hunger that inevitably awaited her at home.

There was too much pressure in the city to grow up fast, start dating boys, become a real "teenager." Until the age of thirteen the only interest Rae had in boys was proving that she could outrun them. She did, however, harbor a secret affection for Melvin Gray, one of her brother's playmates. She displayed that affection by yelling and throwing a bat at him when he struck her out in baseball. Melvin's smooth black skin was the antithesis of the once-prevailing black beauty standard of the fair-skinned, straight-haired boy. Melvin was kind and considerate, even as a child, a miniature Nat King Cole. Rae's extended tomboy period prevented her from expressing her feelings to Melvin, but he became her model of a true gentleman.

She slept deeply and dreamed many peaceful dreams that first night in Aunt Mary Alice's house. Maybe it was the soothing food or the clean country air. Whatever, it was the element Rae needed to begin to feel rooted in life once again.

Shades of winter settled slowly upon the sleepy Georgia town. Late fall blossoms wrestled with the dry leaves of autumn to claim their place within the paradoxical season. Even the birds were dazzled by the wonder of nature, not knowing when to sing, chirping at inappropriate times throughout the day. The red earth hardened beneath Rae's feet, clay crevices grew deeper, signaling the coming of hard winter and an end to the masquerade of springlike weather. Her feet became barometers of the season as they traversed the ageless dirt roads, welcoming the sunrise of each new day. The days numbered seven since she had come, seven country days of motionless time, devoid of routine.

Rae's world existed within the ambit of Slawson Circle. She ventured beyond only to accompany Aunt Mary Alice to town to replenish supplies in her sewing kit—at least that was the reason given for their trip. She suspected that the real purpose was to "show off" for the shopkeepers her great-aunt had patronized much of her life. Rae squirmed as Aunt Mary Alice proudly introduced her "attorney niece." She endured the embarrassment, not wanting to deprive her aunt of the chance to show her world that she had "important" people in her family. They spent hours in town, which consisted of one block of stores on either side of the street, stopping to exchange pleasantries with everyone they met.

They dined at the local Walgreen's store, an event that Aunt Mary Alice termed "eating out." When Rae suggested that they cap off their day with a movie at the local theater across the street, the old woman's eyes clouded over and she promptly declined the invitation, claiming she was tired. Rae later learned that her great-aunt had long been waging her own boycott of the picture show due to inhumane treatment she received there. As recently as the early sixties, the theater reserved the balcony for "colored" and restricted the times that they could attend. Aunt Mary Alice had been denied admission after making extensive preparation for a date with her sweetheart. She never forgot the pain and humiliation of being told that "nigger day" was on Wednesday and Thursday. The segregationist policy of the theater changed with the departure of the family that originally owned it, but Aunt Mary Alice refused to set foot in the theater again.

"Rae, why don't you go and have some fun with the other young folks? You been sittin' 'round the house with me like an old lady and I know you got to be tired of that."

"Well, I wanted to spend some time with you, and I'm not really into partying right now. I've gotten quite a bit of work done on the family history."

"Family history is fine, but you also gotta deal with the present. Now, I'm gonna tell your cousin Luther that you changed your mind 'bout goin' down to The Cafe tonight with him and Leila. That's final. Let's get on outa here while I can still get these old legs to move."

"Okay. Let me pull the car around so you don't have to walk so far."

Later that evening Rae joined her cousin Luther and his wife for a baptism into Duncan nightlife. The Bottom, formerly known as The Cafe, stood at the end of a narrow dirt road, encircled by evergreens towering high into the clear, starlit sky. Except for the remaining dozen or so trees, the forest that once stood as a fortress against invasion by the outside world had disappeared. The standard retinue of brothers hanging around outside greeted them as they made their way through deep ruts in the weed-filled ground.

"Say, baby, you lookin' sho nuff good tonight," a slight man wearing a large-brimmed hat and dark glasses crooned in Rae's direction.

Luther cut him off at the pass. "Shut up, fool, this here's your cousin Rae, Aunt Ida's daughter."

D. J.'s eyes sparkled with faint recognition. "Rae, Babygirl, we haven't seen you since you were a little thing. You sure did grow up nicely. We gonna party tonight, baby. Does Ben know you're here? You know he owns The Bottom."

Rae was swept inside The Bottom in a wave of hugs and kisses. Uncle Ben rolled out the red carpet and treated her like royalty. She was humbled to be back in the place where she partied many times as a young girl, always without her grandmother's permission. Big Mama had insisted that The Cafe was no place for kids, but Rae was never safer. Her teenage aunt would take her to The Cafe under the pretense of going to the store or visiting friends. They inevitably met her aunt's boyfriend, who would ply Rae with ice-cold Coca-Cola's from the red ice chest that kept the sodas at a teeth-chilling temperature. The sound of carbonation fizzing up as Rae removed the bottle cap with the opener built into the ice chest made her tingle. As a reward for silence, they bought Rae fat, juicy hamburgers, smothered with onions and dripping with spicy flavor. She insisted upon eating the whole thing, even though her tiny belly ached and churned.

After she was old enough to sneak to The Cafe on her own, Rae came to study the latest dances that kids who lived in the country seemed to do with an added flair. The basic steps would be the same, but they injected an extra twist or bend into it, provoking a more dramatic effect. By the end of the summer Rae would have several new moves to show friends in Atlanta, guaranteeing her the spotlight for at least the next three parties.

The name had changed, but The Bottom remained the same—from the tall, linoleum-covered counter in the entrance to the uneven wood-plank floor that squeaked in certain areas. The police had frequently threatened to close down The Bottom, citing numerous fire hazards, but the owners would grease the palms of the appropriate city officials, and they would overlook the hazards temporarily. A narrow entrance served as the only exit and there were no windows inside the dance area. An unwashed, barred window behind the counter provided the only view in or out.

Environmental issues were never a concern in Duncan, especially at The Bottom, where smoke pollution nullified the effects Rae's bubble bath and invaded her fresh-washed hair.

Elongated ebony limbs, swaying in perfect time to a funky remake of a fifties tune, miraculously averted collision. The beat of the music was infectious, the sound so clear that Rae imagined the presence of a live band, but there was no band, just folks totally immersed in the groove. Cousin D. J. danced by himself in the middle of the room, then latched on to a post with one hand, hooked the other hand in his belt buckle, and slid into an imitation of a James Brown routine. The crowd waited for a break in his performance, which was not forthcoming, and so they danced around him.

Rae's dance card was full with partners anxious to see if she knew how to get down. She boogied with the best of them. There was no discernible trend to the dancing, the style and intensity varied by age and level of physical conditioning. The only common thread was movement in sync with the music. The African-Cuban beat of the deejay's next selection energized the dancers who formed a line to do a dance unfamiliar to Rae. Their movement flowed shoulder to shoulder and after a brief period of awkwardness the steps came easily to her. Rae thought, This is the best party I've been to in ages, like the old garage parties where we danced non-stop until our parents or the police forced us to turn off the music.

Body heat emanated from every corner. Without ventilation or break between songs, sweat covered her body, causing the already snug outfit to cling like static. She managed to break away from an insistent partner long enough to get a drink. The dilemma of what to drink in a small-town juke joint presented itself when Rae was faced with the choice between beer or hard liquor. Champagne was out of the question, as was wine. She ordered a gin and tonic, which gave Uncle Ben a troubled expression. Apparently, tonic water was not on the menu either. To make things easy, she suggested that he set her up with one of the house specialties, which turned out to be a pitcher of sloe gin fizz accompanied by a basket full of the best fried fish she had ever tasted. "Might as well let it all hang out," she said to Cousin Luther. Rae hadn't tasted sloe gin fizz since freshman year in college, having acquired a taste for less sweet, drier forms of alcohol. Tonight sloe gin fizz seemed appropriate for a stroll down memory lane. Briefly, between bites of crusty fish drenched with hot sauce and wrapped inside white bread, her thoughts wandered back to Daniel. Where is he? What is he doing? She wondered if she had retreated too hastily, but she quickly realized that there was no other choice. A few seconds before the gloom rushed in, her eyes settled upon a strange sight—a white guy sitting quietly in the corner, tapping his foot to the beat of the music. He looked at home, as if he had been at The Bottom many times before.

"Luther, who is the white man sitting in the corner?"

"Oh, that's Sheriff Bingham's son. Comes here a coupla nights a week. He doesn't bother anybody, just keeps to himself and enjoys the music. Every so often he gets the spirit and dances. He knows how to get down, too."

Her tongue probed for the fish bone lodged between her teeth as she realized that she had eaten an entire basket of fish. While trying to brush off the crumbs spilling everywhere, she looked up to find the sheriff's son gazing down at her with focused green eyes.

"Would you like to dance?" he asked in a deep southern drawl. He reached out to Rae with muscular arms protruding from a T-shirt pulled over a tight body. They did not talk as he led her to the dance floor and launched into his routine. Rae thought to herself, This dude dances like a blood—before pulling her act together to keep from being embarrassed. The song ended and the disc jockey slowed the tempo for the first time during the evening. Without hesitation, Rae's partner drew her to him, right arm straight down, left arm pulled behind her, black style. He guided her into a step that was a cross between a slow drag and the dip. The movement began at the knees, their backs absolutely straight, like Spanish dancers. Small circular motions, which Rae interpreted as freshness on his part, were added as they dipped. A quick glance around the room assured her that others were doing a similar dance. Rae rationalized that, if her weak knees were to survive, she would have to ease into it and allow him to support her weight. Relaxing, she sank deeper into the movement, which was now followed by a smooth grind. His knee lunged farther between her legs each time they took a step. He distracted her by repositioning her arms around his broad shoulders and holding her close at the waist. Long, probing fingers pressed into her back as the steps became fewer and the grinding grew more intense. She leaned back from his chest and sensed fully the combustion at the center of their bodies. Hands that knew how to hold and soothe a woman slipped lower on her hips. She was lost in the rhythm of the music. Nipples tensed against the fabric of her dress as he secured his arms under her shoulders. His muscle throbbed beneath the zipper of tight jeans. They lingered motionless on the floor, long after the music stopped. Bathed in the sensuality of their display, the room stood still. She avoided looking at him as she walked back to her table.

Without a word, Luther and Leila knew that it was time to go.

Rae awakened early and phoned Sonya.

"Sonya, it's me, Rae. Now just listen for a minute. I want you to go over to the house and collect the mail and the newspapers. I'm visiting with relatives outside of Atlanta. I needed some time to think. Has anything been happening since I left?"

"Has anything been happening? How can you ask that question and why didn't you let me know you were leaving? I know you've been stressed out about something for the last few weeks, but Rae, this is not like you at all. Poor Carl has been like a madman looking for you. He wanted to call the police, but I talked him out of it. All they would tell me at your office was that you were away on an emergency leave. Do you know how worried we've been after what happened to Latonya Johnson?"

"Any change in her condition?"

"No, and I hear that Daniel is a basket case. He spends a lot of time at the hospital, just sitting and hoping she will come out of the coma. It's going on two weeks since the incident and the doctors are less optimistic as time goes by. Her family is thinking about pulling the plug on her life-support system, which is really a bummer. I ran into Lynn downtown on Thursday and she still doesn't look too swift either. She's gone back to work, but you can see the strain in her face. Surprisingly, she thinks they should turn off the machines because Latonya would never want to be maintained in a vegetative state. They were so close, I guess she would know. It's frightening when something like this happens to someone your own age. . . . Let's talk about something pleasant. When are you coming home? Give me your number in case I need to get in touch with you."

"No, Sonya, I really don't want to talk to anyone right now."

"Girl, you are too scary for me! Have it your way, but do me a favor and give Carl a call. He deserves better than this."

"I'll call him right away. Keep an eye on the house for me and I'll see you in a few days."

Sonya was right. Rae knew she was being unfair to Carl. Several times she had picked up the phone to call him, but put it down. She wasn't ready for the pressure. Carl was so organized and disciplined that he would never understand how she could flake out.

"Hi, Carl, before you curse me out let me explain that I am really sorry for making you worry. I had a lot of things on my mind and had to get away for awhile to pull myself together."

"Where the hell are you? Don't you trust me enough

to come to me when you have problems? Maybe I could have helped you work things out."

"It's not a matter of trust, it was something that I needed to do for myself. I'm visiting my aunt down in Duncan, Georgia. I'll be back in a few days."

"I don't want to add to the pressure, but I missed you, and with all the hassles of getting the company organized, I could have used a little moral support myself."

"I know I've been selfish. When I come back on Saturday, I promise to make everything up to you."

"I'll hold you to that promise. Why Saturday? Can't you come back sooner?"

"No, sweetheart, I have a few things to tie up down here, family matters. Getting away has been great for me, exercising every day and overeating every night."

"Can I pick you up at the airport?"

"Sure, but I don't know the arrival time."

"Rae, you mean you haven't made reservations?"

"Well, I didn't know that I was returning on Saturday until now, while talking to you. See how persuasive you are?"

"Don't flake out on me again. Call me back when you have your flight schedule. I can't wait to see you."

Her final days in Duncan whizzed by as her departure grew nearer. She struggled to prepare herself mentally for what awaited her at home. Rae imagined that astronauts bracing for reentry into the earth's atmosphere must experience similar excitement and trepidation. She had already made the decision to take Carl's offer to become general counsel of New Hope. There was no acceptable alternative.

Fate dictated that she follow a different path to freedom—freedom from a job that stifled her, freedom from a relationship that seemed doomed to failure. Until now, she had thought of freedom as an eternally positive, pleasurable concept, but she realized that it could sometimes be painful, requiring her to eliminate something from her life that she still wanted, but could not have. Rae needed to free her mind from its obsession with Daniel. She had to release him from her dreams.

Chapter Six

"BABY, IT'S SO good to have you home," Carl whispered in her ear as they embraced at the airport.

She welcomed his embrace, glad to have someone to come home to. "I missed you. I have so much to tell you about my trip. It was great, full of nothing but eating, sleeping, and running. Just what the doctor ordered." Rae tried to sound upbeat.

"Something must have agreed with you down there. You look fantastic. You sure you didn't have a man stashed away in Duncan?"

"Be serious. Guess what? I've decided to take the job at New Hope."

"Next to your coming home, that's the best news I've heard in a long time. I need you so much, businesswise, that is. And a little bit on the personal side, too."

"I need a few days to submit my resignation and clean up my house, which I left in a state of total disarray. Will Wednesday be okay? I can't wait to get started."

"Sooner the better. How about a little celebration to seal the bargain? I'm meeting Wilbur Stanley today at six. Want to come along?"

"Not really. I want to catch my breath and go through my mail. What if you pick me up after your meeting?"

"Okay, I'll pick you up at seven-thirty."

Carl's good-bye kiss was not the brush on the lips she had expected. He leaned across the console and pressed against her bosom, holding her securely with one hand. She suspected that he could not be put off much longer. Rae suppressed conflicting emotions as memories of Daniel invaded her mind. She willed her body to respond to Carl. She needed to be held, kissed, and to feel like the most important person in someone's life.

"Let me get out of here, while I can." She smiled, disentangling herself from his arms.

Being back on her own turf felt surprisingly good. She finally allowed the excitement of a new job to overtake her. She gave in to the joy that she was blessed with the opportunity to begin again. Renewed confidence gave her the strength to resist calling Daniel, or maybe it was the fear of rejection.

She had been away for only two weeks, but felt like an alien entering the door to Landis Motor Company. There was a definite chill in the air as she moved self-consciously through the corridors. Outside Rae's office her secretary, Jean, sat with her eyes glued to a memo, never raising her head to acknowledge Rae's presence. Rae gave it little regard, since Jean had always acted "sometimey." The veteran secretary, who had been with the company since the time women were relegated to clerical status, had made public her displeasure with working for a young, female boss. The fact that Rae was black further intensified Jean's animosity.

Jean waited a respectable sixty seconds, then appeared in the doorway, announcing boldly, "The boss wants to see you in his office."

"Bill wants to see me?" Rae asked, referring to her immediate supervisor.

"No. I mean the real boss. Buck Strong, the general counsel."

Word of her return had traveled quickly through the "big house," Rae thought.

"You wanted to see me, Buck?" Rae asked, entering his office. She suppressed the urge to laugh, which surfaced each time she said his name. His frail body, distended belly and flat ass reminded Rae of a pregnant woman carrying all the weight up front. Buck had a well-deserved reputation for sternness, cultivated by his no-nonsense style of management and unwillingness to smile. Striking terror in the hearts of men and women was his forte. Rae knew that this would not be an easy conversation.

"Have a seat, Rae. Let's get right to the point. We were less than pleased with your sudden, unscheduled departure. The success of this organization depends upon the cooperation of all the attorneys, including you. As a result of your action, I've been forced to take disciplinary measures. A letter of reprimand has been placed in your personnel file. You'll find a copy of that letter in your mail basket. What concerns me most is your lack of candor in dealing with the situation. Jean tells me you were extremely evasive in describing the nature of your emergency."

"I realize that leaving so suddenly went against company policy and I apologize for that."

"You've also been withdrawn and uncooperative." Buck raised his bushy, untamed eyebrows in an accusatory manner while waiting for a response to the latest indictment.

"I've been extremely cooperative in all work-related matters. If you're going to spy on me, I suggest you use a more reliable source than Jean."

"I didn't attribute the last statement to Jean. She has always been a trustworthy and competent employee."

"If she's so competent, why'd you boot her out of your office and stick me with her?"

"Look, young lady. I've had enough of your impudence. This is your opportunity to defend your actions. I suggest you take it seriously. We had high hopes for you, Rae. I've been personally monitoring your progress to make sure things went smoothly for you."

"Have you been monitoring the fact that I'm the only attorney at my grade level without supervisory experience? Did you monitor the fact that my salary is lower than my male counterparts' with less seniority?"

"Company policy doesn't allow me to discuss the salaries of other employees. We've considered you several times for supervisory positions, but frankly, your personality doesn't appear well suited. This latest episode confirms it. Anyone who takes responsibility as lightly as you is not ready to supervise."

"That's a bunch of baloney! I worked my ass off for this company. It seems that the only way to get ahead around here is to be a carbon copy of the boss, which is impossible in my case. You give lip service about wanting employees with diverse backgrounds, but that's a joke."

"Calm down. You don't have to act hostile."

"I'm not acting." Rae paused long enough to catch her breath. "I didn't come here to argue with you. My only purpose this morning is to pick up my stuff and submit my resignation."

"Resignation? Nobody's asking you to resign."

"I'm quite capable of making certain decisions on my own."

Buck Strong's initial relief turned to concern as he considered the political fallout from Rae's resignation.

"Well, if you insist on resigning, do me a favor and go over to personnel for an exit interview."

"I don't have anything to say to personnel. I already wasted two years talking to personnel."

"I hate to leave things up in the air in view of your negative feelings about the company."

"Oh, I see. . . . You're worried that I might sue you for discrimination."

"That's certainly not an unreasonable concern considering the ridiculous number of complaints filed against this company by disgruntled minority employees."

"If you spent more time figuring out why employees are so disgruntled, you'd have a lot less litigation to worry about."

"Net it out, Rae. Do you plan to sue or not?"

"The only plan I have, at this particular moment, is to get away from here as quickly as possible."

"Resigning from a stable job in today's economic climate appears to be another of your hasty decisions. Things will look a lot different when the checks stop coming and the bills start mounting."

"I'm sure I can work something out," Rae replied confidently.

"Well, if you need references while looking for a new job, please let us know. You've always received excellent work evaluations. It's your attitude that held you back."

"I wouldn't worry too much about my future or my attitude, if I were you. I've accepted a position as general counsel of a downtown consulting firm. I start on Wednesday."

Buck Strong's jaw dropped to his chest. He stared over the rim of his bifocals at the feisty woman who stared right back at him.

Rae couldn't resist one parting shot before exiting.

"Hope to see you at the annual general counsel's convention in February. Say good-bye to the fellows for me, will you? It's been real, Buck."

Uncontrolled laughter resonated through the prefabricated walls of Landis Motor Company. Some thought it was the sound of an employee gone mad. In reality, it was the spontaneous utterance of a jubilant woman—free at last.

No expense was spared in decorating the offices of New Hope, which occupied the entire seventh floor of the Newman Building. A well-known interior designer had been engaged to do the floor in beige and white tones, accented with lavender. Carl had taken the liberty of ordering furniture for Rae's office. He knew she would accept the offer and gambled that she would be ecstatic about the traditional mahogany desk and chairs. The designer scheduled an appointment with Rae to work out the personal details.

Entering her office on the first day, Rae had to fight the feeling of disbelief that this fabulous office, surrounded by floor-to-ceiling windows on two sides, was really hers. It was a long way up from the stuffy, windowless cubbyhole she had occupied at Landis Motor Company. It was an even higher leap for the poor little black girl from Georgia who had only dreamed about the life she was now leading. She vowed to allow the memories, good and bad, to remind her of where she came from and keep her grounded, no matter how high she ascended into the arms of the magnolia.

Rae hoped the years of deprivation were behind her, that she could begin to enjoy some of the perks attendant to executive status. Although she was classified as an executive at her former job, she had never felt like one. Rae's experience in the corporate world, specializing in finance and business law, had brought ridicule from law school friends who sneered at her choice of specialty. She reasoned with them that not all black attorneys should specialize in criminal law, that some should concentrate on other areas to be ready when business opportunities arose. They did not accept her argument, causing Rae to sometimes question her own choice. She knew that she was good at negotiating contracts, interpreting complex legal provisions and breaking them down into language that could be understood. While her opponents, almost invariably white males, basked in the certainty of their own superiority, she would wear them down through skill and preparedness.

Rae's former associates respected her ability as an attorney, yet they wanted her to leave her self-confidence at the front door of the building. Be excellent, make us money, but don't expect to compete on the same level. The message was clear; the schizophrenia that it induced was intolerable. To stand on the sidelines while mediocre associates passed her by, to be relegated to that special status of no status, was to die a slow mental death. It no longer mattered now that she had found a place where she could excel. She was ready to assume responsibility for her own destiny and for steering the firm down the proper legal course.

Her totally revamped wardrobe blended splendidly with the new surroundings. She went all out with self-adornment, supplementing her already adequate wardrobe with contemporary business suits by Anne Klein, Donna Karan, and Escada. She found blouses and sweaters by Ralph Lauren and Calvin Klein to spruce up old outfits. Her feet never felt better in jazzy Maud Frizon pumps and suede-and-leather sling-backs from Bennis and Edwards. The only item she held back on was a black, quilted Chanel purse. She decided to keep an eye on it until insanity or depression put her in a mega mood to splurge.

The many hours expended by Carl in planning the office space as well as developing a solid business plan were evident. New Hope was the first major consulting firm in the city run by people of color.

The first two weeks blitzed by at fast-forward speed. Carl and Rae spent as much time on airplanes as they did in the office, rarely staying overnight in any one spot. They would arrive home late in the evening and be back in the office by six or seven the next morning. Rae was never more exhausted or more exhilarated, being at the center of a new venture. Working so closely together, she learned a lot about Carl, who seemed somewhat paranoid about business associates. He ran background checks on every officer of the company, including Rae, and insisted on knowing more about his opponents than they knew about him. When Rae kidded him about being a member of the CIA, he was not the least bit amused.

There was little or no time for romance, which was a relief. She wanted to establish a healthy working relationship with Carl before embarking on any other joint ventures. He knew that she was ambivalent about their personal relationship and she appreciated the space he gave her to concentrate fully on her work. Still, she wondered what Carl did at night after the meetings ended. A couple of times she saw him leave the hotel late at night when they were on the road. He hadn't mentioned knowing anyone in the area. She dismissed her curiosity, rationalizing that Carl's outside activities were none of her business.

Working until midnight no longer fazed Rae. It made her stronger and left little time to think about Daniel. Rae had gotten over the morning crying spells when she would wail loudly until her eyes were bloodshot and her voice was hoarse. That sick ritual, performed in private, had given her the appearance of a closet alcoholic and did nothing to improve her situation. Rae dismissed erotic thoughts by pretending she was trying to break the world record for celibacy.

The long hours forced her to rearrange her day to allow for exercise at noon to relieve the strain of nonstop work. She didn't mind skipping lunch, because the late-night dinners were starting to take a toll. Fortunately, the building had a gym in the basement, a convenient perk. Her muscles were in serious need of detensing after a breakfast meeting with a new client who promised to be a handful.

"Hi, Rae, are you doing aerobics today or working out on the machines?" a stockbroker from another office in the building inquired.

"Oh, hi, Faye, I think I'll do the machines. I'm not up for jumping around today."

"Good, I wanted to ask you about someone while we do the bikes."

Rae tensed at the suggestion that she share her one hour of relaxation with an inquiring female. It was too late to escape and she hoped that Faye would be brief.

Faye began skittishly, "I met a really nice guy who works with you. His name is Carl Anderson. The fellows in my office tell me that he's really sharp and that his business has great potential. Is he married?"

"No, as a matter of fact, he's not," Rae reluctantly answered.

"You know, it's not often that you find a young, handsome man with so much going for himself."

"You know that's right." Rae felt the green-eyed monster start to rise.

"We should have lunch together sometime. We prob-

ably have a lot to talk about. I bet we even know some
of the same people. Well, I'm going to move on to the
Stairmaster. Give me one of your business cards before
you leave."

"Oh, sure. I haven't had much time for lunch lately,
but I'm sure we can get together as soon as things ease
up a bit."

"The nerve of that witch trying to use me to get next
to Carl," Rae mumbled to herself, then thought, My
workout is ruined. I'm tighter now than when I came in.
I don't know why I'm letting her upset me so much.
Look at her with that skimpy leotard and fake hair on
her head. If she bends over any farther, her boobs will
tumble out into plain view. I hate women who come to
the gym to do everything but exercise. Calm down,
she's not the kind of woman that Carl would be interested in, but pretty soon he's going to find someone to
spend time with, if I don't get my act together. This
work thing is fantastic, but man does not live by intel-
lectual stimulation alone.

Upon returning to the office, Rae made a point of
stopping by Carl's office, allegedly to discuss a file they
had been working on. She waited through two phone
calls to get his attention.

"What's up, Rae? What did I forget to do this time?"

"What we forgot to do was to take a minute for ourselves to relax."

"I didn't forget. Just didn't want to clutter things up
with my personal desires. I know how hard you've been
working and I really appreciate it. I don't want to lose
you as my general counsel by pressuring you about our
personal relationship. The last time we were together, I
got the distinct impression that I was moving too fast
and so I forced myself to back off until you decide what

you want. You know how I feel. I don't know how you feel."

"It's not that I don't want to be with you. I enjoy your company. What if we leave a little earlier tonight so I can make dinner for you?"

"That's an offer almost too good to refuse, but you know I need to finish reviewing the contracts you put on my desk this morning. I know I won't be finished before nine o'clock. I was thinking about taking the files home with me tonight."

"I've got an idea. What if I bring all the fixings over to your place and you can work while I cook? That way I'll be right there if you have any questions."

"It's a deal. Come to think of it, this is the first time that you will honor me with your presence in my home. I'll see you there at seven."

Rae questioned her motivation for arranging dinner. Immersion in work during recent months had been therapeutic, allowing her to live with the fact that she had not seen or heard from Daniel. She sensed that he was aware of her return. They had communicated, without speaking, a mutual need to go on with their separate lives. Rae knew that she could not persist forever in a nunlike state of existence, but she was reluctant to get involved. Ultimately the fear of making the wrong move became secondary to the dread of being alone forever.

Doubts bombarded Rae as she drove slowly in the direction of Carl's house. She had cautiously avoided his place in the past, preferring to meet him at her home or a neutral spot. Driving through this posh neighborhood, she wondered where Carl got all of his money. The garage door opened automatically as she pulled into the circular drive. Rae was astounded by the grandeur of his home, impressive by bachelor standards or, for that matter, by any standards.

"So this is how the other half lives."

"Come on in here and give me a kiss."

"Not before I get the food started. I know how you are." She laughed, unloading packages. "I need an ice bucket for the champagne. Now go and get your work done so we can eat in peace and socialize a bit when we finish."

"I like that socializing part. Maybe we can skip dinner and get right down to that."

"Don't even try it! Go to your room and let me do my thing in the kitchen."

Sipping champagne while cooking made her totally relaxed by the time dinner was served. He said that he loved her Chinese stir-fry chicken and almond salad.

"I never suspected that you could cook like this. What other hidden talents do you have?"

"Wouldn't you like to know? Let's listen to some music while I clear the table."

"I'll be finished in a few minutes. Leave everything on the counter. The cleaning lady is coming in the morning."

"Nonsense. My mother taught me better than to leave a dirty kitchen."

She was so buzzed by then that she danced through the chores, feeling bubbly and light for a change. Carl's body closing in from behind should not have surprised her. His arm was around her waist, his hand played with her breasts. She resisted only for a few seconds before he found her nipple and began circling it with his fingers. Instinctively the muscles of her vagina began to contract, her hips moved in circular patterns against him. Carl reached down to pull up her leather skirt. Rae's mind struggled to form the words, "Stop, this has gone too far," but the sensations pulsing through her made her mute. He unbuckled her garter belt to pull down her panties, which she stepped out of, then expertly refastened the garter to her sheer black stockings. She felt his stiff penis rubbing against her. Without turning her around he unbuttoned the top of her blouse and slid it down over her shoulders. She moved to assist him in unhooking her bra, but he gently placed her hands on the counter. Carl pulled her breasts outside the bra cups, but left the bra fastened. Her head was pressed forward as he moved closer between her legs, while lowering his pants. His fingers massaged her pubic hair and gradually worked into the opening of her vagina. When he reached her clitoris, she was wet in anticipation. Abruptly he entered her from the rear. She braced against the countertop and widened her stance to allow smoother entry. Gripping her hips tightly, Carl thrust forcefully and deeply into tight spaces. She moved with him as he kissed her shoulders and neck and fondled her breasts. Simultaneous stimulation of her breasts, vagina, and clitoris made her come loudly. Rae was embarrassed by the intensity of her own explosion as she nearly melded into the countertop. She was bruised, her muscles were battered, and she felt raw. Without a word, she pulled down her skirt, straightened her blouse, and fled like a criminal.

Sex scene.

Chapter Seven

"HEY MAN, YOU'VE got to chill out if we're gonna get through this crisis in one piece. I know you got a lot on your mind with your old lady in the hospital and the city council breathing down your back, but it won't do any good for you to end up in the hospital." Gerald spoke to Daniel's back as he studied the tense figure who sat scrunched up in a chair, shoulders tensed, staring into space.

Gerald continued, "We've been through tighter spots than this. Remember the time we hosted the gang summit here and worried the whole time that we might get caught in a crossfire? This fight over funding should be a piece of cake, considering the fact that you started this center with almost no funding. If we got through that shit, we can definitely get through this."

Daniel turned to face Gerald. Daniel's face was showing signs of worry and lack of sleep. "It's different this time, Gerald. For some reason the mayor and the city council are not backing the project. They know that the center has made a tremendous difference in this neighborhood and in the lives of so many brothers who would be on the streets gang banging and shooting dope if they didn't have the center as a refuge. Word has it that my being picked up by the cops for questioning created some concerns about my fitness to act as administrator for the center."

"That's ridiculous. The cops never charged you with nothing. Name a black man in this city who hasn't been picked up or arrested and I'll guarantee you that he's related to the mayor or his bunch of lackeys. What we got downtown is a bunch of fat-assed hypocrites claiming that they want us to become respectable citizens when what they really want is for us to disappear. Sometimes I get so frustrated that I feel like goin' back to my old gangster habits, and I'm not above doin' it, if you want to put a little muscle behind your funding request."

"No, man, that's not what I want. We've worked too hard to resort to that. I've been thinking seriously about stepping down for a while and letting someone else take over, maybe you. That way my personal problems won't stand in the way of the center."

"Get real. You are the center and you know that I ain't no good as the head man. I'm good at what I'm good at, and that's keeping the brothers in line and helping out. This place wouldn't last a week without you."

"Maybe I'm just feeling the effects of the last few months. Let's do this. Use your contacts to try and get to the bottom of why we've suddenly lost favor downtown. Meanwhile, I'll check into some private sources of funding, which won't be easy with the current state of the economy."

"Sounds like a plan for the center, now what about you? You've been walking around here like a zombie. When you gonna lighten up and get a life? What's happening with Rae? You seemed to be getting tight with her before this mess happened with your old lady."

"I decided that it would be better to ease off until this thing with Latonya is resolved."

"That could take years. Every man needs a little comfort every now and then and you can't keep up this vigil with Latonya forever."

"I know, but I don't have a choice right now. I can't desert Latonya and it wouldn't be fair to ask Rae to sit on the sidelines again. The doctors are pushing Latonya's parents to have the life support turned off. I'm the only one fighting it. Maybe I'm wrong, but I sure as hell would want someone fighting for me."

"We need a break. Let's go across the street and get one of those greasy hamburgers. You look like you could use one. I'm buying, so you betta move yo' ass quickly before I change my mind."

"This building isn't big enough for us to avoid each other for the rest of our lives," Carl announced as he entered Rae's closed door without knocking. "Listen, Rae, I'm really sorry about what happened last night. I never wanted it to happen like that. I just saw you standing there and you looked so good that my baser instincts took over. Please forgive me. I know I acted like an animal and I respect you too much to treat you that way."

"I guess we both acted like animals. There is really no need to apologize. Running out like that was silly, but I was embarrassed."

"I hope you haven't sworn off me completely. Maybe you'll give me a second try. . . . Oh, I don't mean it like that. What I mean is that you'll let me show you how gentle and considerate I can really be."

"Well, you cleaned that up nicely. Let's just see what happens. I did have a great time cooking for you and enjoyed your company."

"There was a business purpose to my coming in here, also. You haven't forgotten about our meeting today with Wilbur Stanley? If he decides to take his company public, this could be a major hit for our fourth quarter profits."

"Of course I haven't forgotten. My personal life may be disheveled, but I try to keep on top of business. I've taken the liberty of bringing in a securities expert from the McDonnell firm to consult with us strictly on the securities implications. I'm generally conversant in the area, but I think it's important that we do this one right."

"I agree with you completely. You know I trust your judgment. Let me get back to my office and return a few phone calls before Stanley gets here. By the way, I am sorry for the way that it happened, but I'm not sorry that it did happen. Do you mind if I keep these as a souvenir?" He dangled Rae's black lace panties from his fingers.

"Get out of here, you animal." She laughed as he rushed to close the door, narrowly avoiding being hit by the book thrown at him. Rae sighed in agitation over her recent intimacy with Carl. It was too late to take back what she had willingly given, but her doubts continued to mount. She hoped he would not use it against her as she had seen him use information against others. Although she had no tangible reason to be concerned, regret nagged at her conscience. Rae decided she was being paranoid.

The meeting with Wilbur Stanley was grueling. Many hours of research paid off handsomely as Rae proved herself capable of meeting the challenge of such a lofty undertaking. Wilbur Stanley, in a somewhat patronizing tone, complimented Carl on having selected such a competent general counsel. Despite his obvious loyalty to Carl, Stanley was not to be denied one ounce of service. They would earn every penny of their remuneration working with this "hands-on" businessman who demanded near-perfection from his associates. During the meeting Rae noticed that Carl was being overly solicitous about everything that Wilbur Stanley said. Carl was taking the art of cultivating good business relations to a new level, but maybe she was being hypercritical of Carl because of her own insecurities, she thought.

Late into the evening Stanley mercifully suggested that they break for dinner. Rae's mind screamed to be released from any further discussions of financing or logistics, yet she knew that it would be impolitic to excuse herself from the all-important business dinner. She had learned the hard way that competence was not enough in the corporate world. Either you played the game or got passed over. And so she sat, briefcase in hand, in the back of Wilbur Stanley's limo, sandwiched between Carl and Stanley, as they traded the latest business tidbits. When an opening finally came, Rae inquired about Lynn.

"She's really not doing all that great. She's back in the office part-time since the incident with the Johnson girl, but it seems to have taken a lot out of her. It's a disgrace that the police still haven't arrested anyone in connection with the beating. We're all convinced that it was that boyfriend of hers. Apparently the police didn't have enough evidence to hold him. It's a damn shame that these criminals are allowed to roam free while decent people like us have to live in fear. I may not be able to get him arrested, but I made sure that the mayor knows how I feel about the city funding projects for that bunch of hoodlums."

Rae sat motionless from the moment Wilbur Stanley began his discourse. Heat surged through her body; she searched for air to avoid passing out. She wanted to blurt out how wrong, how ignorant, he was about Daniel, but no sound came from her mouth. Anger raced through her as she watched Carl nodding in agreement with Wilbur Stanley's blanket indictment of Daniel. Rae wanted out of the car, out of the company of two pigs wrapped in brown skin. She hated Stanley for lying about Daniel, but most of all, she hated herself for not coming to his defense. She slid into a shell of self-preservation and remained quiet until they reached the restaurant.

Rae stared in silence at the blood oozing from Wilbur Stanley's prime rib as he hurled orders at any waitress or busboy unfortunate enough to cross his path. She seethed at his excessive references to her physical attributes. Rae's obvious discomfort with Stanley's offensive behavior seemed to go right past Carl, who continued to chow down with abandon. Carl was like a puppet in Stanley's presence, reverently agreeing with every word that spouted from Stanley's vicious mouth. Unfortunately Wilbur Stanley's limitless capacity for Chivas Regal never dulled his acid wit or slowed his ability to keep everyone around him on alert.

Rae played the part of the attentive business associate, but her insides churned. Her eyes looked in their direction and she responded when spoken to, but she could only wonder, What the hell have I gotten myself into?

Stanley insisted on taking Carl home first. The thought of being alone with Wilbur Stanley unnerved Rae. He made his move the instant the door was shut on Carl, placing his sweaty palm on her knee.

"Wilbur, Mr. Stanley, I don't think this is appropriate. I would prefer that you not touch me. You're an attractive man, but I prefer to maintain a strictly business relationship with you."

"Now come on, sweetheart, I do some of my best

business when I get a little pleasure. You're not worried about Carl, are you? I can handle him. Don't blame me for trying. I'm a man. I've had to watch your tight little ass and those see-through blouses for weeks. I can't help but react to that."

"Well, it certainly was not my intention to give you any false impressions; but I don't carry on like this."

"Okay . . . I'll back off for now, but don't forget that there are a lot of things that a man like me can do for a sweet young thing like you."

"Thanks, but no thanks. I appreciate the ride home. Good night."

A whirlwind of activity surrounded the anticipated public stock offering of Stanley Enterprises, Inc. Underwriters to contact, securities attorneys to coordinate, and an endless parade of potential investors all contributed to the circuslike atmosphere pervading the office. Lacking sufficient time to think or review the avalanche of paperwork, Rae was pressed to the limit of her resources. Each night a stack of papers accompanied her home. She reveled in the fevered pace, because it enabled her to avoid confronting the lack of substance in her private life.

She became creative in her efforts to avoid Carl. He attributed her coolness to the circumstances surrounding their sexual encounter. She allowed him to continue in his mistaken belief. After considerable thought, Rae had decided that she was not interested in a repeat performance. Each time Carl suggested that they spend some "quality time" together, she politely refused. Undaunted, Carl was not willing to accept the fact that Rae was slipping away from him.

Rae heard nothing of Daniel's plight with the center, which was not surprising since she had been cut off from the friends and activities that brought them together in the past. Twice she had picked up the phone to warn him about Wilbur Stanley's vendetta. Twice she had hung up before anyone answered. It was no longer simply a matter of missing Daniel. Her pride had taken a major beating and she was determined to maintain some semblance of self-respect, even at the price of loneliness.

After several days of neglecting herself physically, she decided to spend some time in the gym rather than working all night. She had almost forgotten the high of working out until the body, saturated with sweat, transcends the point of exhaustion and enters the realm of total relaxation. Rae felt the toxins excreting from her as she wiped the salty grains from her face and rounded the curb leading to the parking lot. For once she resisted the urge to return to the office for files, rationalizing that she deserved to devote one night exclusively to the betterment of Rae Montgomery. She was so engrossed in thinking about ordering a carryout meal and curling up with a novel totally unrelated to law, that she almost bumped into the tall, dark man waiting under the street lamp.

"Gerald, what are you doing here?"

"I stopped by your office to sell you tickets to a fund-raiser that we're having. They told me you were downstairs at the gym, but the bitch on the desk took one look at me and launched into her 'we don't allow nonmembers' act. So I decided to wait outside for you."

"I'm sorry. I hope you didn't have to wait too long. I got a little carried away with the exercise tonight. What have you been up to? Look, I'm soaking wet. If you have a minute, why don't you swing by the house? You know where it is. I'll write you a check for the tickets and we can chat."

"Sounds good. See you in a minute."

Being home before midnight and having someone there to talk to was invigorating.

"I hope you like pizza, Gerald, because they're the only ones who will deliver this late. So what's the deal with this fund-raiser?"

"We're having some problems getting funding from the city. We've been workin' our asses off trying to find alternative sources to keep the center going."

"Does Daniel know that you're here?" Rae asked, almost afraid of the answer.

"No, he would be upset if he knew. I'm really worried about him. He spends a lot of time at the hospital and the rest of the time he's at the center. I keep tellin' him to call you, but he feels like he's messed with your life enough. Danny blames himself for what happened to Latonya. You know, with his Catholic upbringing and all, he's on a tremendous guilt trip. If he was plain old Baptist like the rest of us, he'd know how to deal with this. Shit happens. I don't know if you heard or not, but last week her parents decided to turn off the respirator. It blew everybody's mind when Latonya kept on breathing. She seems to be hanging in there as of the moment."

"Well, it sounds like she's improving. How did you know where I worked?"

"I have my sources. Danny keeps track of everything you're doing even though he won't call you. We heard about your position at New Hope and we're really proud of you. I always thought you were a real down-to-earth sister, even though you got all those degrees. I'm not real educated, but I read the business page every day and I know that your company looks real good right now."

"My work is the only thing that keeps me going," Rae confided.

"Will you consider coming to the fund-raiser?"

"I can't do that."

"Listen, Rae. I'm not trying to get into your business, or anything, but why don't you cut the brother some slack? My man is crazy 'bout you, but this thing with Latonya has him tied up in knots. He's miserable. You're good for him and he knows it. Danny's under a lot of pressure right now with you on his mind, Latonya in the hospital, and the cops just looking for a reason to bust him."

"Bust him for what?"

"For being a young, black man dedicated to helping other young, black men. They would love to snatch him, even if it's for something as contrived as beating up his old lady." Gerald paused to exhale in frustration. "I have a hard time understanding you and Danny. You two spend so much time doing the right thing that you both end up miserable. Where I come from, we do what feels right and say to hell with the consequences. Granted, sometimes people get hurt, but at least we're enjoyin' ourselves."

"Sometimes I wish that I could operate that way, but they have a way of educating some of that natural instinct out of you." She sighed as she bit into her third slice of pizza. "Anyway, I'm good for eight tickets."

"Whoa, baby, you just bought out my entire stock. We really appreciate it. Is there any personal message you want me to give to Danny?"

"No, no personal message, but tell him that the person who is stopping his action down at city hall is Wilbur Stanley. I'm taking a real risk in telling you this, because Stanley is the biggest client of New Hope."

"You know you can trust me not to reveal the source of my information. I appreciate your help and I won't forget it."

Chapter Eight

SONYA TALKED RAE into attending their ten-year high school class reunion. The invitation, which arrived almost three months earlier, was conveniently shoved to the bottom of her drawer in an attempt to forget that the reunion was imminent and that it had been ten years since she graduated. The sense of dread surrounding her was inexplicable, since there was no real reason for not wanting to attend the reunion. Rae was attractive, in fact she was more attractive now than in high school, having developed a few curves in places that were previously straight lines. She almost looked forward to seeing the girls who, because of their big boobs and big bottoms, were always popular in high school. Some of them would now appear overdeveloped, if not altogether fat. Time sure has a way of equalizing things, she thought.

Despite her lack of sexual allure in high school, Rae had been well liked. She easily won a position on the student council and was active in several clubs. Her only disappointment was failing to be elected as a cheerleader, which was attributable not only to her lack of curves, but also to her reserved demeanor. While other girls rushed to date and engage in sexual adventure, Rae held back, preferring to express herself through sports and in dogged preparation for college.

She was interested in boys, but not to the extent that she would risk pregnancy or do anything that might threaten her ultimate goal of becoming a college graduate. The boy she had thought was the love of her life dumped her for a more mature girl after she failed to "put out."

Rae always believed that education would be her ticket out of the cycle of poverty that had entrapped generations of her ancestors. Each degree and academic honor added a new layer of confidence, but her negative experiences as a poor, black child growing up in the South remained a specter that would haunt every success. There was always the fear that everything she had earned would be taken away. For Rae, freedom could only be found in the arms of the magnolia, where she was safe and in control. When trouble knocked, she would become a young girl again, hanging upside down from a branch of the magnolia tree. Bony legs and arms encircled bark that chafed her skin. She inhaled clean, country air and welcomed warm breezes that blew away the pain. She swung her arms free and hung suspended by the knees from the arms of the magnolia.

In reality Rae's anxiety was no greater than that of others. Rae dreaded the inevitable conversations with classmates who would weigh the significance of their lives with someone else's measuring cup. They would come to the reunion armed with photographs of pets, children, spouses and lovers. Since she possessed none of the aforementioned significant others, Rae's ears were fair game for classmates eager to unload long, involved stories that she could not appreciate. Never before had she questioned whether her life was interesting or fulfilling, but in the days leading up to the reunion she became hypercritical. Maybe she wasn't thin enough. Why was she still single when everyone else was working on their second mate? Maybe she'd take Carl as her date.

Speculation about Rae began the second she pulled up with Carl in his steel-gray Mercedes SEL. She almost panicked, feeling somewhat ostentatious and wishing she had driven her car instead. Her feelings conflicted. She was proud to be with a date driving a beautiful car, but she didn't want to be perceived as flashy. People who used material things to validate themselves, like Cynthia Bernard, wearing a full-length mink coat on the dance floor, were Rae's pet peeve.

That evening she received a lot of attention from female classmates, some of whom had snubbed her while in school for being too bookish. Rae suspected that their sudden interest had a lot to do with Carl, who looked extremely handsome in a new suit and shoes she had convinced him to buy. After being seen in public with Carl for months, she decided that his wardrobe required a major overhaul. Rae had managed to get him shopping by insisting that a man in his position needed to project an image of success, which was impossible to do in a cheap suit and bad shoes. Previous appeals to his vanity had failed, but she knew that bringing it down to a business level would strike a chord.

The big surprise of the evening was Lyle Whipple, an ex-marine, who lectured on the atrocities of war and America's true agenda in Southeast Asia. Lyle, dressed completely in army fatigues, had difficulty keeping an audience, except those unlucky enough to be barricaded in the men's john for ten minutes before being rescued by security guards. Lyle managed to bum everyone out, including classmates who knew that he had never served on active duty. As Lyle was being whisked away, his classmates rationalized that Vietnam was pretty heavy material for a class reunion. After all, they had come to lie a little, fantasize a lot, and get drunk.

An hour into the reunion Rae realized that the entertainment committee had really gotten its act together in organizing the music. Everything was sixties: the Temptations, Smokey Robinson, Mary Wells, Stevie Wonder, and the occasional Mitch Ryder and the Detroit Wheels. It was a blast from the Motown past.

Carl was being dragged onto the dance floor by an aggressive woman in a purple sequined dress. Rae was content to have a moment alone to reflect on her high school days. Across the room she spotted a good friend who she had hoped would attend the reunion. As their eyes met, she knew he had recognized her, too.

"If it isn't Rae Montgomery, the finest woman in all of Claremont High." Rae jumped up to enthusiastically greet her good buddy, Vincent Terrell, whom she had lost contact with after graduation.

"Vincent, sweetheart, I was hoping some of my partners in crime would show up. How've you been? You look great." She beamed with true affection.

"I feel great. I've been over at the district attorney's office working as an investigator for the last five years. It's working out real nicely. I don't have to ask how you've been, because I've been keeping up with your progress in the newspaper. I always knew you would make it big, even though this bunch of assholes didn't have the sense to select you as 'The Girl Most Likely to Succeed.' I know you remember that shit, how I nominated you, but they selected that lame Shirley McKenna, who is now working as an orderly in the hospital. But you showed them, Rae."

"I seem to have a knack for coming in second place. But enough about that. Let's try to be nice tonight. Did you and Delores ever get married? You guys were such a hot item in school."

"No, she left me for one of those high yellow boys, who I understand is now serving time in the penitentiary. You know I get a lot of information over at the D.A.'s office."

"You must know Brad Thompson. He graduated from law school with me and has been with the D.A. for a couple of years," Rae said.

"Yeah, I know that asshole. Nigger thinks he's white. But I just do my job and try to stay away from those fools."

"You never were shy about giving your opinions. Other than Brad, do you think the office has made any progress? For years they've been extremely conservative, almost reactionary."

"Not really. It's as bad as it's ever been. They give lip service in the press about affirmative action, but their idea of affirmative action is to hire Brad Thompson. You know the mayor tried to put pressure on them when we were being accused of discriminatory prosecution, in other words, discriminating in who gets prosecuted. It's still politics as usual over there. They spend too much time on bullshit investigations, like the one where the social worker got mugged, while important shit gets ignored. I don't know why they're so interested in the dude they questioned about mugging Latonya Johnson, but they definitely want to hang his ass. They usually don't give a damn about black-on-black crime."

"Any clues as to why they want him so badly?"

"The pressure is coming from the D.A. himself, but I know that the mayor is leaning on him for some reason. Maybe the dude is dirty, but so far the investigation hasn't turned up much. The investigator working on the case is getting frustrated. When he suggested that they look for another suspect, he got shut down. The D.A. reminded him who was in charge and said that, if he liked working there, he would do things his way. It seems like they're more interested in nailing the boyfriend than they are in solving the crime."

"You know, I'm fascinated by that case. What kind of evidence did they find at the scene of the crime?" Rae tried not to sound too anxious to avoid raising Vincent's suspicions.

"Well, they . . ."

"There you are. I was wondering where you sneaked off to," Carl interrupted at the exact wrong moment.

Rae arranged to meet Vincent Terrell for lunch on Monday, avoiding any discussion of the investigation in Carl's presence. Carl had made tremendous efforts to win her trust, but there remained a residue of doubt about their relationship—where it was going, if anywhere. Whenever she alluded to the possibility that things might not work out romantically, Carl would change the subject, insisting that she would eventually come around. His pursuit of Rae began to border on the irrational. It was clear that her affection for him had peaked and was beginning to wane, but Carl was unable to accept it.

Vincent arrived at Manny's Delicatessen, as did Rae, ahead of the appointed time. The small talk was quickly dispensed with. They both sensed that there were bigger issues on the agenda.

"Rae, I know you didn't invite me here to sample the corned beef. Your boyfriend interrupted us just as we were getting into the grit of the Johnson investigation. I could tell that our conversation wasn't finished. What's on your mind?"

"Vincent, I want all the information you can give me about Latonya Johnson's case. If this will in any way jeopardize your position at the D.A.'s office, just tell me no and I will understand completely."

"I like my job at the D.A.'s office, but you know I'm always up for a challenge. Besides, I trust your instincts and I know you wouldn't ask me to do this unless you had good reason. But I have to ask, why are you so interested in Latonya Johnson?"

"You have to promise me that you won't discuss what I'm about to tell you with anyone."

"That's a pretty tall order, sweetheart. What's little Vincent going to receive in return?" Vincent asked in a crude Cagney accent.

"Just forget it! This was a bad idea," she barked at him, pushing away from the table.

"Hold your horses, Rae. I was just teasing you. You know you can ask me for anything."

Rae relaxed and began to explain. "I was with Daniel LeMond, the man they picked up for questioning, on the night the beating took place. Daniel's not responsible for the beating. I think someone's trying to set him up."

"Are you telling me you're having an affair with Latonya's boyfriend?"

"No ... I mean, yes. I'm not seeing him anymore, but I was at the time. We decided to cool it when things started unraveling."

"Does anyone else know about this?"

"Just Daniel's friend, Gerald Austin, who works at the training center. I have no reason to suspect that he would tell anyone."

"Suspect everybody, including Daniel."

"That's ridiculous. Daniel had no reason to hurt Latonya."

"I would say that having another woman waiting in the wings is a pretty good reason. Was Daniel on good terms with Latonya?"

"Well ... no. They argued before he came to my place that night. He had decided to break their engagement right before the incident took place."

"Are you sure about that or was he giving you a line?"

"At this point, I'm not sure about anything, except that this is messed up!"

"Chill, baby ... and lower your voice. This is a favorite hangout of the boys in blue," Vincent warned her.

"I didn't come here for you to second-guess my choice in relationships. I've been doing enough of that myself."

"I'm not trying to lay a guilt trip on you, Rae. I was just playing devil's advocate, which is the only way to make sure we don't overlook anything."

The Swiss cheese on Rae's corned beef had cooled to the point of rigidity.

"Why do you think Daniel is being set up?" Vincent continued the uncomfortable inquiry.

"It's just a hunch. Latonya had just left Lynn Stanley's house when she was beaten. Daniel had left earlier, right after the fight with Latonya."

"Anything else you want to tell me?" Vincent inquired knowingly.

"Wilbur Stanley, Lynn's father, has been trying to close down the training center where Daniel is the program director. I overheard Wilbur Stanley blasting Daniel, basically labeling him a hoodlum. Stanley insists that Daniel is responsible for Latonya's beating. Why Stanley is out to get Daniel, I have no idea. I know Daniel well enough to know that he was not the one who beat Latonya. That's as deep as I want to get into it right now. Listen, Vincent, you're the only person I've told about this. I'm trusting you with information about my life that needs to be kept private."

"You don't have to worry about me, Rae. I've always loved you like a sister, even though you know I wanted more. I long ago accepted the fact that you wouldn't give me any play," Vincent chuckled. "But seriously, I suspected from day one that there was something funky going on with this investigation or shall we call it noninvestigation. Give me a few days and I'll check back with you. I need to get back to the office and start snooping. Don't worry. You know I'll take care of you. Say, if you're not going to eat that sandwich, I'll take it with me for dinner tonight. You know how it is. Single man, nobody to love me, nobody to rub me, but that's all right."

Vincent strolled out of the deli doing an exaggerated version of the "sporty walk" and humming loudly off-key. Rae sat for another five minutes, watching the chef skillfully carve dripping slabs of beef. She empathized with the animals, getting chewed up and swallowed. Her hope was that Daniel would not suffer a similar fate.

The fund-raiser at the center was a resounding success in terms of the number of people who attended and the level of interest generated within the community. Financially, the event would have negligible impact on the continued viability of the center, due to the low ticket prices and the lack of a corporate sponsor. Daniel was inspirational in his message to those in attendance, predominantly females who had come to check him out in his tuxedo. Gerald had prevailed upon Rae several times to attend, but she declined. It would be too awkward and she was unsure of how she would react to seeing Daniel again. She figured there was nothing to gain and it would just open up old wounds that would not heal.

Daniel's absence had not become more tolerable with the passage of time. Rae still hoped for a glimpse of him on the streets, a chance encounter. But she knew that chance encounters seldom happen, particularly when you want them to. Rae toyed with the idea of engineering a meeting outside of his apartment or at the center. What would she say? "Oh, I just happened to be cruising down Delaney Drive and fancy meeting you here." Her motives would be transparent and she had vowed not to humiliate herself anymore. It comforted her to believe that Daniel was somewhere missing her as much as she missed him. Sometimes she wondered if she had only imagined the intensity of their passion and the magic of their love. The thought that she might never feel that way again would make her cry.

She had to go on without Daniel in her life, as he had gone on without her. Rae's routine varied little over the next few weeks. She concentrated all of her energy on the final phase of taking Stanley Enterprises, Inc. public. The work was grueling, but she felt a great sense of accomplishment in handling such a monumental task. Carl, although generous in his praise of her work performance, was showing signs of irritation with Rae's failure to respond to him. Publicly he maintained the facade that everything was hunky-dory between them. The minute they were alone, Carl would begin to snipe, badgering her for being inconsiderate of his needs. When she finally suggested that maybe she wasn't the right person to satisfy his needs, Carl became apologetic, almost childlike in his insistence that they try to work things out.

As a birthday gift, Carl filled her office with flowers and served cake to the staff, who welcomed the break from the drudgery. That evening at dinner he slowly pulled a blue-velvet jewel box from his pocket and placed it delicately between them. Her hands trembled as she opened the box, containing perfect diamond earrings equaling two carats each. She was stunned by the magnitude of his generosity and relieved that it was not a ring.

"Carl, I can't accept these. It's too much."

"I'll be offended if you don't accept them. You know how I get when you tell me no. Since you're denying me every other pleasure, let me enjoy this one."

Rae felt the noose tightening.

The phone rang as they were opening the door to Rae's town house at the end of the evening. It was Vincent.

"Excuse me a second, Carl, I want to take this in the other room.

"Yes, Vincent, what do you have? I can only talk for a minute."

"The police report indicated that there were shards of broken glass found on the Johnson girl and heavy liquor stains on her clothing. They never located a weapon or whatever it was that was used to beat her up. The strange thing is that she was still wearing jewelry, including a Rolex watch. The only piece missing was her engagement ring. There were scrapes and scratches on her legs, which suggests that someone might have dragged her either during or after the struggle, assuming there was a struggle."

"You seem to have doubt that there was a struggle?"

"I have doubts about a lot of things in this investigation. The only thing that's clear at this point is that she received a severe blow to the head and had several bruises on her body. There was also a bite mark on her breast."

"What do you mean? Why would someone who is mugging her take the time to bite her breast?"

"Doesn't make any sense to me. It appears that the bruise on her breast was made at or near the time the rest of the damage was done. Maybe that's one of the reasons they suspect LeMond, you know, someone close to her. Have you ever known your boy to be into biting titties?"

"Don't call him my boy and you're out of line," Rae fumed. Vincent will never learn when to quit with the joking, she thought.

"I'm sorry, babe. Couldn't resist that one," Vincent apologized. "Oh, yeah, I don't have anything on the old man, yet. But I thought you might be interested in knowing that Lynn Stanley hasn't worked full-time since the incident. She's still on the payroll, but spends most of her time holed up in that big mansion of hers. Stanley visits her daily, and is obviously concerned about her condition. He has a nurse there with her almost full-time."

"Let me call you tomorrow. I have company and this isn't a good time to talk. By the way, thanks."

Walking back to the living room, Rae was consumed with this new information. Carl was oblivious to her distraction as he launched a full-scale sexual assault in front of the blazing fire. She pushed his hand away when he began tugging at her blouse.

"Carl please, this isn't a good time."

"There's no such thing as a good time with you." Carl ignored her complaining as he undressed her fully and positioned her in front of the fire. He deflected her arm as she reached for the knitted comforter draped over the back of the couch. The diamond earrings were the only item he allowed her to wear. For several long moments he stood back and looked at her, caressing her with his eyes. She felt totally vulnerable to his whims.

He unfolded her arms encircling her bosom as a shield against his penetrating gaze.

Carl sank to his knees and ran his tongue down her stomach before lowering her onto the rug.

"Open your legs," he commanded.

She lay completely still as Carl probed with his snakelike tongue. Rae tried to transcend what was happening, closing her eyes tightly in anticipation of the final assault. Daniel's image loomed inside her head. The harder she tried to erase it, the more prominent it became. She pushed Carl's head away and curled into a fetal position on the floor. Carl stood up and hovered over her briefly. Rae could feel the anger in his silence. She was too afraid to look until she heard him move swiftly toward the door. Before she could speak Carl grabbed his coat, announcing before he closed the door, "I'm sick of this game you're playing. Decide what you want, baby, you can't have it all."

Rae lay there naked, in a quandary, before the roaring fire.

Chapter Nine

WINTER'S FURY WOULD not release its hold on this sprawling midwestern city. Driving ice and snow pelted its citizens, constantly reminding them that they were powerless against the brutal forces of nature. The scenery changed from fluffy layers of white powder, blanketing the streets at Thanksgiving, to graying slush mixed with dirt and debris. Rae dreaded another day without sunshine, without a clear view of the sky. The eternal gray haze looming ominously above was an unwelcome guest, lingering for weeks, not days. An unbroken string of below-zero forecasts dulled her sensitivity to the arctic existence.

Her spirit soared the morning the sun broke through the clouds, warming her heart, if not the atmosphere, and enticing neighbors out of hibernation. An intense ray of sunlight beamed through a crack in the drawn curtain, settling upon closed eyelids, inviting Rae to awaken and enjoy the beauty of the day. The firmness of the icicles decorating the eaves trough convinced her to abandon the impulse to push open the storm windows to receive the natural air.

Ebbing faith was renewed in her ability to complete the transaction with Wilbur Stanley by week's end and to get through the final phase of this marathon endeavor. The strain was exacerbated by the growing distance between her and Carl, a distance which, according to Carl, could only be bridged by her commitment to him. His once subtle approach to winning Rae was replaced with a ramrod determination to possess her. Carl's pressure was often unspoken, but it permeated every second of every minute she was in his presence.

The dilemma made her think about work alternatives. She loved her job, but the situation with Carl was becoming intolerable. He had done a one hundred and eighty degree turn regarding his claim of being able to separate his business and personal life. Rae decided to postpone making a decision until after the closing, which was scheduled for Friday, three days away. As a grand finale to the efforts of the staff, outside counsel, accountants, and other business associates, a party was planned at the offices of New Hope for immediately following the signing. A preclosing was scheduled for Thursday to ensure that no details were left unattended that might spoil Friday's festivities.

Rae and Carl worked late into the evening, poring over stacks of documents, making sure nothing was left to chance and generally avoiding eye contact. She declined his dinner invitation, offering as an excuse her general state of exhaustion.

Quiet music on the car radio soothed her through the drive home. The magnificence of the night sky was equaled only by the beauty of the morning's sun. She drove through the streets marveling at the brilliance of the moon, the closeness of the stars. The galaxy paraded its finery in breathtaking splendor, filling her with satisfaction at having witnessed this moment in time. Her personal life was in shambles, but she was determined to get through what she hoped was a temporary period of adversity. She couldn't feel sorry for herself. A fool could have predicted the outcome of her situation with Carl.

Under the same sky that brought Rae peace and tranquility, a shadowy figure entered the courtyard of the training center, his presence imperceptible except for the sound of footsteps crackling in compacted snow. The calmness of his gait belied the purpose of his mission. Entering the building, he spotted the silhouette of a man seated at a dimly illuminated desk. His back to the door, engrossed in a newspaper article, the man at the desk did not hear the stranger close in on him, did not see the pistol as it was drawn from the assassin's waistband.

Thinking that his friend had returned with dinner, Gerald turned, laughing, to share the article. Instead he stared, mind and body frozen, down the barrel of a gun. He felt the bullet rip through his face before he could utter a sound. The victim had no time to respond, to control the final moments of life. His only movement was the twitching reflex of his feet. The swivel chair spun away before the bullet that entered his brain stilled him.

Dispassionately the assassin returned the weapon to his waistband, rearranged his black leather coat, and walked slowly, but deliberately away. The magnitude of his violence was betrayed only by the force with which he flung open the swinging doors, knocking Daniel and the dinners he carried to the ground. Surprised by the impact, the assassin lost his footing and fell on the icy walkway. Daniel sprang to his feet and advanced toward the intruder, but retreated when the killer reached for his gun.

Scrambling inside the swinging doors, Daniel rounded the corner to the office and locked the door, yelling at

Gerald to get down. Instinctively he armed himself with a baseball bat and extinguished the light with a ball hurled across the room. He stepped behind the door, clutching the bat. Within seconds the gunman blew away the lock and eased into the darkened room. A major league swing from Daniel's bat knocked the killer to the floor, causing him to discharge one misdirected round into the carpet. With his back on the ground and both hands locked securely on the gun, the assassin fixed his deadly aim on Daniel's paralyzed figure, steadied himself, and pulled the trigger. In slow motion, Daniel experienced, in the half second before the click of the gun's hammer, pieces of unfulfilled dreams. The killer squinted in disbelief at his gun held at arm's length, then at Daniel standing before him, unharmed. The gun had jammed.

Propelled by a surge of adrenaline, Daniel rushed the fleeing felon with his upraised bat, abandoning the chase when it became apparent that the intruder was in full retreat.

Even before he called out to Gerald in the darkness, even before he felt the warm, sticky substance oozing from his friend's head, he knew that Gerald was gone. A pool of blood flowed freely into the crevices between the tiles.

Fifteen minutes after Daniel's frantic call to 911, the police arrived. Vincent Terrell, hearing the report on his police scanner, arrived minutes before the police. He found Daniel sitting on the floor, obviously in a state of shock. The beat cops aggressively questioned Vincent's presence at the crime scene until a detective from the homicide division intervened on Vincent's behalf. Detective Cleveland ordered the policemen to secure the crime scene and remove all but essential personnel from the area. A group of eight curious policemen dispersed

from their immobile position peering down at the life-
less body. Vincent was relieved when Detective Cleveland, with whom he had worked on prior assignments,
took charge of the officers, instructing them to preserve
all physical evidence and minimize contamination of
the crime scene.

An angry crowd had gathered outside the yellow
plastic tape used by the police to cordon off the center.
Heated verbal confrontations ensued when police removed curious onlookers from the walkway leading up
to the center. The milling crowd buzzed with resentment
and frustration at seeing the police surround the center.
They were unaware that a homicide had occurred inside, unaware that one of their own had, once again, become a victim.

The crowd hissed and moved dangerously close as
police prepared to take Daniel downtown for further
questioning. A young boy from across the street tugged
at Daniel's sleeve, his eyes begging. "The center won't
close down, will it, Danny? You'll be back, won't you?
Please . . ." The boy's mother pulled the persistent
youth away from the patrol car, but not before shouting
to the wind, "This shit never changes, it never does. Get
the kids all excited and then disappoint them."

As the patrol car pulled away, the coroner's investigator entered the building to conduct his clinical evalu-
ation of the homicide victim. Daniel had left in time to
avoid witnessing Gerald, his friend, reduced to an object of scientific inquiry. Methodically the coroner's investigator took his scalpel and made an incision on the
right side of the body, below the rib cage. A thermom-
eter was jabbed up and into the liver to gauge the temperature, which would determine the official time of
death. Upon completion of the examination, the body
was wrapped in a body bag, strapped down on a gurney,

and wheeled into a county van. By now the crowd of onlookers had dwindled to a dedicated handful who braved the freezing temperatures. At last the curtain came down on the all-too-familiar scene of death, the crowd dispersing to their homes to wonder out loud when the violence would end.

Vincent's call came at eleven-thirty P.M., as Rae was turning off the reading light.

"Rae, you'd better get down to the police station. There's been a shooting at the center."

Her heart stopped beating.

"One of LeMond's coworkers, Gerald Austin, was shot to death. LeMond was brought down to headquarters to make a statement. I don't think he's a suspect, but he asked me to call you."

"I'll meet you at the police station, Vincent. I'm on my way."

Rae barged into the detective's office where they were questioning Daniel and insisted on speaking with Daniel alone before he answered any more questions. The hurt on Daniel's face made her heart go out to him. Suddenly she felt the impact of Gerald's death, realizing that she, too, had lost a friend. As Daniel struggled to recount the horrifying incident, Rae tried to remain calm. Rae insisted that the police end their questioning and allow Daniel to get medical attention.

"One final question, Mr. LeMond. What happened to the lamp in the office where the shooting took place?"

"I knocked it down with a baseball. I knew the guy had a gun and I wanted the advantage of darkness."

The preliminary police investigation corroborated Daniel's version of the facts, but they requested that he make himself available for further questioning, if needed. He had provided them with a detailed description of the murderer and agreed to cooperate in creating a composite sketch of the suspect.

The only words Daniel spoke as they walked toward her car were "Rae, that bullet was intended for me. I'm usually alone there at night, but Gerald agreed to help me catch up on some reports. He wanted barbecue and we flipped a coin to see who would go around the corner to pick it up. I lost the toss."

Tears dammed up for hours poured out the moment they entered her town house, his temporary shelter from the savage violence that had threatened his life and claimed the life of his best friend. Daniel shook spasmodically from the trauma, the acute realization that life's slender thread was broken without warning and without reason. Rae was helpless to alleviate his suffering. The cumulative impact of Gerald's death, Latonya's beating, and their estrangement swept over them like a tidal wave, engulfing them, taking them under. Daniel and Rae sat close and cried until fatigue overcame Daniel. He lapsed into a fitful sleep, his body curled tightly in the far corner of her bed.

Rae stood alone in the kitchen, thinking over a cup of tea. One of them would have to be rational in order to survive the crisis. She could not help but wonder why trouble seemed to be following their footsteps.

Throughout the long night she paced the floor, trying to assess the next move. Rae could not shake the irony that Gerald, who had tried desperately to bring her and Daniel back together, had caused their paths to cross again. Despite the awful circumstances, being close to him felt natural, as if they had never been apart.

When the phone rang at six-thirty in the morning, she knew it was Vincent.

"I apologize for calling so early, but I figured you would be up. It might be a good idea to keep Daniel

away from his apartment and the center for a few days,
until we catch up with the triggerman. I have a suspicion that Daniel was the one he was gunning for. This
was not just some thug or junkie off the street that
killed Gerald. It looks like a planned hit. The preliminary ballistics report suggests that the triggerman used
a .22 caliber automatic with hollow point bullets."

"Why would anyone want to kill Daniel?"

"I don't know the answer to that question. I'd like to
come over and talk to him to see if we can do some investigating of our own. We can't leave this entirely up
to the police, if we want to get quick answers. Is he up
yet?"

"No, and I want him to rest. . . ."

"I'm up." Daniel startled her as he answered from the
doorway.

Vincent agreed to meet them at Rae's house in twenty
minutes.

There was a moment of awkwardness between them.
She broke the silence by issuing him towels and a
toothbrush and busying herself in the kitchen with
breakfast. A call from Carl at the office disrupted her
thoughts.

"Why the hell aren't you here, Rae? We're two days
away from the biggest closing of this firm's short career
and you choose today to lollygag," Carl scolded.

"Lollygag! I've worked my ass off for the company
and you accuse me of lollygagging. Look, I don't want
to argue with you. I'll be in a little later this morning.
I had a personal emergency that could not be avoided.
Whatever it is can hold for a couple of hours," she
snapped back.

"I suggest that while you're taking time to handle
your personal emergency that you spend a few moments

reassessing your priorities. Personal problems are just that—personal problems."

"Is that all, Carl?"

"For now it is. We'll continue this discussion when and if you decide to grace us with your presence."

Rae hung up without saying good-bye. "That son of a bitch," she mumbled, exhaling aggressively to calm down. She had too many things on her mind to let Carl's asininity distract her.

Vincent demolished the huge breakfast of grits, bacon, and eggs while Daniel toyed with his coffee and juice. She couldn't blame him for not eating. It was difficult to muster up an appetite under the circumstances. Rae rarely prepared such a large breakfast, but couldn't think of anything else to do. In her family they always ate big during important events, like weddings or funerals. Once again, it struck her that Gerald was dead and would soon be buried. The knowing glance that passed between them told her that the same thought had entered Daniel's head. Daniel looked away quickly, resolutely replacing sorrow with anger and a determination to get the man responsible for Gerald's death.

Suddenly gripped with fear for Daniel's safety, Rae wanted to shield him from the evil that had already claimed one life, but they would not give in to Rae's protests to let the police handle it. In her heart she knew that the police could not or would not do justice. Her offer to accompany them was summarily rejected. Vincent insisted, and Daniel agreed, that Rae should go to work.

"Promise to call me if anything comes up," she pleaded.

Daniel turned to her as they prepared to depart. "I don't think I took the time to thank you for everything you've done. I know it was presumptuous of me to call on you after everything that has gone down. Gerald thought very highly of you and he was right. Don't worry about me. I can take care of myself. I'll call you later."

"How are you going to call me? You don't have my number at work."

"Yes, I do. I just never used it." He kissed her on the cheek and turned to leave as she prayed to God to watch over him. When the door was closed Rae reminded herself that nothing had changed between her and Daniel. These were unusual circumstances and she should not assume that he was back in her life to stay. Daniel needed her now, but maybe not tomorrow. She had to gird her emotions against another setback, but what she really wanted to do was to hold him and comfort him, forever.

Chapter Ten

RAE'S RESOLVE TO be strong evaporated the moment she laid eyes on the line of honorary pallbearers encircling Mount Zion Baptist Church. The men, wearing black berets and shirts emblazoned with the center's emblem, resembled a squadron of soldiers. Expressions of sorrow and anger were not masked beneath their dark sunglasses. As she walked into the church vestibule, which was overflowing with mourners patiently standing on weary feet, her uncertainty at coming washed away. Gospel sounds swept over her, replacing the sting of the criticism she had received from Carl for abandoning the office celebration.

Only fragments of the eulogy were audible from her position in the vestibule, yet the moaning and sighing pervaded the overflow crowd, which now spilled into the streets. The chill of wintry air was no match for the energy generated by the mourners who had gathered to say farewell to Gerald. She felt faint. Inside, the cries and intermittent shouts of Gerald's family and friends pierced the air as the choir sang "I'm Going Home to See My Lord."

The lump in her throat grew larger as they were ushered into the sanctuary for the final viewing of the body. As she drew near to the open African-mahogany casket, draped with wreaths and garlands of flowers cascading over the sides, her knees buckled. The damage done to Gerald's smooth ebony face unleashed anew her outrage at this savage crime. An involuntary gasp rose from her throat. She swallowed bitter tears that flowed freely.

Daniel rescued Rae from her position in front of the casket and escorted her to a seat among Gerald's family. Embarrassed by her loss of control, she buried her face in his shoulder and wept through another gut-wrenching solo. The mourners were stirred into a fit of hysterical sadness, which did not subside until they exited into the cold, crisp air.

The reflection of sunlight against the snow blinded her swollen eyes. Daniel left Rae's side to assist Gerald's mother, limp with grief, into a long, black limousine. He was surrounded by a cadre of young men from the center whose purpose was not merely ceremonial. They served as security against the violent forces that had caused them to be here today. Renewed concern for Daniel's safety sent a chill through Rae's body and she gripped his hand as they climbed into the back of Vincent's car.

Rae was impressed by Daniel's calmness during this difficult time. They sat in silence until he emerged from thought.

"Rae, Gerald was one of the smartest brothers that I know. I was too dumb to take the best piece of advice he gave me. He said I would be a fool to let you go, but I stood by and watched you being swept away by that slick dude down at New Hope. . . ."

"Oh, th-that was . . ." she stammered to explain.

"No, let me finish. I didn't interfere because I figured you have a right to carry on with your life, even though mine is at a standstill. The time that I spent mourning for Gerald, I was really mourning for myself. Losing my best friend, feeling responsible for a woman that I haven't loved for a long time, and not being able to be with you, it was all too much. And then it hit me that Gerald would want to kick my ass for carrying on like that. I heard him as clear as day say to me, 'Quit this shit.' I cannot rest until I find the man that killed him. I'm going to resolve this thing with Latonya. She lapses in and out of the coma, but she is improving. The doctors say that once she stabilizes, they'll perform neurosurgery to remove a blood clot caused by the blow to her head. She can't talk very well or walk. When she is awake she communicates a little by squeezing my hand. She will require massive physical and occupational therapy to begin to function again, but they're not sure how complete her recovery will be. The most surprising part of this ordeal is that none of her friends, not even Lynn Stanley, have cared about her recovery. Not once has Lynn visited her since she's been in the hospital."

"I'm really shocked to hear that."

"Yeah, I was a little surprised myself. I tried to convince Latonya for years that she was hanging out with a bunch of insincere, bourgeois leeches, but she refused to cut them loose. I'll do as much as I can for her until she improves. Until that happens, I won't ask anything of you, except to remember that I want you back."

"It's been enough for me just seeing you and being able to talk to you again."

Daniel smiled for the first time since their reunion.

The interment was anticlimactic after the funeral. They were drained emotionally and quickly drifted toward separate destinations to privately reflect upon the life and death of a man who had touched them all in a special way.

Daniel and Vincent dropped Rae off at her car. She cautioned them to be careful. Rae had promised to return to the celebration in progress at the office, a promise she was tempted to break. She was so engrossed in her thoughts that she never saw the white Cadillac turning the corner behind Vincent and Daniel as they headed for the freeway.

The Cadillac cruised at a safe distance, one lane over and several car lengths behind Vincent's Ford Taurus. Unaware of the white shark stalking them, they rode the freeway figuring out their next move to capture Gerald's killer. "You know, Danny, the police are speculating that there's a drug connection because of the violence against Latonya and the shooting at the center."

"Why is it that every time someone black is a crime victim, we suddenly become a suspect in a drug scam. This makes me sick!"

"Hold on, man. Don't get upset with me. You know they have a limited understanding. Whaa . . ." Vincent reacted just in time to avoid crashing into the pickup truck that stopped abruptly in front of him.

"What the hell . . ." Vincent swore as he swerved to avoid impact.

Daniel turned his head to respond to Vincent, but from the corner of his eye caught a glimpse of the killer in the Cadillac, sailing past the Taurus.

"It's him, it's him," Daniel roared into Vincent's ear, while dangerously turning the steering wheel into the next lane to pursue the Cadillac.

"The white Cadillac . . ." were the only words needed to propel Vincent into frantic pursuit. Rush-hour traffic created a tight maze for the chase, as the stalker became the stalked. The assassin's plan to follow and lie in wait until Daniel was alone was sabotaged by the sudden traffic tie-up that allowed Daniel to recognize him. The Cadillac wove in and out of bumper-to-bumper traffic, wreaking havoc on the nerves of unsuspecting commuters. One motorist crashed into the vehicle ahead of him when he noticed the white Cadillac bearing down behind him at a reckless rate of speed. Miraculously the driver of the Cadillac avoided crashing into anything, except the center highway divider, which sparked fire as metal ground against cement. In a desperate dash to avoid the slow, but persistent Taurus, the killer crossed three lanes of traffic to cut into the nearest exit. Unable to merge quickly enough to make the exit, Vincent pulled into the emergency lane, threw the lever in reverse, and drove backward to the exit, tires squealing, nearly out of control.

So frantic was their exit from the freeway that they barely missed colliding with the black-and-white patrol car that trailed the Cadillac, sailing west down a major thoroughfare at ninety miles an hour. The police were as unrelenting in their pursuit as the Cadillac was in its flight. The speed was so great, the intensity so high, that astonished bystanders expected the cars to lift from the street and take flight. The lead vehicle was brought to an abrupt halt as it veered to the left, balanced on two wheels, and came to a booming stop at the base of an ornate street lamp.

Daniel bolted from the seat of the Taurus before it came to a complete stop, ignoring Vincent's pleas to wait until it was certain that the killer no longer presented a threat. He sprinted toward the wreckage of the Cadillac, sailing past the police and then reaching in to grab the injured occupant who sneered obstinately through his pain. The police restrained Daniel from striking the killer who was pinned inside the automobile, unable to reach his weapon. Breathless, Vincent raced to the smoldering automobile and pulled Daniel away. Daniel explained to the police that the man trapped in the car was the suspect in a murder case. The police assured Daniel that the suspect wasn't going anywhere until the fire department arrived to pry him out of the car.

Nosy spectators filled the streets when it appeared safe to approach the twisted mass of metal and steel. Sirens blared as police and firemen began the task of unraveling the trail of destruction left by the killer. Several innocent bystanders had been injured while fleeing from his path, but no one was killed.

Two hours later, Alfredo Manuel, suffering only from minor scratches and bruises, was booked and charged with the murder of Gerald Austin.

The relief that Daniel experienced was incomplete. Something was missing. They knew that Alfredo Manuel was merely the instrument of destruction and not its mastermind. Vincent and Daniel vowed to continue their probe until all the pieces fit together. Daniel tried unsuccessfully to reach Rae with the good news, but was informed by her secretary that she had left the office for the day.

Chapter Eleven

RAE STAGGERED INTO the vestibule of Carl's house, feeling unnaturally high from the two glasses of champagne she drank at the office. Rae's long limbs folded into the nearest seat, as she struggled to collect herself. Carl extended a glass of champagne in her direction.

"Ready for a refill, Madam General Counsel?" His lips were smiling, but his eyes were not.

"No, thanks," Rae responded, slurring every syllable. "I don't feel so good. Do you mind if I lie down?"

"Go ahead. I'll check on you in a minute."

Wilbur Stanley smiled slyly at Carl as they watched their unsuspecting victim stumble to the bedroom. The loud music and rowdy crowd were no match for the drug-induced stupor that overcame her. After two more hours of entertaining, Carl and Wilbur Stanley were ready for the main event of the evening. Remaining guests were ushered out to their cars, some unwillingly, while Carl checked to make sure that Rae remained under the influence of the barbituate he had slipped into her drink. Indecision gave way to anger as Carl looked down at Rae, sprawled helplessly across his bed. He rationalized, She made me do this. She could have had everything, but she betrayed me. If I can't have her, then I don't give a damn who does. Stanley wants to check Rae out, then so be it. After all the time and money I put into her, she should be good for something.

Rae's wrist fell limp as Carl ran his hands over her inanimate body, the body he had touched, but never possessed. Ambivalence over the act he was about to commit caused Carl to hesitate, saying to himself, "It's really a shame. You're so beautiful."

"What are you waiting for, man? Get her clothes off," Wilbur Stanley demanded as he entered Carl's bedroom, spilling drops of Chivas Regal with each step.

"Shhh," Carl cautioned. "She might hear you. Stand back in case she wakes up unexpectedly."

"Not likely, with the number of pills I gave you," Stanley said with a smirk.

"I only gave her half. Don't forget, this isn't our typical slut," Carl reminded Stanley.

"Yeah, but they all got the same pussy and tits," Stanley chortled as he seated himself in the corner, awaiting the show.

The sun beaming down overhead alerted Rae that she had slept past noon. Her eyes strained against the light as she stretched and took a deep, cleansing breath in an effort to shake the lethargy clinging to her. Carl entered his bedroom smiling, much too cheerful for her current state of mind.

"I hope I didn't make a fool of myself last night. I don't know what happened, but the champagne really got to me," she apologized.

"No problem. The party broke up shortly after we got here and I let you sleep it off. Here's a little breakfast in bed for my favorite lady and the morning paper to start your day."

"Thanks, Carl. That's very thoughtful. Let me wash my face first."

Her legs were shaky and her head pounded as she made her way across the plush, off-white carpet. Carl had hung her clothes neatly in an antique chest, her favorite piece of furniture in the room, and dressed her in his black silk robe.

The bags under her eyes startled her as she dared to glance in the mirror. She decided to take a quick shower to remove the stale makeup and wake herself up. The warm, steamy water felt good on her skin, but could not cleanse the guilt she felt for being here with Carl. Sleeping with Carl was the last thing she had wanted to do. To make matters worse, she couldn't remember if she had done anything. Emerging from the bathroom, she noticed the tension in Carl's shoulders as he stood reading the paper.

"What is it, Carl? What's happened?" she asked, afraid of the answer.

"Oh, nothing important. Looks like they found the guy who did the shooting over at that training center."

She grabbed the newspaper from his hand and began reading the story.

Suspect Arrested in Training Center Homicide

Police have arrested a suspect identified as Alfredo Manuel in connection with the homicide of Gerald Austin, which occurred earlier this week at the Medgar Evers Training Center on the city's east side. The arrest took place after a high-speed chase, which caused minor injuries to several bystanders. The suspect eluded the police for several blocks before his vehicle crashed into a street lamp, ending the drama. Shortly after the crash, police were informed by a witness that the man pinned inside the vehicle was the suspect in the Austin murder. Firemen were called to the scene to pry the suspect from the wreckage of his late model Cadillac sedan. The suspect suffered only minor injuries in the crash. Ironically the arrest occurred on the same day of the funeral for Gerald Austin. Police have declined to give any further details of the arrest, since it is the subject of an ongoing investigation. Alfredo Manuel was booked on murder charges. The arraignment is scheduled for Monday.

Before the paper could hit the bed, she raced to the chest for her clothes.

"What's this? No time for breakfast? That article sure got you going."

"I don't have time to talk right now. I'll explain later."

"Don't bother. I understand more than you think I do. I think you get a kick out of dashing out of my house like Superwoman."

His comment puzzled her, but she was too distracted to stop and discuss it. Rae zoomed through the city streets, oblivious to speed limits and lucky to make it home without running over anyone. She thought, I am really something, staying out all night drunk while major shit is happening.

A note slipped under the door awaited her arrival. Daniel had tried to reach her with the news, but couldn't find her. He had left a number where he could be reached.

Vincent answered the phone.

"Vincent, it's Rae. Is everything okay? Is Danny all right?"

"Yeah, he's fine. We had a rather productive time yesterday, but I'll let him tell you about it. He's right here."

"Hi, Rae. Listen, everything is fine. No one is hurt. I tried to call you, but you had just left the office."

"I'm sorry, I . . ."

"You don't have to explain. You're a big girl and I expect you to have a life of your own. I was just disappointed that I couldn't share my excitement with you. Anyway, Vincent helped me find another apartment. I don't think it's safe to go back to the old one."

"But you can stay at my place."

"No way. That's too dangerous, in more ways than one," Daniel insisted. "You know I'll have to testify at the trial and it's best that I keep a low profile until things settle down."

"Does that mean I won't be seeing you?"

"No, I couldn't take that. I'll stop by later and fill you in on the details."

She was pissed that Daniel wasn't jealous or anxious to see her. Vincent came back on the line. When the conversation ended, Daniel made popcorn and pulled out a six-pack of beer before taking a seat next to Vincent on the living room floor of his new apartment.

"What exactly are you looking for in the newspaper?"

"I have no idea, but my instincts tell me there's a clue somewhere in here."

"In the sports page?" Daniel questioned.

"Probably not, but you can't be too careful with these investigations." Vincent laughed at himself. "I'm bullshitting you, man. Thought I'd check to see how my team did last night before I get seriously into my Sherlock Holmes mode. Why don't you put on one of those Sly Stone compact discs to create the proper paper-reading atmosphere."

Daniel questioned his sanity for spending the next two hours dealing with Vincent.

"You want another brewsky?"

"No man, I have to drive home."

"So what's gonna happen now that we have the suspect in custody?"

"Thanks to my keen intuition, my never-ending perseverance, not to mention my excellent power of persuasion, yours truly has managed to get himself appointed as the official investigator on the murder case. The D.A. will talk with Alfredo Manuel's attorney. If they can cut a deal, we may know fairly soon who ordered the hit. If not, we keep digging on our own. What are you going to do in the meantime? Pick up where you left off with Rae?"

"That's a loaded question. I wish it was that easy."

"You worried about Carl?"

"Oh, you know him?"

"Yeah, we met at the class reunion. I wouldn't worry too much about Mr. Black Executive. He's an empty suit, if I ever saw one."

"So, Vincent, what's your angle on all this? What are you after?"

"Same thing you're after, but I don't stand a snowball's chance in hell. I don't have your looks or Carl's money. Rae and I have been friends for a long time. Whether I like it or not, we've reached an understanding that friendship is all that will ever come of it. Is friendship enough for you?"

"No."

"At least you're honest. I gotta get out of here. I'll talk to you in the morning."

"Right." Daniel closed the door and sank into memories of the hours spent wrapped inside Rae's softness. He wanted desperately to feel her again. She was the one who made him care about something other than the myriad social causes he had dedicated himself to.

He realized that his life as Latonya's appendage had been a way of avoiding personal decisions. Latonya had made all the decisions, submerging them in a social enclave that contradicted his political philosophies, but gave him the entrée he needed to get his programs funded. Daniel had lingered in the cycle of hypocrisy, repulsed yet unable to break away. When his chance for happiness came, he missed out by floundering in a sea of uncertainty. He didn't want to miss out again.

Chapter Twelve

ALFREDO MANUEL'S FLOOR-LENGTH black leather coat and matching attire were traded in for the standard blue jumpsuit issued at the county jail. Manuel's .22 automatic pistol recovered at the scene of the car crash fit the description of the murder weapon. His black alligator cowboy boots, which were seized as evidence, matched footprints found inside the center and on the walkway leading up to the center. Detective Cleveland had done an excellent job in preserving the evidence by maintaining a detailed evidence log and taking ample photographs and prints at the crime scene.

Alfredo Manuel knew police procedures well, having made his living as a paid gunman from the age of eleven. He knew enough to maintain his silence, especially among the other prisoners, who sometimes received favors by acting as informants. The coldness of Manuel's red eyes streaked with broken veins made him an unlikely subject for light conversation. He refused to eat at first, figuring that he would be released very soon. His rap sheet was three pages long, with charges, but no convictions, as an adult felon. Alfredo Manuel was as skillful in evading the law as he was in the use of weapons.

Anticipation turned to agitation when Manuel's private lawyer failed to appear. He had resigned himself to spending the weekend in jail, but expected the man who hired him to send an attorney to prepare him for the arraignment on Monday.

Manuel's mind flickered with anger as he sat in the crowded holding cell, waiting for his case to be called. A thin, well-dressed female approached the pen, balancing several files in her arms.

She called out, "Alfredo Manuel. Hi, I'm Cindy Spelling with the Public Defender's Office. I'll be representing you this morning."

"Fuckin' *puta*, you ain't representing nobody. I got my own lawyer." Manuel pounded his fists and spat a thick wad of saliva, which trickled down the screen of the cage. Two bailiffs removed him forcibly, his curses trailing off into an echo as he was returned to his cell.

His body shook with rage as the realization set in that he had been abandoned by the person who hired him to lay open the head of Daniel LeMond. He had done exactly as instructed and could not be blamed because the wrong man sat at the desk that night. For the first time he felt like a real prisoner, with no one on the outside to help him.

His concentration was broken by the sound of the guard's gravelly voice announcing, "Alfredo Manuel, your lawyer is here to see you, if you're up to it now."

"What lawyer?" he asked, hoping in vain that his client had come through for him.

"The P.D., Ms. Spelling. Want to see her or not, boy? We got a lot more inmates to deal with than you," the guard added impatiently.

Manuel hung his head in resignation and answered, "Yes, I want to see her."

Cindy Spelling appeared far too fragile to be a jailhouse lawyer. Her pale-pink cashmere jacket almost matched the color of her flawless skin. Cindy's polished appearance clashed with the harsh environment in which she met her clients. Criminal law was the profession she had chosen, having passed up opportunities to practice a more genteel, though less emotionally challenging, brand of law with cronies of her father, a retired superior court judge.

Alfredo Manuel shored up his machismo image by surveying Cindy Spelling from head to foot.

"What can I do for you, baby?" he said with a sneer.

"No, it's not what you can do for me that we are here to talk about, Mr. Manuel. You have a very serious murder charge hanging over your head and it doesn't appear that you can walk away from this one as you have from the prior charges against you. The prosecutor is coming after you for the big M. They seem to think that they have enough evidence to make it stick."

"What do they have?"

"Well, they haven't revealed everything. That won't happen until later. I have read the police reports and it appears that they found a gun in your car, which they believe is the same gun used in the killing. They have your shoes that match footprints made at the scene, and more importantly, there is a witness who can place you at the scene of the homicide. I'm not here to prejudge you, but to defend you. Now, if you're willing to cooperate, I'll see what I can do for you."

"Man, you got a lotta fire for such a little broad. What do we do now?"

Cindy Spelling cringed at his reference to her as a broad, but realized the futility of arguing semantics with him. "First, you go to the arraignment and enter a plea. I assume that plea will be not guilty, is that correct?"

"You got it."

"Then I'll talk to the D.A. and find out what he has in mind and we go from there. I think you should know that there are a lot of people out there paying close attention to this one and the D.A. is under heavy pressure to wrap this case up quickly. Is there anything you want to tell me before I talk to the prosecutor?"

"No, I'd rather wait until tomorrow."

"By the way, I noticed from your record that you were previously represented by an attorney named Phillip Moreland. Is he the lawyer you were expecting to come to your defense this time?"

Without responding, Alfredo Manuel winked at her impudently as he was led away by the guard. Cindy Spelling grumbled to herself, "I don't know where this jerk gets off trying to belittle someone who is being paid to help him. Sometimes I wonder why I do this job, but then again, I do it so well." She smiled, packed her expensive leather briefcase, and walked out.

Immediately following the arrest of Alfredo Manuel, Vincent Terrell had launched his own investigation of the suspect. There was little doubt that Manuel was the one who pulled the trigger that killed Gerald Austin. There was also little doubt that Alfredo Manuel acted merely as a paid assassin, carrying out a badly executed murder contract. Phillip Moreland's name featured prominently in the criminal record of Alfredo Manuel. Vincent had a strong suspicion that if he could determine who Moreland was working for, he could establish the motive behind the killing. Vincent knew that it would not be as simple as researching the information in *Martindale-Hubbell*, the reference book concerning attorneys and their principal clients.

Phillip Moreland was a high-profile criminal attorney with close ties to well-financed crime figures. His firm, through political maneuvering, which often bordered on extortion, garnered a substantial quantity of city and county legal business. Attorney Moreland, impeccably attired in custom-tailored suits and sporting slicked-back hair, often bragged about taking his street savvy into the courtroom and beating the good old boys at their own game. Cunning was his middle name and he treated the pimp and the professional to an equal dose of intimidation. Only legitimate clients would be listed on the client reference list for the Moreland firm, but it was the unnamed clients who were the bread and butter of his organization. They paid the rent on his lavish office space and put gas in his Rolls-Royce.

After years of trying to establish grounds to disbar Moreland, the State Bar had given up on it. Moreland was a master at going right to the edge of violating the rules, such as tampering with his clients' trust accounts, without falling over. Vincent recalled the negative publicity the firm had received several years ago when a disgruntled client barged into the law office with a sawed-off shotgun, demanding a long-overdue settlement check. When the receptionist confronted the deranged client, he blew a hole the size of a grapefruit through her chest. Having overheard the ruckus, Phillip Moreland barricaded himself inside his office until police arrived to restrain the rampaging client. In his quest to find Moreland, the gunman had killed a total of three people. Phillip Moreland, the survivor, had escaped unscathed.

Vincent Terrell headed for the best place in the city to obtain information, the Fox's Lair, home of the best prime rib and a happy-hour haven. They were all there, the up-and-coming attorneys, judges, a small contingent of sports figures, and the most beautiful women in the world angling to hook up with any of the aforementioned groups. A quick survey of the room revealed that Moreland was not present, but several attorneys from his office were seated at his favorite table near the back of the restaurant. Moreland always insisted on being seated facing the door to keep his eye on everyone in the room. Vincent purposefully seated himself at the bar next to a paralegal from Moreland's office, someone he knew from school.

"There he is, my main man. What's been happening?"

"Aw, nothing much, just trying to stay ahead of the crowd," the paralegal responded, heartily slapping hands with Vincent.

"You guys been as busy downtown as we've been at my office?"

"Yeah, man, Moreland snatched some new contracts from the city and we been bustin' our butts to stay on top of it."

"Where is the boss man, he's usually here at happy hour, isn't he?"

"He's been meeting a lot with one of our clients who just closed a big deal last week. Speak of the devil, they just walked in. You can always tell when the boss man comes in because the ladies rush to the rest room to powder their noses, ha, ha."

The joke was wasted on Vincent who spun on the bar stool to observe Phillip Moreland enter the Fox's Lair with his friend and client, Wilbur Stanley.

Vincent's first call was made anonymously to Cindy Spelling who was working late, reviewing files for tomorrow.

"Ask your client, Alfredo Manuel, about Phillip Moreland and Wilbur Stanley." Click ... Vincent hung up before Cindy could say anything.

Damn, I wonder what that was about? she thought,

quickly jotting down the names still fresh in her memory.

Vincent's call to Rae began with an apology. "Listen, I know I shouldn't call you at the office, but I need to talk to you this evening."

"Is something wrong with . . ."

"No, he's fine, but I have some new information I want to run by both of you. Is seven-thirty a good time for you?" Vincent asked.

"Make it eight-thirty at my house," Rae suggested.

"I'll bring Danny with me. See you then."

"Your theory doesn't make much sense to me. Why would Wilbur Stanley want to kill me? I've known him for a long time. He doesn't like me, but he has no reason to want to kill me," Daniel queried as he paced around the living room of Rae's town house.

"Remember the warning I sent to you a few months ago through Gerald? I warned you that Wilbur Stanley was behind the push to shut down the center." Rae forgot that she had sworn Gerald to secrecy.

"So you were the source. Gerald gave me the information, but refused to divulge the source. I didn't believe it then and I'm still having trouble understanding why a high roller like Stanley would waste time bothering with someone like me. In fact, he was the one who helped me get funding for the center when I was starting out. Everybody knows that Wilbur Stanley has a direct pipeline to the mayor. Latonya talked to Lynn and Lynn talked to her old man. He wasn't thrilled about the idea, but Lynn always gets what she wants."

"You obviously pose a threat to him in some way and we've got to figure out what that is," Vincent said reflectively. "Have you had any arguments or disagreements?"

"We always did a lot of verbal sparring. We don't see eye to eye on many issues, but there was never anything serious. Except ... except the night that Latonya was attacked. He was at Lynn's house when Latonya and I were arguing. I was trying to convince Latonya to leave with me, but she refused. I grabbed her arm and Stanley jumped in and insisted that I leave immediately. We didn't trade blows or anything, but I was pretty ticked off with that whole crew."

"If it's true that Stanley is behind the killing, then that means Daniel is still in danger. He can just hire another hood to do what Alfredo Manuel couldn't do." Rae turned to Vincent.

"I already thought of that. The best way to protect Danny is to go on the offensive by putting the finger on Wilbur Stanley. That way we neutralize his power."

"I think you're right, Vincent. Don't you agree, Daniel?" Lost in his own thoughts, Daniel failed to acknowledge Rae's question.

"I knew you would agree with that approach and so I already put the plan in motion. By tomorrow morning Alfredo Manuel's attorney will be asking the right questions to get the attention focused on Wilbur Stanley. If you're ready to leave, Daniel, I can drop you off at home," Vincent offered.

Rae was definitely ready for them to leave. She was feeling distant from Daniel, whose thoughts were obviously focused elsewhere.

Daniel was too immersed in his own thoughts to notice Rae's agitation. He would spend the night thinking about his relationship with Wilbur Stanley and trying to unravel the mystery of "why."

A record two days and two nights in custody at the county jail had begun to wear on the patience of inmate number A-728, Alfredo Manuel. His lucrative business had accustomed him to a better style of life. Rest would not come easily. His heavy eyelids fluttered fitfully as he fought against sleep. Just after midnight he succumbed to the inevitable sleep induced by the rhythmic drone of the toilet drain in the adjoining cell. Just after midnight the prisoner approached him, jagged blade in hand, intent on canceling Alfredo Manuel's date with tomorrow.

All through the night the name Wilbur Stanley danced in Cindy Spelling's head. Cindy knew she had heard it somewhere, before the anonymous phone call. It was like playing a game of Trivial Pursuit, but someone forgot to provide the answer. She bolted upright in the bed as the chimes of the grandfather clock signaled twelve-thirty. The suddenness of her movement startled her sleeping husband. She assured him that she was merely restless and insisted that he go back to sleep. On the excuse of getting a cup of hot cocoa, Cindy visited the study where she rummaged through old newspaper articles until she uncovered the one that had dogged her sleep. There on the front page of the business section was a photo of Wilbur Stanley, Carl Anderson, and several other business people announcing the sale of Stanley Enterprises, Inc. The article made her impatient to uncover the connection between a respected businessman like Stanley and a thug like Alfredo Manuel.

Cindy's preoccupation with this new information caused her to swerve out of control in her BMW while exiting her exclusive suburban neighborhood. Sweat beaded under her arms as she assessed her near slide into the steep ravine. The cream-colored leather seats felt suddenly sticky and warm, at odds with the subzero temperature. She cursed the car dealer for not installing the sheepskin seat covers before delivering the car. She was on a mission and neither sleet nor ice would dampen the enthusiasm that she felt about her work for the first time in several months. Lately she had found herself questioning her motivation in continuing to work as a public defender when there were several other opportunities available to her. Her physician husband had stared disbelievingly when she accepted the position after graduation from law school. His attitude was almost as surprised as when she announced her intention to attend law school at age twenty-six after two babies and six years of marriage. Cindy had decided that there were more important things in life than entertaining doctors' wives.

Great, she thought, I'm the first attorney making it down to lockup this morning to "order up" my client. She felt that this was going to be a productive day.

"Hey, Gus. Give me Alfredo Manuel, if you would."

"I'd like to, Ms. Spelling, but he ain't here. You'll have to try the infirmary. Looks like your boy got involved in a little scrape last night."

Gus's words were lost in the wind beneath Cindy Spelling's billowing cape as she sprinted toward the jail infirmary.

"Alfredo, who did this to you?" she pressed impatiently while surveying the heavy bandages wrapped around the left side of his face and shoulder.

"I don't know. He didn't leave his calling card."

"Quit being a smart-ass. Somebody tried to kill you and I want to know why."

"I couldn't see him. It was dark, but somebody had to let him in my cell. Probably one of your nice guards trying to earn a little extra money to send his kids to college."

"The main question that you need to answer is who

put him up to it. Don't you see that it's a vicious cycle? They pay you to kill somebody and then they pay somebody to kill you. You're a smart guy. I'm sure you realize by now that your friends, or shall we call them business associates, have deserted you. You're in this alone and unless you let me help you, they'll come after you again. Now, I know who Phillip Moreland is. What is Wilbur Stanley's involvement?"

"I don't know what you're talking about."

"Okay, I see that you're going to allow yourself to be used as the sacrificial lamb. I'm withdrawing from your case. You don't need a lawyer, you need a bodyguard."

"No, wait, please. I need your help. What's the best deal I can get, if I cooperate?"

"Right now you're facing the death penalty or life without the possibility of parole, if they convict you of murder for hire. If no special circumstances are found, the maximum penalty is twenty-five years to life. We can negotiate for manslaughter, but the prosecutor will probably not settle for less than second-degree murder. We're talking somewhere between fifteen years to life."

"I can't spend my life in here."

"We can ask the prosecutor to recommend a reduced penalty, but the actual sentence is up to the judge.

"Now what about Wilbur Stanley?"

"Stanley hired me to kill the dude who runs the training center, Daniel LeMond. He was supposed to be there alone that night. His friend was there instead and I popped him by mistake."

"Why did Stanley want Daniel LeMond dead?"

"I never ask why. I just do what I'm paid to do. Will I have to testify against Stanley?"

"Of course, you're the only person who can link him to the murder."

"And how do you propose to protect me while I'm in this joint?"

"I'll have you placed in protective custody during the trial and I'll see what I can do about getting you beyond Stanley's reach thereafter."

"My instincts told me to pass on this hit. This is the first time I've gone after a dude who wasn't as dirty as me or the man that I was working for. From now on I'm gonna stick to drug dealers, hustlers, and political con men. They don't get no protection from the Man Upstairs."

"Are you saying that you've done this before for Wilbur Stanley?"

"I ain't saying nothing, except that, if he hadn't tried to fuck me over, I would never have turned him in. I ain't letting the state fry my ass while that freak runs around free as a bird. I want that son of a bitch in here with me so I can collect on the debt he owes me."

Chapter Thirteen

WILBUR STANLEY SHIELDED his eyes against the flash of cameras and the shouts of reporters pushing and shoving to catch a glimpse of this powerful man being led into the courthouse by his attorney. Phillip Moreland locked his paralyzing stare on an attractive female reporter who had unwittingly shoved her microphone into his face.

"I'm going to say this one last time. As I indicated to you in my office this morning, we will have a statement for the press following the arraignment. Be kind enough to allow my client and me to proceed to the courtroom to answer these absurd charges. And you, young lady, had better get control of that microphone before I charge you with assault with a deadly weapon." The group roared with approval as the always-colorful Phillip Moreland began his routine of working the crowd. He would entertain, dazzle, and seduce them. Like puppies, the yipping reporters trailed Moreland and the unusually reticent Wilbur Stanley into the courtroom.

Moreland had advised his client to tone down his mode of dress and to forsake the heavy diamond-encrusted jewelry that had become everyday ornaments. Moreland appeared exceptionally suave in his hand-tailored charcoal-gray suit, reserved especially for this occasion. On the other hand, Wilbur Stanley seemed to have aged considerably in the two days since he was notified of the arraignment. He stood drawn and shrunken before the judge as the charges against him were read. How could this happen? This was his city, his courtroom, his judge, and his district attorney who were indicting him like the common criminals he had preached against with great passion and conviction. How could the mayor let this happen? Had the mayor lost control of these officials Stanley had helped to get elected?

Amid the circuslike atmosphere of the courtroom, Wilbur Stanley stood mute, eyes glazed with disbelief as his attorney entered a plea of "not guilty." The common people had arisen early to get a seat to witness the man whose wealth they envied and whose power they despised being charged with first-degree murder and conspiracy. Overnight Stanley's cronies had become lukewarm in their loyalty to him. The issue was too hot in the community and they would be criticized if they wholeheartedly supported Stanley. The mayor had launched into a swearing rage when he heard from the district attorney that charges against Stanley were imminent.

The assistant district attorney initially assigned to prosecute Alfredo Manuel had leaked the story of the allegations against Stanley before the district attorney could muzzle him. Vincent sat in rapt attention as the assistant district attorney detailed the information against Stanley and bragged how he had blown the story wide open, giving little credit to Cindy Spelling and no consideration to how he was damaging his future with the D.A.'s office. His future as a prosecutor ended the moment his boss got wind of the story, but not soon enough to stop the calls to the news media, to supporters of the training center, and to Gerald Austin's family.

Spectators gasped in disbelief as the judge ordered Stanley released on a one million dollar bond, a mere pittance in view of his profit from the sale of Stanley Enterprises, Inc. An elderly woman hissed in disgust as Stanley was allowed to walk free down the courthouse steps where Phillip Moreland held a press conference, while his client was whisked to his chauffeur-driven limousine.

"What we have witnessed here today is a travesty of justice. We won't talk about Wilbur Stanley's fine reputation in this community or the many dollars that he has contributed to help the poor and the oppressed. We have seen an innocent man accused of a crime that he did not commit and his reputation tarnished on the basis of lies told by a two-bit criminal." Phillip Moreland had begun his sermon, but was interrupted by a question from a sharp reporter.

"Mr. Moreland, isn't it true that Mr. Stanley retained you in the past to obtain Alfredo Manuel's release from jail?" The reporter caught Moreland off guard.

"Gentlemen, gentlemen, and ladies of course," he said, stalling for time. "Our purpose today is not to put Mr. Stanley or me on trial here on the courthouse steps. I suggest, first of all, that you check your sources before you make slanderous statements that could subject you and your employer to substantial liability. Let me conclude by stating that my client will resist these false and malicious accusations through every legally available avenue."

The reporter whispered to his colleague, "And some not so legally available."

Phillip Moreland swept past the hounding reporters and entered the limousine in a huff.

"Somebody is fucking with us, Wilbur. They're feeding information to the media that they would be too stupid to know without some help. We need to get to the bottom of this quickly," he advised the visibly shaken Wilbur Stanley who sat cowering in the corner as they sped away.

Tension hung in the air at New Hope like smog in southern California on a hot summer day. The few employees who had not received advance warning about the charges against Wilbur Stanley were alarmed to see security guards at the elevators checking identification as they arrived for work. No one, except staff, was allowed to enter the offices without express clearance from the president, Carl Anderson.

On the advice of Vincent Terrell, Rae reported to work as usual, although she longed to witness Wilbur Stanley brought to justice. Carl was not his confident self when he assembled the staff to explain the reason for the added security.

"As many of you already know, Wilbur Stanley, one of our main clients, has been charged in connection with a homicide that occurred a couple of weeks ago. The news media is extremely anxious to get any information it can about Mr. Stanley, whether or not it has any bearing on the charges against him. Our official corporate policy is 'no comment.' You are not to discuss Wilbur Stanley or his dealings with this firm under any circumstances. The penalty for any infractions against this policy is instant dismissal. We have retained additional security to protect you against media intrusions. In the event you notice strangers in the office, please report them immediately to the head of security. Mr. Stanley is a trusted business associate as well as a longtime friend and I expect you to keep that in mind during his time of need. Remember that he is innocent until proven guilty and also remember that his business has contributed greatly to keeping you all employed. Thank you for your attention and now let's get back to business."

Rae expected Carl to be supportive of Stanley, but she felt that he had gone overboard in attempting to put a "gag order" on the employees who would inevitably have a high level of interest in the Wilbur Stanley affair. Just last week Stanley was in the office dispensing orders and partying with total abandon. Rae had already glimpsed Stanley's dark side and convicted him in her mind, an untenable position in view of her position with the company. All day she sat glued to her chair, dreading the inevitable confrontation with Carl, searching for a way to explain that his confidence in Wilbur Stanley was not well placed.

Rae's decision to seize control of the situation led her to his office where she tactfully closed the door and instructed his secretary to hold all calls until further notice.

"We need to talk about the situation with Wilbur Stanley. The whole office is buzzing about it and yet you have not mentioned one word to me, your general counsel," she began.

"What is there to say about it? It's a criminal matter that has absolutely nothing to do with our business relationship with Wilbur. I thought I made it perfectly clear to the staff, which includes you, that we are to maintain neutrality in this matter."

"So now I'm staff, am I?"

"You know perfectly well what I mean. You have never liked Wilbur Stanley and I am sure that you were thrilled with the new developments."

"Like has absolutely nothing to do with it. I have always respected him as a businessman, but you know that on a personal level he's a viper. From day one he tried to treat me like a piece of ass and you did absolutely nothing to discourage him."

"I figured that Little Miss Independence could take care of herself."

"I can take care of myself. Are you so blinded by the dollars that you can't see that this man has participated in a murder?"

"Now watch yourself, sweetheart. You're an attorney. I shouldn't have to remind you of the old 'innocent until proven guilty' theory. Don't be so naive that you let your emotions mess up a good thing."

"And what good thing might you be referring to? Certainly you're not referring to our relationship."

"Of course not. You messed that up a long time ago. I'm talking about your job. Wilbur Stanley's business has paid my salary and yours, which is quite generous, I might add. Really, Rae, I thought you were more sophisticated than this. If you're going to be in the big league, you'd better learn how to play the game. You let your little schoolgirl crush on that lowlife at the training center ruin all this." Carl made a sweeping gesture with his hand.

"How do you know about Daniel?"

"I know everything about you. You betrayed me, Rae. Betrayed me after I invested a lot of time and effort in you. You know I had to thoroughly investigate the woman I was planning to marry, the woman who would bear my children. I gave you plenty of time, but you couldn't get over him. I have to give him credit. He totally messed up the plan."

"The plan? I am not a plan! I'm a human being. You can't decide my life for me, as if I were a machine. You were the one who foolishly insisted that we could separate our business and personal lives. I admit that I was partly to blame. I wanted this job so badly that I tried to make things work between us. When I tried to be honest with you, you wouldn't listen. I wasn't about to make the biggest mistake of my life and commit to you for the sake of a job. I thought you were a decent man, but I was wrong about that, too. You're insane, insane with power, as insane as your friend Wilbur Stanley. You think you can control everyone and everything around you. I feel sorry for both of you." Rae stared in disbelief at the man she had almost trusted. Carl had made her feel guilty for not being able to love him. Now she realized that her instincts had served her well. She backed away from him, moving toward the door, afraid to ever turn her back on him again.

Miraculously she survived the long drive from her office to the district attorney's office. Rae was in a state of total confusion. Without offering an explanation to anyone, she had grabbed her coat and purse and had run from New Hope as swiftly as her legs would carry her. One quick stop at a pay phone to call Vincent brought no results. She proceeded in the direction of his office, desperate to talk to the only person who could appreciate her dilemma.

Pulling into the parking lot, she saw Vincent getting out of his Taurus. Rae drew his attention by wildly honking her horn while searching for a space in the crowded parking lot. Vincent's brow furrowed in an expression of concern as he sensed her manic excitement. Rae blabbered unintelligibly as she attempted to roll down the window of the car. Vincent came around to the passenger side and sat next to her.

"Slow down, Rae. Now tell me what's happening."

Recounting her argument with Carl, Rae expressed

her suspicion that Carl might be involved in the murder. "If Carl knew about Daniel and me, maybe he put Wilbur Stanley up to putting the contract out on Daniel."

"Whoa . . . Let's not jump the gun. Sure the guy is an asshole, but we don't have anything at this point linking him to the killing. I'm sure he was jealous when he found out you were giving the goodies to Danny boy, but that doesn't make him a killer. Did he say or do anything specific that would point to his involvement?"

"Yes. He said that Daniel had messed up his plan. The nut had everything figured out—marriage, children, and who knows what else. He's really tight with Wilbur Stanley and I think they're both crazy enough to try anything. I was at Carl's house the morning I read about the arrest of Alfredo Manuel. When I told him that I would call him later to explain why I had to rush out, he told me not to bother because he understood more than I thought he did. Can't you see, he knew about Daniel all along, even though he never said anything. I think he's had me under surveillance."

"What I see is that this has gotten you all hysterical and you're starting to see ghosts. I thought you had stopped seeing Danny after you went to work at New Hope."

"Well, I had . . . I have. After the thing happened with Latonya, we sort of mutually agreed to separate. Carl and I hung out together, but there was never any commitment on my part. He wasn't too happy with that, but my heart wasn't in it. I hadn't seen Daniel for months before Gerald died. Even now we're just good friends."

"That's a bunch of crap. I feel the vibes between you two every time you're in each other's company."

"Vibes or not, this is a very confusing time for both

of us and shit just keeps happening. I think we're cursed."

"Notice how I got you to calm down by mentioning Daniel's name." Vincent gave Rae a much-needed friendly hug and asked her to wait while he ran inside for messages. Rae had to agree with him that she was in no condition for driving.

They headed for the bar. Rae asked in passing if he would help clean out her office at New Hope.

He exploded. "Clean out your office! What the hell for? Carl didn't fire you. You're not going anywhere, at least for the time being. We need you on the inside to see everything that goes on. If your hunch is right, and I'm not sure that it is, how else will we get the goods on Carl? He's not going to come out and confess to you or the police."

"But I'm afraid of him now. It will be too eerie being around a man that I suspect of murder."

"He doesn't know that you suspect him. He just knows that you don't like his friend, Wilbur Stanley. I'm not asking you to sleep with the man. It might be a good idea to avoid being alone with him until we can straighten this thing out."

"I doubt seriously after today's conversation that he'll be pressing me for any private moments. I ought to have my butt kicked for getting involved in any of this. It's all because of men. From now on I am swearing off men."

"Let's hurry up and get some alcohol in you. You're starting to crack up."

Happy hour extended into the wee hours of the morning. Vincent and Rae talked a lot about high school days, intentionally avoiding the subject of Carl. She knew that Vincent's secret agenda was to pump her up for the task before her, to remind her of what a brazen bitch she had to be in order to face the Carl Andersons and Wilbur Stanleys of the world. Rae's ego needed reinforcing, having suffered greatly from the acknowledgment that her big career move to New Hope was fizzling fast.

Quiet voices deep inside goaded her to let it all out, cry like a helpless baby, but she knew this wasn't the time for self-pity.

As a young girl she had succumbed to pressure and allowed a boy's teasing to bring her down from her place high up in the arms of the magnolia tree, where she was secure and strong. The boy teased that only tomboys climbed trees and perched on branches. She had allowed him to shame her into deserting her position of expanded vision. Once Rae was down on the ground, the boy had little to offer her, save taunts and tales of what little girls should be and ridicule for what she was not. Having reached the ground, she could no longer ascend to the space where new growth blossoms and where birds feed their young. She became ordinary, earthbound, without freedom to feel the wind against her face. Sympathy and tears would have to wait.

Chapter Fourteen

CINDY SPELLING SAVORED her position of power as she met with Ralph Lundin, the assistant district attorney assigned to prosecute Wilbur Stanley. She had locked horns with Lundin on a prior occasion. Despite Cindy's herculean efforts to secure an acquittal for her client, the outcome was predictable. The jury was not inclined to acquit a felon with several priors, whether or not he was guilty of the crime with which he was currently charged. Ralph Lundin had been like a shark in pursuit of her client, wrongfully accused of burglary.

In contrast, Lundin seemed almost cavalier in his approach to the murder charge against Wilbur Stanley, focusing instead on the lack of credibility of the principal witness, Alfredo Manuel. It was clear that Lundin, who openly aspired to become the next district attorney, intended to treat the Stanley case with kid gloves. Secretly he was incensed that his boss had saddled him with a case where he had so much exposure at this politically sensitive time. Like all prosecutors, he hated to take on a case where there was a risk of defeat. He approached Cindy cautiously, as was his style in all matters, complimenting her on her excellent defense strategy in their recent battle. Cindy doubted whether he could have mustered the compliment had he not been victorious.

"As you well know, the preliminary hearing is going to be critical because of the nature of the evidence against Stanley. I have an investigator working full-time on the case, but our case hinges on the allegations of your client. I'll need to interview Manuel in order to properly prepare for the prelim."

Cindy pivoted in her high-backed executive chair, superior in quality to the county's standard issue furniture. She paused long enough to give Ralph cause for concern before responding, "No problem, as long as I'm there while he's being questioned. Let me warn you, Ralph, that I will not tolerate any attempt by you to put my client on trial. Keep in mind that he is your witness, but first and foremost, Alfredo Manuel is my client. I will not allow any questions that go beyond the scope of Wilbur Stanley's involvement in the homicide."

"That goes without saying, Cindy." Ralph feigned a smile. "I anticipate that Phillip Moreland will move to have the preliminary hearing in closed court to avoid prejudice to his client. I hate like hell having to face Moreland in court. You know what a barracuda he is."

"Maybe you should withdraw from the case, Ralph, if you feel intimidated by Moreland. He's not invincible, nobody is."

"That was a low blow. You know that I'm not intimidated by anyone. What I meant is that he is a master at manipulating the media and you know that his favorite twist is to insinuate that there is something racist about the prosecution."

"I wouldn't worry about that too much. There are more people incensed by the killing and the violence in their community than there are people who support Wilbur Stanley. I think you should capitalize on the rich and ruthless versus the poor and oppressed angle. That's really what this is all about. Did you talk to Daniel LeMond?"

"I haven't had a chance, but he's at the top of my list. He's the guy who tracked down your client, isn't he?"

"Yes, and he may be the only one who can tie this whole thing together."

"We did pull a background check on LeMond that revealed that he is not as poor as he pretends. Did you know that he's from a very wealthy family?"

"You're missing the point, Ralph. The fact is that he is working for the poor, despite the circumstances of his birth. Some of us do not define our mission in life on the basis of how many dollars our daddy has in his pocket."

"Touché, Ms. Spelling. I think this poverty law thing is starting to wear on you."

"Seriously, Ralph, how well you present your case is important. A lot of eyes will be watching to make sure that you go after Wilbur Stanley with the same zeal that you exhibit when you prosecute your everyday, run-of-the-mill suspect. This is the first and probably the last time that I will wish you success in your efforts. Do let me know if I can assist you in any way." Cindy smiled in satisfaction at having put the screws to Ralph Lundin who slunk back to his office to lick his wounds.

A few days later Daniel was complaining to Rae: "I can't believe they gave the case to that prick, Lundin. Of all the D.A.'s in that office, they had to pick the biggest Nazi in the bunch. We might as well concede defeat, if we have to depend on him for justice."

"You have a right to be upset, Daniel, but you know how political the district attorney's office is. Ralph Lundin does have the reputation as one of the best trial lawyers in the office and I'm sure that once he stops dragging his feet everything will work out," Rae assured him, while remaining unconvinced herself.

"Here I am, best friend gone, my life in danger, and dependent upon some geek to protect my interests. I hate this feeling of powerlessness. Maybe we should sue Stanley ourselves."

"A civil action by Gerald's family makes good sense, but if they let the State pursue the criminal action first, we will gain a lot of information at the State's expense. No matter how the criminal proceedings turn out, a civil action is a viable option."

"Do you think there's a possibility that Wilbur Stanley will get out of this?"

"It's possible."

"Lundin seemed to be disappointed with the information I gave him. He said it was a lot of hearsay and supposition on my part. He was upset when I refused to disclose the source of my information about Stanley trying to shut down the center. I told him to subpoena the mayor and ask him why our funding was cut off. That really ticked him off."

"If necessary, you can use my name."

"Are you kidding? Lover boy over at New Hope would really appreciate that. I can see the headlines, 'General Counsel Snitches on Principal Client.' "

"Some things are more important than a job."

"I never thought I'd hear Miss Gucci/Fiorucci say that."

"Look. Just because things aren't going your way doesn't give you the right to attack me. I have my own problems, which I'm sure you have been too busy to notice. I've gone out of my way to be supportive and I'm not altogether sure why." Rae's voice began to crack as her anger intensified. Patrons in the intimate restaurant glanced furtively toward their table as they sensed the escalating argument.

"Oh, baby, I'm sorry. I got carried away with everything that's been happening." Daniel reached for her hand to smooth things over, but she recoiled from his touch.

"Do you think you're the only one that bad things have been happening to? I have sat around for months being the understanding fool while you played Prince Charming to Sleeping Beauty. You don't even appreciate how hard it is for me to do my job while siding with you against a man who is the bread and butter of my firm. This thing is tearing me apart from the inside and I have no one to turn to because you have other priorities."

"I thought that I was doing you a favor by giving you space. I know you're seeing Carl Anderson, and I didn't feel that I had the right to interfere with that. I tried to avoid creating a conflict at your job by not making demands on you while this is going on. Does Carl know about our relationship?"

"We don't have a relationship, remember? And no, he doesn't know about our past relationship." She lied because Vincent had insisted that she not reveal to Daniel her suspicions about Carl.

"We have a major communication problem. We've been skirting the issue of 'us' for long enough. What do you want, Rae? I didn't try to get next to you because I thought you would feel disrespected."

"I don't want anything, except to get my Gucci purse and get out of here," Rae said. She grabbed her things and dragged her bruised ego out the front door of the restaurant with such fury that the windowpanes rattled for seconds after her departure.

"But we haven't had dinner. We need to talk," he

yelled after her, hastening to pay the tab before pursuing her clicking heels.

"Where are you going? The car is the other way. Let me take you home and we can have a nice, calm discussion. You won't solve anything by running out like this. At least slow down. You know I can't keep up with you."

Purse swinging, coat flying, Rae continued to walk fast and hard to work out her anger. She knew better than to say anything because it would come out harsh and dirty. She must have walked half a mile with him maintaining a safe and silent distance behind her, realizing that she would not respond until her anger subsided. Once her breathing resumed a normal pattern, Rae turned to walk in the direction of the car. Daniel tested her resolve by slipping his arm around her shoulder, which she summarily shrugged away.

Dead silence prevailed as they rode pensively in the direction of her house. His detour caused her to break the silence.

"Where are you going?"

"I thought we could use a neutral zone to talk," he explained, pulling into the parking lot of a downtown hotel known for its entertainment. Rae sat alone in the lounge, listening to jazz and ordering drinks while he made a phone call. Women appraised him with desire in their eyes as he reentered the room.

"Rae, I have a confession to make. Part of the reason I've been acting like an ass and saying things to you that I don't mean is that I'm jealous of you and Carl. I have tried to act like a liberated man and not stifle your freedom, but it is kicking my butt. Every time I think about you with him I literally kick the walls, and you know the walls are not too sturdy in my apartment. I've just taken the liberty of getting a room upstairs. I'm not trying to be disrespectful. The room has double beds and I promise to leave you alone, if you want. I just wanted to spend some time with you tonight. I don't want to be alone. I've been alone so much lately that I can't take it anymore."

His fingers traced the lines in her palm. Then he gently squeezed her hand. She would not look at him. Rae focused on the bass player, hugging his instrument close to his body. As the set ended, Daniel took her hand and led her to the upstairs elevator. Over her objection that she had to work in the morning, he ordered sandwiches and champagne from room service.

"I promised you a celebration tonight and all I've done so far is make you sad. Let me make it up to you and I'll make sure you get home in time for work."

Their evening began as it should have several hours before. They ate and talked until the hour dictated that they turn in. He flipped a coin to see who would get the bed near the window. She lost, but he gave it to her anyway. Rae undressed in the bathroom, slipping into the soft, fluffy robe supplied by the hotel. Crawling under the covers, she felt shy. Daniel kissed her on the cheek, tucked her in, and thanked her for putting up with him before retiring to his side of the darkened room. Rae lay there in the dark for what seemed like an eternity, feeling dumb for having initiated the separate sleeping arrangement. She could hear him turning under the covers in the bed next to her. He was naked and tired, but too restless to sleep.

"Are you asleep?" Daniel asked.

"No."

"Are you sleeping with Carl?"

"Not tonight."

"Can I sleep with you?"

His answer came in the way she reached for him as

they climbed out of bed. Rae opened the robe to shield
him. They stood skin to skin for the first time in
months, their fingers intertwined. Daniel's kisses began
tenderly. His hands skimmed the outline of her body,
causing the hair on her arms to stand on end. Her robe
dropped to the floor. He sat in a chair and pulled her
down in his lap, facing him. Her thighs straddled Daniel's firm, muscular thighs. Rae's mouth found his and
they kissed hard, their tongues probing desperately. The
tension of his erect penis pulsed beneath her as he
sucked each breast. He exhaled deeply when she raised
up to allow her fingers to play in circles below his
waist, then eased slowly downward to take him in. She
remembered how perfectly they fit together, how he
was the inverse mold from which her body was formed.
Grabbing onto the back of the chair, she moved in tan-
dem with him, selfish in her satisfaction, taking everything as quickly as she could.

Rae fell against him in apology. Daniel responded by
lifting her to the edge of the bed and kissing her thighs
before entering her. Her legs were raised over his shoulders, secured against his chest, as his hips led into her
repeatedly. At last they reached that level of commu-
nion where hostility and doubt dissolved and nothing
stood between them, except the quiet harmony of their
breathing.

Daniel, completely satisfied, collapsed on top of her.
Tenderly he asked if he was crushing her. She dared
him to move.

The lovers basked in the joy of their reunion until the
talk became too serious. He tried to bait Rae into discussing Carl, but she evaded his questions. The cloak of
jealousy fell over him when it became clear that she
would not satisfy his curiosity. She wanted to keep him
guessing.

"I'm going back to my bed if you insist on acting like this," Daniel threatened.

"No problem with me," she answered nonchalantly.

He rose, in a huff, and jumped into the other bed. Rae waited fifteen seconds and jumped in behind him.

"That other bed was getting kind of messy," she teased him as they began messing up his bed.

Chapter Fifteen

THE WARM GLOW within Rae's heart was fueled by lengthy conversations about nothing during hours spent in front of the fire enjoying Daniel's company. Her state of bliss was marred only by Daniel's growing frustration in his efforts to reopen the center and his anxiety about the impending preliminary hearing, which threatened to become the media spectacle of the year. The city took notice when the mayor was summoned to appear at the hearing.

"Mayor Barnett, can you comment on being subpoenaed to testify at Mr. Stanley's preliminary hearing?"

"Yeah, I can comment. It's bullshit, pure bullshit. Who ever heard of the mayor being called to testify in a case that doesn't involve him?"

"But, Mr. Mayor, the prosecution is alleging that you succumbed to pressure from Wilbur Stanley to cut off funding for the Medgar Evers Training Center."

"Now you know me better than that. That's a damned lie. When have you ever known me to succumb to pressure from anybody? This city is facing a major financial crisis, which means that many programs, no matter how popular, will have to be cut. Private sources are going to have to do their part and fill the gaps. What does cutting funds have to do with this ridiculous murder allegation anyway? I think the D.A. is stretching to prove his case and in the process is tarnishing the reputation of one of the finest citizens in this community. Those responsible for this witch-hunt will be held accountable for their actions."

"Are you threatening the D.A. for doing his job?" The reporter egged him on.

"This interview is over. I don't have time to talk to people who ask stupid questions."

"Mayor Barnett, Mayor Barnett . . ." a chorus of reporters pursued the feisty mayor, veins popping from his forehead, nostrils flaring as his bodyguards cleared his entrance into the courthouse.

The atmosphere inside the courtroom was electric. Reporters unable to squeeze their way inside the packed courtroom crowded the corridor. Contrary to the expectations of Ralph Lundin, the defense did not request a closed court, fearing that such a move would be perceived as an admission that Wilbur Stanley had something to hide. The decision infuriated the mayor, who loathed the idea of being grilled in public about his connections with Wilbur Stanley. The mayor was less concerned about answering questions regarding the training center. He had taken great care to follow the proper procedures to eliminate the funding. All important discussions on the subject were held in private, during dinner and over drinks. Out of curiosity the mayor had asked Stanley why a rinky-dink operation like the training center was of any importance to him, but Stanley had declined to answer. He didn't care that Stanley used up political favors on insignificant matters, so long as campaign contributions continued to flow.

The mayor's testimony added little to the prosecution's case. As expected, the mayor categorically denied receiving any requests from Wilbur Stanley to terminate funding for the training center. Phillip Moreland declined to cross-examine the mayor, figuring that to do so would only reinforce the prosecution's theory of cronyism between the mayor and Wilbur Stanley.

The prosecutor, Ralph Lundin, scanned the courtroom nervously, as if searching for land mines planted by the defense. Lundin was unusually well-dressed for the preliminary hearing where he could set the stage for a much-needed victory in his quest to become district attorney. Lundin's initial discomfort with handling the case had been replaced with enthusiasm once he realized that his campaign was lagging due to his lack of visibility among the electorate. During his five years in private practice and ten years with the district attorney's office, Lundin had scored an impressive string of victories, but he knew that elections are not won solely on the basis of past victories. Since he began exploring the possibility of running for office, Lundin noticed that a change had taken place in the mood of the voters. His platform needed to be crafted cautiously to give his candidacy broader appeal. A straight law-and-order platform no longer assured him dominance in the election. He would need a few votes from within the inner city to guarantee his election. Inch by inch the opposition, left smoldering during the last decade in the ashes of conservative fire, had found enough converts among the recession-racked electorate to threaten Lundin's lock on the election. Lundin needed a clear and decisive victory to kick off his campaign.

Ralph Lundin called Alfredo Manuel as the second witness. "Mr. Manuel, you have testified that you were hired by Wilbur Stanley to kill Daniel LeMond and that you mistakenly shot and killed Gerald Austin. When did Mr. Stanley hire you?"

"Three days before the shooting."

"Describe for the court the circumstances surrounding your hiring by Mr. Stanley."

"I got a call from my contact who told me that Mr. Stanley had a job for me and to meet him that evening at the Fox's Lair to discuss the deal. When I got there he told me who I was to hit and when I was to hit him, but he blew it because he told me that LeMond would be there alone. He paid me half the money, twenty-five hundred dollars, and told me I'd get the other half when the deal was completed. That is, when LeMond was dead."

"Did you ever meet Mr. Stanley face-to-face, prior to this assignment?"

"Yes, my contact set it up. I told Stanley that I could handle jobs for a fee. We agreed that all instructions and money would flow through my contact."

"Did Stanley hire you to do other business prior to this assignment?"

"Yes, I did a few jobs for him."

"Was the procedure for payment and receipt of instructions handled in the same way for those prior assignments?"

"Yes."

"I have no further questions for the witness."

Phillip Moreland took three deliberate steps toward the witness, then paused to assess his prey.

"Mr. Manuel, have you been given anything in return for your testimony against Wilbur Stanley?"

"Well, yes."

"What was it?"

"The charges against me were reduced to second-degree murder and I was placed in protective custody."

"Why do you need protective custody, Mr. Manuel?"

"Because Stanley tried to kill me."

"Are you suggesting that Mr. Stanley came into the jail and tried to kill you?"

"No, he had someone inside try to stab me to death."

"How do you know that, Mr. Manuel?"

"Because that's the way he works."

"Aren't you attributing an awful lot of power to a man who, according to your own testimony, you only met once? Isn't it true, Mr. Manuel, that you don't know who tried to kill you and that your entire testimony against Mr. Stanley is based on speculation?"

Ralph Lundin sprang to his feet. "Objection, counsel is asking the witness a compound question."

"Objection sustained. Rephrase your question, Mr. Moreland."

"Isn't it true that you have no actual knowledge of who stabbed you?"

"I guess so."

"Isn't it also true that you never spoke directly with Mr. Stanley regarding a hit on Daniel LeMond?"

"Not directly."

"How would you describe your occupation, Mr. Manuel?"

"I'm an enforcer."

"Can you give us a little more detail?"

"I carry out orders given by people who hire me."

"These orders entail performing illegal acts, is that correct?"

"Of course it involves illegal acts. They wouldn't need me to do legal acts." A repressed snicker spread through the courtroom.

"Who is your contact, Mr. Manuel?"

"I'm not saying."

The judge interceded, "Mr. Manuel, you will answer the question or be held in contempt of court."

"So what. I'm already looking at years in the slammer. A couple more days won't hurt. I don't snitch on nobody who deals fairly. I wouldn't be here testifying against that bastard Stanley if he hadn't tried to fuck me up."

"Mr. Manuel, you would say anything about anybody to get yourself out of a first-degree murder charge, wouldn't you?" Phillip Moreland tried to keep him on the ropes.

"No. I'm not like your boy over there, I got some sense of honor."

"When did you suddenly acquire this sense of honor? Was it at age eleven when you committed your first robbery or at age twelve when you stabbed a kid in the elementary schoolyard? . . ."

Lundin bolted from his chair. "Objection. Mr. Manuel is not on trial. Any alleged prior criminal acts of Mr. Manuel, particularly juvenile acts, are irrelevant and inadmissable."

The judge angrily interceded, "Mr. Moreland, you are way out of line and you know it. Don't try my patience here. Objection sustained."

"I withdraw the question, Your Honor." Moreland gloated over the damage he had done and proceeded to the next question. "How long had you tried to meet Mr. Stanley before he agreed to see you?"

"About a year."

"Were you not introduced to Mr. Stanley as a private investigator?"

"Yes, I was."

"You have testified that instructions were given to you secondhand through an unidentified contact, is that correct?"

"Yes."

"Would you tell us specifically what was said to you

when you were given instructions regarding Daniel LeMond?"

"My man told me that LeMond would be alone at the center at a certain time and that the old man wanted me to go in and silence him."

"Go in and silence him. Had your contact used those exact words before, say in connection with previous employment?"

"No, not exactly."

"How did you know what he meant by the term silence?"

"I'm a professional, I've been in this business for a long time."

"If you're such a professional, how did you manage to shoot the wrong man?"

Anger spewed from the humiliated witness who shot back, "That wasn't my fault. I did what I was told to do. They owe me." Moreland moved in on his prey.

"Isn't it possible, Mr. Manuel, that your contact was referring to someone other than Mr. Stanley when he referred to the 'old man'?"

"I knew who he meant." Alfredo Manuel began to stammer, caught in the web of the master legal technician.

"Does your contact refer business to you from other sources?"

"Yes."

"Isn't it true that some of those other sources are older males who could also be referred to as the 'old man?' The fact is, sir, you didn't know who was hiring you to do what and the only thing that you gave a damn about was whether you got paid!"

Manuel lunged from the witness box, reaching for the throat of Phillip Moreland who had drawn dangerously close to launch his intimidating questions.

Evading the choke hold of the towering bailiff, Alfredo Manuel screamed, "You fancy black bastard, you are no better than I am. I'll kill you for trying to fuck with me." Manuel was dragged away hurling threats in a mixture of Spanish and English. His starched shirt provided by the D.A.'s office was pulled above his head by the bailiffs grappling with his flailing feet and arms.

Sweat beaded on the brow of Phillip Moreland, still clenching his perfect capped teeth as he rearranged his silk suit. Grease mixed with sweat trickled down from his chemically processed hair to his forehead. Moreland welcomed the judge's decision to adjourn, ending the morning session on the exact dramatic note he had orchestrated.

Rae had ignored Vincent's suggestion to stay away from the hearing. Sitting glued to her chair in the courtroom, she was appalled by the serious damage done to the credibility of the prosecution's principal witness. Rae dreaded the inevitable attack that would be leveled against Daniel when court reconvened. Making her way to the door of the attorney's conference room, she recognized the desperate voice of Ralph Lundin. He was being loudly reproached by a woman in the room with him. Rae's timid knock on the door was drowned out by the volume of their argument, which halted the instant she entered the room. A red-faced Cindy Spelling stood shoulder to shoulder with Lundin.

"I'm Rae Montgomery and I have information that can help you in the preliminary hearing."

She was rushed into a seat at the small conference table and began to tell her story of Wilbur Stanley's vendetta against Daniel.

An hour later she was sequestered outside the courtroom until other witnesses, including Daniel, completed their testimony. She was fighting an internal battle to keep her nerves intact. A hush fell over the courtroom as she was called in. The media people leaned forward in anticipation of her surprise testimony; the defense braced itself for the axe that was about to fall. Until this point the prosecution had failed to show any evidence of Stanley's ill will against Daniel. Rae could not answer why the malice existed, but could testify that it did exist. She knew that without her testimony the prosecution could fail in its attempt to establish probable cause. Without her testimony Wilbur Stanley, the man she believed to be responsible for Gerald Austin's death, might not be brought to trial. With this massive motivation as her armor, she took the longest walk of her life down the narrow aisle to be sworn in as a witness.

Rae's appointment as general counsel of New Hope had featured prominently in local business news. The fact that she was instrumental in the sale of Stanley Enterprises, Inc. added spice to the already sizzling story. Several reporters hounded Rae as she fought her way out of the chaotic courthouse. Taking the risk had paid off, at least in the short run. Wilbur Stanley would face charges of murder and conspiracy. Rae prayed silently that she had done the right thing by testifying.

"Miss Montgomery, will your testimony today affect your firm's relationship with Mr. Stanley or your position as general counsel of New Hope?"

"No comment." Overwhelmed by a sea of reporters and overzealous spectators, she was unable to comment because of the gag order issued by the judge. Rae settled in next to Daniel in the car. The cameras continued to click. She was too tense to relax, despite his reassurance that she had done an honorable deed by risking her own privacy and security for the sake of justice.

"I'm really proud of you, Rae, even though you broke your promise to stay out of this."

"How could I stay out of it when the prosecution was going up in smoke?"

"I know, I know." Daniel patted her shaking hand.

"Aren't you at all concerned that all this publicity might get back to Latonya?" Rae asked.

"It's out there now. It's all out in the open. Frankly, I'm relieved." Daniel squeezed her hand, lighting up her world with his smile.

She had one stop to make before going home to unwind. Word of Rae's testimony had reached New Hope faster than she did. Rae proceeded directly to her office, ignoring the stares and whispers of employees stunned by her appearance in the office. She called her secretary in to prepare a letter of resignation. When the task was completed, the secretary turned to leave without comment, but upon reflection spoke up.

"You have my respect for what you're doing. Most of us in the office, except Mr. Anderson, of course, think that Wilbur Stanley is guilty. We hate to see you leave."

Carl stormed into the office before Rae could say thanks.

"Did you consider the damage to the firm when you launched this vicious campaign against Wilbur Stanley?"

"I considered everything and everyone before I made my decision. I told the truth and you know it. You were in the car the night Stanley made his statements about Daniel and the center. You don't care about anyone, except yourself and how much money you can make."

"What I know is that your little idealistic ass is blowing it for everyone," Carl fumed as he advanced toward Rae, whose only protection was the desk between them. Instinctively she grabbed a tortoise-shaped crystal paperweight from the desk, aimed it at his head, and prepared to release it. The door was flung open before she could launch her weapon. Fortunately Daniel had ignored Rae's instructions to wait in the car and sprang on top of Carl like an angry lion. Security hastily intervened to break up the scuffle, but not before Daniel left the imprint of his fingers around Carl's neck. By now the entire staff had assembled in the doorway to witness the debacle. Several staffers gathered around to see if Rae was all right. Rae played it to the hilt, leaning on Daniel and claiming alarm at the vicious manner in which Carl had attacked her. No one came to Carl's assistance, except his security guards who asked if he wanted Daniel arrested. Shaken, but eager to avoid more adverse publicity, Carl insisted that the incident was a simple misunderstanding and urged everyone to return to work. The guards ordered Daniel and Rae to leave. She reminded them that she was general counsel of the firm and would leave when she was ready. Rae turned to Carl and informed him in a detached, confident voice that her resignation would be on his desk in ten minutes.

Daniel and Rae left New Hope that afternoon, their hands firmly clasped together. The unreality of her shattered career and her newfound celebrity as a witness for the prosecution combined to throw Rae's world into a tailspin from which she would not soon recover.

Chapter Sixteen

RAE'S FIRST FEW days of unemployment were therapeutic, giving her time to catch her breath and clean up her house. She began making fancy meals, which she and Daniel consumed by candlelight. After the third straight day of baking bread, she realized that she needed something more to do. Rae feared that she would gain a hundred pounds and go stir-crazy in the process of becoming an icon of domesticity.

She understood completely Daniel's frustration at not operating the center. Daniel had decided to postpone reopening the center until after the trial. Gerald's death created a vacuum in his spirit, which he was having difficulty coping with. Funding had all but dried up after the shooting and he knew that a totally revamped approach was mandatory to nurse the program back to financial health.

He begged her to have patience and not do anything foolish, like taking a mediocre job. "Don't blame yourself for what happened at New Hope. You did an excellent job there and you know it. This will all be over in a couple of months. If it's the money, I can help you."

"No, it's not the money. I just feel helpless, sitting here and doing nothing all day."

"You're not doing nothing. You're taking care of me."

"Yeah, for how long? Until Latonya gets out of the hospital?" The much-dreaded topic was out in the open again.

"No. I made a promise to you that I intend to keep. Latonya is making steady progress, according to her doctors. They expect to transfer her from the hospital to a rehabilitation center soon. The frustrating part is that she still doesn't remember what happened to her. Every time I bring up the subject, she gets weird—like she's scared of something. I don't want to put unnecessary pressure on her, but I need to know. It's a bad feeling having people looking at me suspiciously, like I'm some kind of woman beater."

"Anyone who knows you would never think such a thing. People have short memories. They're probably trying to figure out what you're doing with me rather than thinking about the incident with Latonya."

"Our relationship isn't much of a secret since the preliminary hearing and your departing performance at New Hope. It's you that I love and you shouldn't have any doubts about it. I'm doing for Latonya what I would do for any friend.

"Look, you and I have had to deal with a lot of crap recently. Why don't we take a vacation to someplace warm—maybe the Yucatán Peninsula in Mexico."

"It sounds tempting, but I really should stay here and try to get my life back in order."

"Forget order for a minute. I need to get away from here and so do you. Is it a ticket for one or tickets for two?"

Her decision took five seconds. "Tickets for two."

She barely had time to retrieve her Spanish dictionary from a box in the basement before Daniel returned with tickets in hand. Fretting constantly that she needed more time to prepare her out-of-season wardrobe for the trip, she still managed to arrive at the airport early the next morning.

Juxtaposed with her sense of excitement was quiet fear that the trip might dull their passion. Maybe he had only wanted her because she was the forbidden fruit, she thought. She was afraid not to be afraid in case of disappointment. Why couldn't she accept the good things while they were happening instead of worrying about the boogeyman lurking around the corner?

The quaintness of the airport at Cancún excited Rae's sense of adventure. The absence of trams, moving sidewalks, muffled announcements over the public address system, or elaborate arrival and departure boards immediately caught her attention. The people of Cancún appeared busy, but not frantic; friendly, but not obtrusive. Sixty miles beyond the city of Cancún was Akumal, a place better described as a village—and their first rest stop on this two-week trip. Their villa had all the necessities, including air conditioning and excellent service, but none of the trappings of first-class American hotels. The only telephone was in the lobby of the hotel and cable television had not reached Akumal.

Entertainment consisted of sitting around grass huts on the beach that served as bars. The threat of "Montezuma's revenge" restrained Rae from ordering the elaborate tropical drinks that were favored by uninformed foreigners. *Cerveza* became the drink of the day, although she never drank beer before. But Rae needed no intoxication, so intoxicating were the unlit beaches and the gentle brush of waves against the shore. She soaked up the relaxed atmosphere surrounding her and savored the respectfully distant attitude of the guests. They were all there for different reasons, but they had one reason in common—to leave the headlines and unpleasant world events behind them.

Rae also soaked up too much sun. Daniel was attentive, but not sympathetic to her distress at overexposing herself. Rae had hit the beach with a vengeance. She became a sun junkie, starved for heat, defrosting from the chill of a brutal midwestern winter, and determined to get more black, more beautiful as rapidly as possible. She grimaced as Daniel smoothed the ointment over her roasted upper chest, which had received the severest burn.

"From now on I'll regulate your sun-worshiping hours. Some people don't know when they've had enough," he kidded her.

"Don't make fun of me and get your hands off my butt. That's not where the sunburn is."

"No. But it's where something else is." He cooled the pain with moistened lips, carefully avoiding the affected area while giving maximum attention to everything else. She moaned, not from pain, but from relief. Her concern that their passion would be lost had been completely unfounded.

After four days of languishing on the beach at Akumal, she was left with the constitution of a dishrag, too limp to find out what was happening with the rest of the world and too satisfied to care. Nighttime on the beach brought a display of phosphorescent waves that streaked across a jet-black sky, sprinkled with lanterns of pointed light. They walked slowly down the beach, feet pulling through heavy sand, not knowing where the sky began or where the water ended.

Invigorated by the restfulness of the preceding days, they awakened ready to venture deeper into the interior to explore the ancient Mayan ruins. A paperback purchased in Cancún, detailing the many theories about the decline of the Mayan civilization, kept them company during the long drive through the countryside. Rae studied the history of the Mayas with enthusiasm. She was fascinated by the distinct physical attributes of the people living in the remote areas. Their sloping foreheads and compact stature were very similar to those of the people in the photos in the book.

Rae talked nonstop about the people and the culture they were exploring. "Apparently the Mayas abandoned their cities and fled to the rain forests around A.D. 900. We're headed for Chichén Itzá, which was subsequently occupied by the Toltec warriors from Mexico." By the time they reached Chichén Itzá, Daniel was ready for a break from the history lesson.

The city screamed with ancient culture from the sacred cenote, a deep cavern surrounding an underground water source into which offerings of jewelry, precious metals, and human bodies were once made, to the pyramids towering high into the sky. At the pinnacle of each pyramid stood a temple. Steep and narrow steps led up each side of the pyramid, making it difficult for novices like Rae and Daniel to climb without using their hands. Their guide, spouting details of ancient religious rituals, goaded them to the top to hear his lively narrative. She was dizzied by the view and astonished that the priests, who had climbed the stairs to offer gifts to the gods, had to walk erect. The pyramid at Chichén Itzá was not the first one that they visited, but it was by far the most impressive.

A highlight of the ancient ruins was the ball court, a stadium measuring approximately twenty-five feet by seventy-five feet with sloping walls along the sides. Standing inside the court, she visualized the enthusiasm of the crowd, cheering their team on to victory. The fantasy faded when the guide recounted how the victor was sometimes sacrificed to the gods. She quietly hoped that this was one of the many tall tales imparted by their guide, who had a penchant for embellishing the truth.

They stopped along the road in the cities of Uxmal and Coba. Sporadic showers caused the tourists barely a pause before the moisture evaporated under the unrelenting sun. The leanness of the pigs running free in barren yards attested to the poverty of the people.

Twenty miles beyond Uxmal they stopped at a roadside stand to purchase lukewarm Cokes from a vendor whose shelves offered little else. Brown-skinned children playing in the yard paused to whisper to one another while pointing at Daniel. An elderly woman with a deeply creased face peered out from behind the tattered rag covering the doorway to her thatched hut. Her squinting eyes stared in bewilderment as she approached Daniel, one finger pointing at his head, speaking in a raspy voice, *"El pelo, el pelo, nunca he visto pelo como lana del cordero."*

Rae responded, *"Es bien; usted puede tocar el pelo si quieres."* Daniel looked at Rae suspiciously as the old woman drew near to touch his hair, the likes of which she had never seen. They knew then that they had ventured off the beaten path.

Continuing their journey, they noticed several groups of Mexicans, mostly women and children, walking alongside a narrow two-lane highway. Rae was attracted to the clothing worn by the women, invariably white or brightly colored and remarkably spotless despite the fact that the women had walked through dirt and mud. A bus full of eastern European tourists passed by them, then pulled off the road and detoured down an almost hidden path, overgrown on either side with trees and untamed foliage. On impulse they decided to follow the bus. The path was lined with people heading to a single destination. Their excitement peaked when they realized that they had stumbled upon a bullfight. Daniel's previous suggestion to visit the bullfights in Cancún had not appealed to Rae. The concept of going to a stadium to watch men kill animals had struck her as barbaric. But it seemed different, almost natural, to be standing in the center of nowhere, outside a bullring constructed by the locals. There were no ticket takers or refreshment stands to commercialize the event. Inside an uneven, rickety fence preened six proud matadors, obvious heroes to the adoring crowd. Their garments were as regal as, but significantly more worn than, the brilliantly colored outfits of the matadors Rae had seen on television. Without hesitation she rushed, camera dangling from her neck, from one side of the bullring to the other, oblivious to the unfriendly sounds emanating from the crowd. The bullfighters willingly posed before her lens, encouraging her to capture them from every angle. She focused the lens on the women and children seated on the opposite side of the ring. Deep frowns upon the faces of the matriarchs in the crowd let her know that something was wrong. Their stares and whispers chilled her as it suddenly dawned on her that she was the only woman on the side of the ring with the matadors and other men from the village. Their hissing swelled until she meekly returned to the women's side of the fence. With the exception of two women from the tour bus, Rae was the only woman not wearing a dress. Her cutoffs salvaged from law school days had seemed ideal for traveling across the barely populated countryside, but were highly inappropriate to the occasion. Smiling apologetically, she hastily retreated to the car, thankful that the women, who looked like sisters with a bad attitude, had not jumped on her for being a culture klutz.

Their final two days were spent in the city of

Cancún. They had enjoyed the taste of rural existence, but wanted to experience the comfort of a plush hotel before returning home. Rae longed to step out of a shower without feeling sand beneath her feet. A rush of anxiety flooded her as she realized that the extreme relaxation would soon be replaced by trials (in the literal sense), tribulations, and career decisions. Daniel had helped her relax, as only he knew how, and she wanted to savor the remaining moments of tranquility.

But Montezuma would not allow it; he wanted his revenge. Rae had been fastidious about everything she had eaten in the outlying areas, but mistakenly believed that it was safe to relax precautions in Cancún. Daniel was genuinely concerned about her condition, but could not fully appreciate how an otherwise healthy woman could lie facedown for hours with her head hanging over the side of the bed, too weak to move. Rae refused to venture more than a few feet from the hotel.

During the entire flight home, Rae clutched the airsickness bag. A stockpile of medicine was conveniently stored in her overnight bag. Steadying herself against Daniel as she maneuvered through the airport, she ignored the curious glances from other travelers, suspicious that she had consumed one cocktail too many on the plane. For the first time she envied the senior citizens in wheelchairs being pushed through the terminal. Her only consolation was that she had lost five pounds, but her deeply bronzed face and slender torso could not make up for the ferocious storm raging inside her belly.

Rae was amazed at Daniel's attentiveness. He catered to her every need and made sure that she wanted for nothing. She applied gentle persuasion by exaggerating her illness when he hinted at spending the night at his apartment. Her place was decidedly more comfortable than his, but he was concerned about overstaying his welcome. He looked relieved when she convinced him to stay the night.

Chapter Seventeen

SONYA TALKED RAE into going to dinner despite Rae's protest that she was too "leperlike" to be seen in public.

"Girl, you can't start hiding out because of the trial. That thing could drag on forever. The least I can do is make sure you're well fed and you know how my cooking is."

Sonya knew how to make Rae laugh. "Remember the time you served spaghetti at your dinner party and nobody would eat it? The spaghetti was stuck together in a big, white blob and the sauce was so thin that it ran like water. It was months before we stopped calling you Chef Boyardee." Rae laughed until she could hardly catch her breath.

"Why didn't you invite Daniel to have dinner with us?"

"I just felt like doing a girl thing tonight. Daniel and I have been together so much during the last couple of weeks that we both needed a breather. You know how it is having a man around all the time."

"Can't say that I do." Sonya smiled wistfully. "How did you manage to keep this thing with Daniel a secret for so long? I really felt left out when I found out about it in the newspaper."

"I hated not being able to tell you, Sonya, but there were other people to consider. I wanted to be able to tell the world how I felt, but the circumstances were never right."

"Daniel was the reason you made the sudden trip to Georgia, wasn't he?"

"Yes. I figured that Latonya needed him more than I did at the time. Waiting around in the wings and risking getting my feelings hurt was never my style. I also needed time to consider Carl's job offer. Obviously, I didn't think about it long enough."

"Since you brought it up, what is happening with Carl? Is he kaput since you took the stand against Wilbur Stanley?"

"He was kaput before I took the stand. Carl is living proof of the adage, 'All that glitters is not gold.' He was extremely nice in the beginning. Then he started applying the pressure and I started backing up. Carl turned out to be a real control freak. I put up with it as long as I did because I was feeling guilty."

"About what?"

"About using him."

"Are you kidding? Men use us all the time and don't feel shit. I'm not suggesting that Carl was like that, but he was using you, too. Obviously, you had something that he wanted. I wish somebody would use me just a little bit, if you know what I mean."

The waiter interrupted to take their order.

"Anyway, the situation with Carl got pretty scary near the end, but that's all behind me now. I'm glad you called me for dinner. I needed to get out."

"So is this it for you, girlfriend? I know Daniel is fine as wine, but is he the one, you know, the man of your dreams?"

"I don't know if he's the man of my dreams, but he is definitely the man of my here and now. You know how cynical I had become about men. I had more or less dismissed the word 'love' from my vocabulary. I won't jinx myself by using that word now, but I will say that I am happier than I have ever been. I haven't felt this way about anybody since I was a teenager. Frankly, I had resigned myself to never having that feeling again, which makes it even better. The strangest part is that it's happening at a time when the rest of my life is in total upheaval. To say that I'm on an emotional roller coaster is to put it mildly."

"What about your career?" Sonya asked.

"I don't want to rush into anything. I want to make sure that the next move is the right move, one that I can live with for a long time. I've saved up a few dollars over the years and can afford to spend a couple of months thinking things over."

"Are there any wedding bells on the horizon?"

"Absolutely not. I don't want to think about it until the dust settles. Any discussion of marriage would probably make Daniel run for the hills. He's been engaged to Latonya for half of his life." Rae laughed before completing her thought. "He probably needs some time out, too."

"When does the trial start?"

"It's scheduled for the end of the month, but it wouldn't surprise me if they ask for a delay."

"Why would Wilbur Stanley want to delay it? I would want to get this mess over with as quickly as possible."

"No, I meant the prosecution may request a delay. They certainly didn't have their act together at the preliminary hearing. Much of the testimony against Stanley was circumstantial or hearsay evidence. The rules of evidence will be a lot stricter at trial and Phillip Moreland will be better prepared because he's had a chance to preview the prosecution's case."

"You don't think Stanley will wiggle his way out of this, do you?"

"I sure as hell hope not. What I'm trying to say is that it's not a slam dunk. In my heart I believe the man is guilty, but the burden of proof is on the prosecution."

"After all the shit he's pulled, he deserves to be convicted of something."

"I thought you liked Wilbur Stanley. What are you talking about?"

"Like is not an appropriate word to use when discussing the Stanleys. I like going to Lynn's parties, but that's the extent of my like for her. She has always been the supreme bitch. That freaky father of hers has hit on every woman he's ever met, including me. He's attractive enough and rich enough, but he acts like a real grease ball with women."

"I'm glad to hear that I wasn't singled out for his affection. Let's talk about something more pleasant. What's happening with you?"

"Nothing that begins to rival your spicy life. But I did meet a guy two weeks ago. We've been out a couple of times. I'm not totally sure about him."

For the next hour Rae listened attentively to her precious, long-winded friend provide the details of her latest romance.

The waiter interrupted again to place a bottle of champagne next to their table. Rae didn't remember ordering champagne.

"Compliments of the gentleman at the bar." The waiter nodded in the direction of the bar.

Rae turned to acknowledge her gratitude, then exploded. "That bastard! Who does he think he is?" She bolted from the table, ignoring Sonya's pleas to wait. She blew past the stunned waiter and approached Carl angrily.

"What do you think you're doing?"

"Thought I'd stop in to say hello to my favorite girl."

"I am not your girl and I'd appreciate it if you would leave me alone. I don't want anything to do with you."

"But I miss you, sweetheart. I didn't know what to do with myself while you were off vacationing with Danny boy."

"If you don't stop following me, I'll call the police."

"And tell them what? That I bought you a drink in a public place?"

"Uh . . . Is everything okay?" Sonya interrupted.

"No. Everything is not okay. This creep is following me around like some kind of psycho. Let's get out of here."

"Now is that any way to talk to a nice guy like me?" Carl grinned devilishly.

Rae kept moving until they were outside in Sonya's car.

"He looks like trouble to me," Sonya said.

"Trouble is putting it mildly. Drive fast before he follows us again. I can't believe him. He's crazier than I thought."

Rae kept her appointment to meet Ralph Lundin at the D.A.'s office the next morning.

"Miss Montgomery, so nice to see you. Come right in. I know we've gone over this before, but I thought you might have remembered something else or come up with new information. I need all the help I can get with this one."

"No. I was hoping to see some progress with the information you already have."

"I would like to talk further with Mr. LeMond, but I get the impression that he's not too fond of me. Maybe you could get him to cooperate by explaining that we are all on the same side."

"I don't know that he would ever consider himself to be on your side, but I'll try to get him to speak with you again. How is the investigation coming?"

"You understand that I'm not at liberty to discuss everything, but I can say that things are proceeding in the normal manner."

"That's a long way of saying that nothing is happening."

"You cut right to the point, don't you?"

"I don't have time for bullshit. I lost a very lucrative job by getting involved in this trial and I don't want to see my efforts wasted."

"I assure you, Miss Montgomery, that your efforts have not gone unappreciated. I am aware of the impact of your testimony at the preliminary hearing. But you know as well as I that we're going to need more for the trial. Did Wilbur Stanley ever threaten to do physical harm to Mr. LeMond?"

"Not in my presence. He only threatened to close the center down. Stanley kept insisting that Daniel was the one who beat up Latonya Johnson, but no, he never threatened to hurt him."

"Let me assure you that we have our best investigator working on the case. Vincent has a reputation for leaving no stone unturned. If there is anything to find, he'll find it. Oh, there he is now. Vincent, can you step in here for a second? Vincent, this is Rae Montgomery, one of our witnesses in the Stanley murder case. Miss Montgomery, this is Vincent Terrell, the investigator that I was telling you about."

"Miss Montgomery and I have met. I interviewed her briefly, at your request."

"Oh, yeah. With so many things going on at the same

time, I forget who is doing what. Vincent, you might want to interview Miss Montgomery again to update her statement. Also, you should probably give Daniel Le-Mond a second shot. No pun intended. He might speak more freely with you. I don't think you'll be disappointed with Mr. Terrell, Miss Montgomery."

"I'm sure you're right," she said and smiled.

"I'll walk Miss Montgomery to the elevator," Vincent offered politely.

"I'm starting to get nervous about this trial," Rae said as soon as they were out of Lundin's office. "Is anything happening?"

"Not as much as I would like to see happening. We have less than a month to come up with something or there is a good chance that our boy Wilbur Stanley will walk. Lundin is serious about getting a conviction. He's given me the go-ahead to devote seventy-five percent of my time to the investigation. I know you're concerned, but don't throw in the towel yet. You look worried. Is something else bothering you?"

"I hate to be a crybaby, but Carl Anderson is following me around. I was having dinner with Sonya last night and he showed up unexpectedly."

"What did he say?"

"Some crap about missing me. I think he's trying to scare me."

"Maybe the boy still has a 'love thang' for you. I wouldn't worry too much about him. If he gets too far out of line, we can get a restraining order. Did you tell Danny what happened?"

"No. I don't want to upset him. You know how excited he can get."

"If we hang tough a little while longer, I believe we can pull this case together."

"I wish I felt the same optimism as you," Rae answered halfheartedly as the elevator door closed between them.

Shadows from the half-closed blinds reflected Daniel's somber mood when Rae returned home.

"What are you doing back so soon? I thought you were going shopping?"

"I didn't feel like shopping. Why should I buy new clothes when I don't have anywhere to wear the ones I already have?"

"I want you to quit moping around the house so much and get out and have fun with your friends."

"Look who's talking. Why are you sitting here with the blinds closed, looking so serious? What's that you're reading?"

"I'm reading Reverend Thompson's eulogy from Gerald's funeral. I asked him to send me a copy after the service. He said some powerful words that day and I thought I might be able to use them as a source of inspiration at some time in the future. Well, the day has come when I need inspiration. You remember the eulogy, don't you?"

"No, I could barely hear anything. I was stuck in the church vestibule. Let me see that." Rae sat in her favorite chair and began to read aloud.

Who among us can say that they are happy with their life? Gerald cannot, but I can say it for him. He was happy with his life and he told me so, two weeks before a senseless act of violence took him away.

I grieve today not for Gerald, who had found that greatest gift in life, but for the family and friends among us who will miss him for all the days of our lives.

I've known Gerald since he was a little boy, bad

by all societal definitions, but actually too quick and too bright to be reined in by the limits of what was offered to him. I didn't know him through the church, at least not initially. That boy refused to come to church even though his mother did her best to make him attend. I knew him from the many times that I intervened on his behalf with the juvenile authorities, who didn't know what to do with him, except to try and break his spirit.

Too many times Sister Austin came running, begging for help, trying to save her baby from the drugs and the crime that flourished around him. Too often Gerald returned to the streets, looking for validation, trying to find his manhood in all the wrong places.

And then one day, after we had all written him off, Gerald came to my office for a visit. The steadiness of his hands, the clearness in his eyes, and the calmness with which he spoke told me that our prayers had been answered. He thanked me for the many times that I stood by him, even when my faith in him was waning. He thanked me for ministering to his mother who had raised him alone, under difficult circumstances. I asked if he would join the church and he said no. I told him I wasn't worried, that God was already working a blessing in his life.

When I saw Sister Austin later that week, we talked about the wonderful change that had taken place in Gerald's life. She attributed that change to his work at the training center.

Sometimes a man needs someone to take him in, just as he is. That was all that Gerald needed. The spark ignited in him and the light of his enthusiasm shone upon hundreds of young men who needed someone to take them in. Although his work at the training center has been cut short, the impact of his presence will be everlasting.

Young men deprived of meaningful work will turn to the devil's work. Young men without a sense of dignity will disrespect their community, their homes, their families, and themselves.

This community is in a crisis, people. The Medgar Evers Training Center is one of the few institutions within this city that is facing the crisis head-on. It is a tragedy that the center has been the scene of violence and bloodshed, the same violence and bloodshed that they have fought against. It will be an even greater tragedy if we allow this violence to end their work.

We must support the program director in his efforts to obtain funding, we must make our voices heard down at city hall. We must ensure that this program, which can save the lives of our young men, is maintained. That is the greatest tribute that we can pay to Gerald Austin. Let your sadness be channeled into activism, let your grief be a motivating force. Don't worry about Gerald. He had found his peace within and now he will sleep in eternal peace.

Rae remained silent for a few moments after finishing the text, touched by the vivid memories that it evoked.

"Daniel, how did you meet Gerald?"

"He came to the center right after it opened. I was struggling to put the sign up by myself. Gerald was leaning against the fence, toying with a toothpick in his mouth when I noticed him enjoying my predicament. Teetering on the ladder and trying to hold the sign in place at the same time, I yelled over to him that I could use some help. His only answer was 'Sure you can.' He just stood there looking cocky, not moving an inch to help.

"Some little kids, maybe nine or ten years old, ran into the yard, asking me what I was doing. I told them that we were starting a job training program for young men. They wanted to know if there would be any sports activities and I said yes, if that was what they wanted. Their eyes lit up and they literally started jumping up and down before running off to tell their friends.

"Gerald stood there a few moments longer, sizing me up. He finally approached the ladder and told me to get down, which I did. He climbed up, told me to hand him the hammer, and proceeded to do in five minutes what I had spent an hour trying to accomplish.

"I tried to get him to come inside when he finished, but he brushed me off, saying he had more important things to do. I was hoping he would come back the next day, but he didn't.

"I spent the first two weeks at the center without any clients. The city had not referred anyone to the center as they had promised to do and the people in the neighborhood ignored me, even the kids who had come by the first day. I wasn't from the neighborhood and I guess they needed to check me out.

"Gerald drove up one day in an old Thunderbird and stopped to shoot a few hoops with me. I asked him if he would be interested in working at the center and he said no, that he had a job. When I asked what he did, he said that he was a businessman. He asked if I wanted to play one-on-one for money. I said sure, but if I won, that instead of money, I wanted him to bring some clients to the training center. It gave me a chance to explain to him what I was trying to do. I think it surprised him when I won the game.

"True to his word, he sent a couple of teenagers over

the next day. He probably had to pay them to come. Gerald started hanging around under the pretense of waiting for his friend who lived up the block to come home. He was around so much over the next few weeks that I finally convinced him that he should get paid for his time. I'm sure the pay was far less than what he could make hustling on the streets.

"His cockiness gradually turned into caring for the guys we worked with. We eventually developed a close bond, despite the differences in our backgrounds. The rest is history."

"You don't talk about your family very much," she said, curious about his background.

"There's not much to talk about. I have a mother, a father, and a sister who live in Philadelphia."

"You know what I mean. I know who you are now, but I don't know much about your past, which seems to be a closely guarded secret. I want to know more than just the names of your family members. I want to know what they are like, what they do. Don't get nervous. I'm not trying to get you to take me home to meet your mother. I just want to understand you better, which has a lot to do with your background."

"In this case you're wrong. My past has nothing to do with what I am today. If you must know, my father is a doctor and my mother and sister are socialites. I am the black sheep of the family because I refused to follow in my father's footsteps. They had it all planned out for me, but I refused to go along with the plan. I studied sociology and psychology instead of medicine. They threatened to take away my trust fund, established by my grandfather, who was also a doctor. I told them to go ahead. They backed off."

"So that's why you have such contempt for money."

"I wouldn't call it contempt."

"Well, those of us who haven't had much of it respect it greatly. Materialism is bad in any language, but it sure helps to have some spending power."

"I know, and that's why I've decided to use some of my trust fund to get the center going. Will you help me? I don't want to get bogged down in the business end."

"Sure, I'll help you. It's not like I have a lot of other things to do."

"Great. Let's talk about it some more. I'm going to check on things over at the apartment. I'll see you tomorrow."

Daniel rushed out and Rae realized that talking about his family had unnerved him. She wondered if there was a connection between Daniel's background and his attachment to Latonya. Rae needed to know more about his life, even at the risk of alienating him. They were spending a lot of time together and it was clear that their relationship was getting serious, but without any sense of direction. It seemed strange to Rae that she had fallen in love with a man whose insecurities stemmed from too much privilege, while her own insecurities were rooted in the absence thereof. Rae sensed that she was way out on an unsteady limb that could snap at any moment.

Chapter Eighteen

DANIEL SHOOK HIS head in amazement when Rae unveiled her proposal for the grand reopening of the training center. With the help of his clients, they would renovate the building and establish a fitness-and-health center. The new facility would incorporate a laundry and dry-cleaning operation and a cafeteria to sell breakfast, lunch, and snacks. The long-range goal was to branch out into a retailing business selling essential workout items such as socks, T-shirts (emblazoned with the center's specially designed logo), and exercise equipment.

As a follow-through to the mayor's pitch for private-sector funding, they would pursue donations of exercise equipment from the manufacturers. Next, they would approach the manufacturers of sports shoes and clothing who received a substantial share of their profits from African-American youth. In exchange for their donations of seed money, the manufacturers would receive product endorsements to help counter recent negative publicity about kids committing criminal acts to obtain expensive sportswear. Information could be distributed to the community encouraging support for those manufacturers who contributed to the program. The manufacturers would also be asked to provide jobs for a specified number of program graduates.

"I believe that a valid criticism of the center's training program has been its inability to provide job placement for those young men who are ready to move on," said Rae. "By providing an expanded number of jobs within the center, and providing outplacement services to those in need, the center could become a focal point for employment opportunities. I envision clients from the center becoming personal trainers, aerobics instructors, masseurs, waiters, cooks, salesmen, and security guards. The ultimate goal of the plan is to achieve financial independence for the center. If we work it right, you'll have enough paying customers partaking of the center's superior services within a two-year period. We still need to do a lot of work on the budget, which will be one of the main selling points for corporate sponsors."

Daniel was intrigued by the breadth of the idea. His only concern was that the center not turn away the very people he was trying to attract.

"Everyone enjoys nice things. We should make the center as attractive as possible and the services as efficient and economical as possible to draw from all elements of the community."

"When do I write my check?" Daniel graciously offered.

"Not yet. Your money will be used primarily to do the renovation and construction work. People are more likely to donate if they see that you've already put your money where your mouth is. We need to solicit bids from architects and builders to get a handle on how much money is required. I also need to take care of some legal matters. By incorporating the project and structuring your contributions as loans, you can receive favorable tax treatment when repayment is made."

"Do you think I'll ever be repaid?"

"I wouldn't advise you to do this unless I did. It's one thing to be magnanimous; it's another thing to be foolish. How do you think millionaires can afford to make huge contributions to the charities of their choice? They do it in such a way that the contribution helps them rather than hurts them. I'll give you the name of a tax attorney and accountant who will help you with the financial end. There's no reason why both you and the center can't benefit from this deal."

"It sounds like we have a lot of work to do. What's your timing on all this, captain?"

"I know this won't make you happy, but we need at least six months before we get rolling. That doesn't mean we can't begin planning right away. I can get the paperwork done in a few days, but there is one thing I want to settle first."

"What's that?"

"I want a commitment from the city for a long-term, rent-free lease on the building."

"What! You know the kind of response we've been getting from the city. They're not going to give us anything but a hard way to go. Besides, I don't want to deal with that bunch of bastards."

"If you're going to be in business, you've got to stop thinking with your heart and start thinking with your head. The mayor has publicly proclaimed his support for the concept of the center, although he claims to have no money to fund it. It will not cost the city a dime to give us that space. The property is located in a target enterprise zone and we're proposing to do the very thing they claim to want us to do. We can get some of the brothers from the center and a large contingent from the church to go down to the next city council meeting to request the lease. I'll make sure we get on the agenda and that the media is well aware of our plans. The mayor and the city council will be in no position to tell us no. You don't have to say a word, if you don't want to. I'll make the presentation as the attorney for the center."

"Don't be disappointed when they turn you down."

"Now look who is being the pessimist."

Gerald Austin's mother, Reverend Thompson, and dozens of well-dressed church folk deliberately seated themselves at the front of the council chamber. Rae augmented her carefully prepared plan for reopening the center with testimonials from several community people, including young men who had received training at the center. The mayor craftily attempted to disrupt their presentation by questioning the safety of participants in center activities. Rae torpedoed his question by pointing out that the only known incidence of violence at the center had been perpetrated by an outsider, allegedly hired by one of his close business associates. Supporters clapped and shouted their approval of her response to the mayor, taming him into taking a less aggressive and less adversarial approach to the balance of their presentation. By a vote of four to three, the proposal for a long-term, rent-free lease of the center was approved. The mayor abstained from voting on the issue.

Jubilation erupted on the steps of city hall after approval of the plan. Their moment of joy was preserved in pictures by a corps of press photographers who captured Reverend Thompson sending up a prayer of thanks to God, church sisters doing the holy dance, and Mrs. Austin, tears streaming down her face, joining in an embrace with Daniel and Rae. They were on a roll, but the real fight lay ahead of them.

The pictures appeared the following morning in the "View" section of the *Tribune*. Phillip Moreland's bran muffin dropped into his coffee when he spotted their smiling faces featured prominently in the news. He immediately phoned Wilbur Stanley who sat crouched over his breakfast of Chivas Regal. An incoherent Stanley, unable to appreciate the significance of the article, hung up on Moreland midsentence.

In a quiet suburb of the city, Latonya Johnson was wheeled to the balcony of her room in the rehabilitation center.

The nurse politely asked, "Can I get you anything else, honey, before I check on my other patients?"

Very slowly Latonya's sluggish tongue formed the word "paper."

The nurse bent forward to understand her barely audible utterance, before responding, "Oh you want a newspaper. I'll be back with your paper in just a minute, sweetheart."

Looking at the newspaper was a treat for Latonya, whose condition had not permitted her to enjoy this basic pleasure for many months. She could not read easily, but enjoyed looking at the pictures and seeing what was happening in the world. The process of turning the pages was tedious. Half an hour passed before she turned the page to see Daniel's face, pressed close to the face of a woman. Seeing Daniel's face alive with hope and happiness that did not include her hurled her into a state of rage. Her body convulsed, thick saliva rolled from her lips, struggling in vain to form words of disapproval. The attending nurse, engrossed in flirtation with the doctor on duty, was slow to discover her patient slumped on the cement floor of the balcony. Despite her weakened condition, Latonya had pulled herself up by clutching the edge of the table before collapsing. Her blanket lay in a crumpled heap, ripped at the seam by the unexpected power of her hands.

"You were fantastic at the city council meeting yesterday. I don't know what I would have done without you. You had them eating out of your hands. It's great having you working with me."

"Wait a minute. I'm only helping you get things organized. I'm sort of thinking about going into private practice after we get your project off the ground. What do you think?"

"I think it's a great idea. You have the right stuff to be good at whatever you do. You're smart, no, let's make that brilliant, and you're very organized, which is more than I can say for myself."

"What you lack in organization you make up for in commitment and sincerity, which is something that I'm learning a lot about being around you."

"I think that means we complement each other. Come here and give me a big hug."

Rae hugged him and couldn't quite manage to get back to doing the dishes until the phone rang.

"Can you get the phone for me? My hands are wet," she asked sweetly.

Daniel's face went blank as he listened to the voice on the other end. Rae knew immediately that something was wrong.

"Danny, what is it? What's wrong?" She almost yanked the receiver from his hand before he hung up.

"It's Latonya. She's had a relapse. I need to get out there right away."

"Of course. Do you want me to drive you?"

"No. I'll be okay. Listen, I'm sorry to run out on you like this, but . . ."

"Don't worry about me. Just go and drive carefully. I'll be here when you get back."

Rae fiddled around in the kitchen for a few minutes after he left before accepting the fact that her appetite was gone. Bored with circling the room looking for who knows what, she settled into a chair with a book, pretending to read.

She thought, This is déjà vu. I've played this scene before in the not-so-distant past. She knew the choices were to wait, or to wait, and so she waited.

Daniel approached the circle consisting of Latonya's parents, the attending nurse, and the doctor on duty. He felt like an intruder. Mrs. Johnson managed a weak smile of acknowledgment, while Mr. Johnson signaled his contempt by rolling his bloodshot eyes. Mrs. Johnson introduced Daniel to the group as Latonya's fiancé. The doctor explained to Daniel that Latonya had fallen from her chair and was suffering from what appeared to be emotional distress. They had given her something to calm her down, but couldn't figure out what caused the problem.

The nurse interjected, "She was having a really good day, good enough to sit out on the balcony to get some fresh air. She even asked to see a newspaper. I wasn't gone for more than a minute. When I came back her blanket and paper were on the floor and there she was lying on top of it all."

Daniel knew instantly that the newspaper was the source of the problem.

The doctor's voice came back into focus. "That's all we can tell you right now, except that it doesn't appear that she has suffered any additional physical damage. She is still awake and alert, but not as communicative as she has been. The best thing to do is to keep her calm."

"Can I see her?" Daniel inquired of the doctor.

"Sure, but make it brief."

Mr. Johnson turned toward Daniel on unsteady feet. The smell of alcohol spouted from his mouth with every syllable. "Young man, we know all about your carrying on with that lawyer lady. I'm sure that's why you stopped coming to see my baby as often as you did before. Don't you do nothing to upset her 'cause she can't take it. You're no good. You get my baby all messed up like this and then you leave her. I may be old, but I can still handle you." His slurred words and stumbling feet caused his wife to break down in tears.

"I'm sorry, Daniel. My husband doesn't know what he's saying. He's had a little too much to drink. Latonya is his pride and joy and he can't stand to see her hurt. You go on in to see her for a moment. I think she'll like that."

Daniel had to collect himself before entering Latonya's darkened room. Her body was still. He thought she was asleep, but she turned her head to face him as he came near.

"Hey, I hear you had them jumping around here." Daniel tried to sound cheerful. "We need to talk, Latonya. You feel like talking?" She shook her head and reached out for his hand. He could see the tears forming in the corners of her eyes. "Well, if you don't want to talk, I'll do the talking for both of us. I think I know why you're upset. If you're not ready to deal with it, we can talk about that later. There is one thing we need to discuss right now. Do you know who attacked you? If you could face that issue, it might speed up your recovery. Physically you're doing fine, but I think you're in denial about what happened. Will you talk to me, Latonya? Tell me what happened," Daniel pleaded.

"I can't remember. I can't," was all she said as her tears began to flow.

"It's okay. You don't have to talk until you're ready." Daniel smoothed her hair with his fingers, then sat down on the bed beside her. Latonya held his hand tightly in hers until she fell asleep.

Two hours later Daniel phoned Rae to say that he was on his way home, his home. The despair in his voice convinced her to save the questions until later.

"Daniel, you are not responsible for what happened to Latonya and the sooner you come to grips with that, the sooner you'll be able to get on with your life. Latonya and her father are dealing in emotional blackmail and it's not fair to you. I feel bad about what happened to Latonya and I sympathize with your position, but if you're going to be with me you have to tell her, now."

"I think she already knows."

"How?"

"She was reading the newspaper with our picture in it when she went into convulsions. She didn't say anything last night, but I could tell by the way she looked at me that she knows something. Her parents know about you. It was just a matter of time before she found out. I'm sure they became suspicious when I stopped spending as much time visiting her."

"Has she discussed the incident?"

"Barely. She says she doesn't remember much about that night. The police tried to question her, but she was totally unresponsive to them. Without some assistance on her part, they'll probably close the case. Her father thinks that I'm a piece of shit. He blames me for what happened to her."

"Her father is a drunk. Aside from her parents, you are the only person who stood by her through this ordeal. Snap out of the guilt trip. You might want to think about discussing this with a professional."

"You mean a psychiatrist? I don't think so. I can handle my own problems. What's this note?"

"Vincent is coming over to discuss the Stanley case with you. He called an hour ago and said he would stop by this afternoon."

"I don't know what else there is to discuss. I've given them all the information I have."

"I realize this case is starting to wear on you, but you have to keep it together. You owe that much to Gerald. Vincent is trying to come up with new angles. What they have right now may not be enough. That may be him pulling up now."

"Hey, man. How's it going?" Daniel greeted Vincent.

"It could be better. I've been running into a lot of dead ends. I'm sure Rae briefed you on why I want to talk to you. My personal assessment of the case is that unless we come up with better witnesses, Phillip Moreland won't have any trouble convincing a jury to acquit Wilbur Stanley. The case is weak. So far, we haven't been able to establish a decent motive. All we have is a wacked-out gunman who had no direct contact with the defendant. We need to explore other avenues to see if we can shake loose some new information. When you look at all the elements of this puzzle, the one missing piece is why Wilbur Stanley wanted you dead. I want to talk to the person who might be able to provide the missing piece. I want to talk with Latonya, nothing as formal as a deposition, but just ask her a few questions."

"Absolutely not! Why do you need to bother her? The woman can barely speak. She's incapacitated," Daniel snapped at Vincent's suggestion.

"We would be negligent if we didn't talk to everyone who might have information. She's out of the hospital, recuperating in a rehabilitation center. We should let her doctor decide if she's able to answer questions," Vincent suggested.

"Your timing could not be worse. Latonya had a relapse yesterday after seeing a picture of me in the newspaper."

"What were you doing in the picture, announcing wedding plans?" The moment he said it, Vincent knew his comment was in poor taste.

Rae jumped in to save Vincent's hide. "No, it was a photograph taken after our meeting down at city hall. Daniel and I were in a photograph with Gerald's mother, Mrs. Austin. Daniel thinks that the photo triggered Latonya's relapse."

"The way you two lovebirds have been parading around town, Latonya would have to still be in a coma to not know what's happening. You knew you would have to deal with this sooner or later. You lucked out and postponed it until later."

"Amen," Rae chimed in sarcastically.

"Thanks, Vincent. All Rae needed was more ammunition to use against me."

"I'm not looking for anything to use against you. I just want you to deal with this thing realistically," Rae added, emotion rising in her voice.

"Look, guys, I didn't mean to start a family feud," Vincent attempted to apologize.

"You didn't start anything. We were talking about this before you got here."

"Why don't we give Latonya a few days to recover

from this latest episode and then decide how to handle the situation. Danny, let me know when she's able to talk."

The thought of Daniel sitting by Latonya's bedside made Rae jealous. The thought of being jealous of an invalid made her cringe.

"Give me a call at the office tomorrow, Rae. I want to talk to you about some other matters."

"Okay, Vincent. I'll give you a buzz." She walked him to the door, seriously contemplating leaving with him.

Chapter Nineteen

A MOROSE WILBUR Stanley sat on the screened-in porch, squinting through cloudy eyes at the algae-covered duck pond. Oppressive humidity, unusual for this early in the spring, drove him to the open air. A fan in need of repair whirred noisily in the corner, barely facilitating his labored breathing. The air, heavy with moisture, drained his flagging energy. It was as if the walls inside his modest home, surrounded by several acres of land, had begun to suffocate him.

He was protected against invasion by the outside world, but could do nothing to escape the demons inside his head. Mail and newspapers accumulated at his high-rise apartment in the city, which he had abandoned the day of the arraignment. The few friends who called to inquire about his well-being were turned away. Phillip Moreland was confident that trial delays would allow public sentiment against his client to die down, but the healing salve of time eluded Wilbur Stanley.

Wilbur Stanley sank deeper into a morass of self-pity. He looked older than his sixty-seven years. His downward spiral appeared irreversible, despite constant assurance from Phillip Moreland that the prosecution was running scared for lack of evidence.

"Need anything, Mr. Stanley? Can I get you a sandwich? You haven't had anything solid to eat in two days. A man your age needs something decent in his stomach. Let me bring you a little bit of that smoked sausage my wife made. You always liked her sausage." His assistant, Lester, turned toward the kitchen to prepare his meal without giving him the opportunity to say no. Twice daily he brought trays of food to the man who had employed him for thirty years. Lester's concern intensified each time he emptied the trays of untouched food that sat for hours in front of his boss.

The blankness of Stanley's eyes did not betray the vivid scenes from the past parading through his mind. Wilbur Stanley's steely nerves and unstoppable drive had propelled him to the top of real estate in the late fifties, a time when discrimination severely limited opportunities for blacks. An early proponent of the concept of leveraging, Stanley had amassed an impressive portfolio of real estate investments. His strategy was to buy up entire blocks of distressed properties and renovate each property for sale to those who could not afford or were not allowed to buy elsewhere in the city. Stanley provided financing at high rates of interest to buyers unable to obtain conventional bank loans. Traditional methods of collecting on the usurious loans were unavailable, consequently Stanley hired a squad of "collection agents" to assure receipt of payments.

As a favor to a friend facing foreclosure, Wilbur Stanley had purchased his first nursing home in a suburb twenty miles outside the city. The business was rapidly transformed into a profitable operation. A chain of nursing homes was acquired in rapid succession, culminating in the multimillion dollar sale of Stanley Enterprises, Inc.

With money came the respect and adulation that he craved. Women vied for his attention, which he generously bestowed upon them, but his affection was reserved for one special woman. A Creole lady with doelike brown eyes and prominent cheeks had captured his imagination from the first time he saw her, dominating the dance floor at the Paradise Ballroom. Young Wilbur Stanley declined to compete with the horde of hopefuls that fought for Adele's attention. After observing her from a distance for weeks, he announced matter-of-factly to her that she would soon be his bride.

Struck by the boldness of his approach, she thought of him constantly after their introduction. Her girl-friends quickly gave Adele the lowdown on Wilbur Stanley who, with his money and power, was considered a prime catch. Methodically and without romantic fanfare he took her as his wife following a brief courtship.

Adele's fiery, spirited personality clashed with Wilbur's stern, businesslike attitude. She thought that marrying Wilbur would raise her partying to a new plateau, giving her more money to spend and more time to spend it. He lavished her with gifts of furs and jewels, but was selfish in his desire to keep her away from the fast crowd. Contact with family and friends whom he considered undesirable was prohibited. The irrepressible Adele devised elaborate schemes to evade him and his corps of bodyguards assigned to watch her. Even as Adele's belly grew large with Lynn, he could not control her impulsive nature. Childbirth slowed her for two weeks before she reimmersed herself in the nightlife that she thrived on.

Her tolerance of Wilbur's strictness lasted another two years before a devastatingly good-looking hustler convinced Adele to follow him to Chicago where he immediately put her to work on the streets. The drugs he fed her diminished her concern for the two-year-old daughter left behind. No thought or explanation was given to the man she had married for all the wrong reasons.

Seven years later Adele, burned out and in bad health, returned to the home of her husband and child. Her once-supple body was emaciated and rotting teeth appeared beneath drawn lips. The shine in her huge brown eyes had dulled and been replaced by a permanent yellow film. All that remained was Adele's nervous giggle when she begged, "Wil, let me in."

Wilbur Stanley closed the door quickly in Adele's face before Lynn could finish asking, "Daddy, who is that at the door?"

He answered calmly, devoid of emotion, "Nobody, honey, nobody."

Wilbur Stanley had watched Lynn grow into her mother's eyes, eyes too big for the romping toddler whose world consisted only of him and select playmates deemed good enough to be in her company. Friends warned him that he was overprotective with Lynn, but he was intent upon shielding her from the bad influences in the world. Sometimes when he held Lynn in his lap, he became lost in those eyes, thinking of his radiant, lovely bride. If he looked beyond the eyes, he knew Lynn was not Adele. Adele's body was long and graceful, a dancer's body. Lynn was solid and thick, like him. The personalities of the mother and daughter were more dissimilar than their physical appearances. Adele's sense of gaiety had eluded Lynn, who exuded a constant air of sadness, even as a child.

"It's awfully muggy out here, Mr. Stanley. You should come inside and let me turn on the air conditioner."

"I'll come inside in a minute, Lester. As soon as I finish my drink."

Lester shook his head as he walked away, knowing he would have to return to remind Wilbur Stanley, oblivious to time, to come in.

Chapter Twenty

SPRING HAD ENTERED with a whimper, its arrival eclipsed by the events of the day. The weather was as unpredictable as Rae's fluctuating sense of security. One minute she was excited about the new opportunities available to her, the next minute she was depressed about the lack of a steady job. She avoided being dragged down with emotional baggage by devoting her time to the plan for reopening the center. Rae and Daniel worked well together as long as they channeled their energy into the project. Disagreement flared whenever they discussed Latonya or the impending trial, which was scheduled to begin in a few weeks.

Rae had spent so much time researching the legal issues that she felt almost competent to try the case herself. The many hours spent in the law library would pay off when she opened her own practice, she rationalized. She ran into Cindy Spelling one afternoon coming out of the county law library.

"Oh, hi. Do you remember me? I'm Rae Montgomery. I testified at Wilbur Stanley's preliminary hearing."

"Of course I remember you. It was such a madhouse that day that I'm surprised you remember me. I was on my way to lunch. Care to join me?"

"Sure. Why not."

They drove to a mom-and-pop Mexican restaurant a

few blocks away before they began discussing anything of substance.

"Cindy, I'm concerned about the trial. I know it's not your case. Based on the conversation that I heard between you and Ralph Lundin, I suspect that you might have a better feel for what's going on than he does."

"Ralph and I certainly have our differences. I'm also concerned about the case, although the outcome won't have any impact on my client. Two things worry me. First, there are obvious weaknesses in the prosecution's case and second, my client's rather volatile nature doesn't help. But Ralph Lundin is a good attorney, and his itch for the top spot in the D.A.'s office will force him to work hard to get a conviction. This is a weird position for me to be in, hoping for a conviction. But I smell a rat and I think the rat is Wilbur Stanley. Unfortunately, Alfredo Manuel is not the best witness in the world. You saw how he made a fool of himself at the hearing. Despite his lack of endearing qualities, I believe he is telling the truth."

"I believe him, too."

"How's Daniel doing?"

"So-so. He's frequently on edge. We're working on getting the center reopened before the end of summer. I'll be calling you soon to buy tickets to our fundraiser."

"I'd be happy to help out. Are you planning on working with him at the center?"

"No. I'm helping him get organized and then I'll be opening my own practice."

"That's fantastic. What will you specialize in?"

"It will be a general practice, but I'd like to concentrate on business law. Starting out, I'll take whatever comes in the door."

"I admire your courage in coming forward the way

you did. I don't think people appreciate how hard it is to turn your back on a job you've worked hard to get. It's especially difficult for a woman. Private practice is looking more appealing every day. My job at the public defender's office is becoming routine. I'm not enjoying it as much as before. I've been thinking about going out on my own, but operating as a solo practitioner is not the easiest thing in the world. Let me know if you would consider taking on a partner."

"I never considered the possibility of a partnership, Cindy. It might make sense to join forces with someone who has the criminal law experience that I lack. I'll keep that in mind. Let's give it some serious thought once this trial is over."

They left the Mexican restaurant feeling ten pounds heavier, but emotionally lighter, sensing that they had sown the seeds of an excellent business opportunity.

The parklike grounds of the rehabilitation center provided a symphony of sounds for Latonya's ears. She sat serenely in her chair, resisting her mother's suggestion to return to the room.

"All right, just a few more minutes, honey. I have to get you back in time for lunch. It's so peaceful out here that I hate to leave."

The rustling of unraked leaves was like cymbals to the soprano chirping of fluttering birds. Tiny fish shot up from the stream, breaking the calm, then dove swiftly, piercing the water's surface.

Mrs. Johnson moved uneasily, unsure of what she was about to say. "Latonya, I need to talk to you. I don't want to upset you, but it's time we talked about Daniel." Latonya's grip tightened around the arms of the wheelchair as her mother began the dreaded conversation. "I don't understand why you clam up when Daniel comes to visit. He's been real good to you throughout this crisis. You know that he has a girlfriend, don't you?" She shook her head to register disapproval of the subject, but her mother would not be deterred. "Listen to me: You can't keep him by pretending to be worse off than you are. You're still young, baby. There will be other men in your life. Right now you need to concentrate on getting well. May God forgive me if I'm doing the wrong thing by being honest with you. I know you better than anybody, including the doctors. You can get better, Latonya, but you've got to do it for yourself. It's killing your father to see you like this, unresponsive and uncooperative. I'm not condoning what Daniel did, taking up with another woman. . . . But when you were in a bad way, he sat next to your bed for days at a time. He fought to keep the life-support machines turned on, even after the doctors told us there was no hope. I thank God that we listened to him and not to the doctors." Mrs. Johnson sank to her knees and sobbed, her head resting on Latonya's lap. A torrent of repressed tears streamed down Latonya's face as she lovingly stroked the face of the woman who had comforted her through it all.

Rae's plan was to stop by the training center to check on the progress of the renovations. Although Daniel was supervising the construction, she couldn't resist the temptation to watch over their shoulders to make sure no shortcuts were taken at the expense of safety or aesthetics. Her car was headed in that direction when she got the urge to stop by the house to review brochures on available office space. The conversation with Cindy Spelling really had her humming.

She mumbled to herself while standing at the door, searching for the right key on the massive key ring, "I need to get rid of some of these useless keys, starting with the keys to New Hope. I doubt seriously if I'll need them in the future."

Voices could be heard from inside. "Did I leave the television on?" she wondered out loud. "No. Daniel must have come home early."

Finally Rae conquered the stubborn lock, then called out to the empty living room, "Danny ... Danny are you home?" Looking around apprehensively, she walked into the bedroom where the volume was booming on the television. The close-up view of a triple-X–rated movie on the screen mesmerized her. The camera zoomed in on a man's penis sliding in and out of a woman lying very still on a bed. The man pulled away and turned to face the camera, blocking the lens with his chest. The camera scanned upward. Panic seized her as she realized that the distorted, leering face too close to the camera was Carl's. She was paralyzed, watching in disgust, as the camera probed the most private parts of the female's body, posed in suggestive angles on the bed. The woman's body was limp, but hands, Carl's hands, spread her legs and propped up her knees to allow an intimate view. The screen faded to darkness, then sharpened to focus on the woman's face. Her features became distinct. Rae gasped as the face became her face. The camera pulled back from the close-up to capture the full length of her body, stripped of clothing and jewelry, except for Carl's diamond earrings. Rae watched in stunned silence as Carl rejoined her on the screen.

She dashed to the VCR and pounded the power switch with her fist, unable to endure another second of the filth parading across the screen. The total violation of her privacy, the invasion of her home and being, incapacitated her. Rae did not move or speak until shrill echoes from the phone jarred her from the stupor. Haltingly she picked up the receiver. A garbled voice on the other end offered a deal. "Your testimony for the tape, sweetie. You have a beautiful ass. Your boyfriend will enjoy seeing how photogenic you are. Hope not to see you in court." Click.

Rae squatted in the middle of the floor, knees hugged against her chest, beaten down by degradation. She was too horrified to move. Minutes passed in a blur before she crawled to the phone. "Vincent, get over here. No, it can't wait. I need your help, now."

Her stomach bloated under the weight of the latest burden. She swallowed the fluid rising in her throat and breathed deeply to control the urge to throw up. Rae needed time to secure the revolver from the closet before relieving her stomach of the Mexican meal. The gun trembled in her hand as she kneeled beside the toilet, sweating and heaving until the foul-smelling bile gushed out. Shaking legs pushed up from the soiled floor and carried her to the basin where she splashed cold water on her face with one hand, the other hand still clutching the revolver.

Rae sat on the couch and watched the door. She was a stranger in her own home. When the buzzer sounded she approached the door cautiously, breathing a sigh of relief as Vincent's face appeared.

"Okay, sweetheart, what did Danny boy do this time?"

"It's not Daniel. Vincent, someone broke into my house and played a videotape on my television. They left before I got home, but turned on this tape of Carl and me—naked."

"I didn't know you were into that kinky stuff."

"This is serious!" Rae screamed, quieting him with her emphatic pronouncement. "I didn't know the tape was being made. It looked like I was out of it. The only thing I can think of is that the tape was done the night of the party at Carl's. We were celebrating closing the Stanley deal and I remember feeling so woozy that I had to lie down. That's all I remember until the next morning when I woke up with a king-size headache."

"Somebody must have slipped you a Mickey. You think Carl shot the video while you were asleep?"

"That's the worst part. Someone else might have been there because Carl was in portions of the video, which didn't appear to have been shot from a tripod."

"It may not be as bad as you think. Let's take a look at it. . . ."

"No, no, no!" she screamed. "I don't want anyone to see that garbage. They threatened to show it to Daniel if I testify. You've got to help me. I want to kill that bastard Carl," she cried.

Vincent tried to comfort her by putting his arms around her shoulders, but she instinctively jumped away, as if his touch held electricity. "Can't you see he's trying to ruin me? I can't stand this anymore, I can't."

"Come here, Rae. It's me, Vincent," he spoke in a soothing tone. Rae studied him like a confused child before walking into his arms, weeping loudly. "Settle down. It'll be all right. I'll take care of it. No one's going to bother you and Daniel will never find out. I want you to go into the kitchen and make some tea while I look at the tape. I'll be there in a minute."

Ten minutes later Vincent walked quietly into the kitchen with the video stuck in his pocket.

Too embarrassed to raise her eyes to his, she asked, "Pretty bad, huh?"

"I can't lie about it. What you have here is a copy, which means that I need to get the original. Pour me a cup of that tea, if you would." Vincent paused to prepare his tea and to think. "There's two ways to deal with this. First, there's the legal way and then there's my way. What's your preference?"

"I don't want to get you in trouble. You've already done more than you should have."

"Don't worry about me. It will be my pleasure to take care of it. How do you want to handle it?"

"Handle it your way. If I go to the police, it will be all over town."

"Now you're talking. Put the gun away and then come back and talk to me."

She was anxious to get rid of the gun, which was making her more nervous. When she returned to the room, Vincent sat next to her on the couch.

"I'm going to stay here until Daniel gets home. I know it will be hard, but I want you to act like nothing has happened. I don't want Daniel going off the deep end and messing things up. Stay close to him until I phone you tomorrow. I don't think they'll come back into the house, but just in case, I'm calling a locksmith. I'm really sorry this happened. I should have listened to you when you warned me about Carl. He was as cool as a cucumber when the D.A. took his deposition. That son of a bitch was probably sitting there plotting this vicious episode as he answered the questions. Let me shut up. I don't want to get you riled up again. Why don't I get us a real drink while you turn on some music."

Vincent approached the house on foot, a solitary figure walking the tree-lined streets of Carl's exclusive neighborhood. The absence of vehicles parked along the curb and the lack of debris littering the streets bore no resemblance to Vincent's neighborhood. He had counted on the noise from competing ghetto blasters, the rumble of domestic arguments in progress, and the banter of children playing well into the night to provide cover for his assignment. Deafening silence amplified the squish of his sneakers against the smooth pavement and the rustling of his trench coat as his arms moved in cadence with his steps. He tried to hold his arms still, but realized how unnatural it felt to walk with rigid arms. His getaway car was parked a few blocks away to avoid detection. Vincent knew that his well-traveled Taurus would be a red flag in this neighborhood where women drove Mercedes Benz station wagons to the grocery store.

He timed his arrival to coincide with Carl's meeting at the Downtown Economic Club. Years of investigating criminal behavior made simple his entry into the luxurious bachelor pad. His shoes squeaked against the Italian marble floor in the vestibule. A well-lit African-mahogany statue startled him as he rounded the corner to the living room. "Shit," he whispered to himself. "I thought Kunta Kinte had caught my ass." He allowed himself to be distracted momentarily to appreciate the beauty of Carl's surroundings. The walls were not typical plaster, but a textured gray stucco, gracefully accented by understated wallpaper in complementary tones. No lights hung from the ceiling or the walls, but were inconspicuously recessed overhead or cleverly blended into the fixtures. Vincent considered turning on the lights, just to see how they worked, but discarded the idea when he recalled the purpose of his visit. He moved quickly to the videotape cabinet, resisting the temptation to continue his leisurely tour. A survey of the contents of the cabinet disclosed that the object of his search was not there. After his search of the other rooms failed to produce the video, Vincent bid adieu to the African warrior statue and moved toward the front door.

He paused momentarily to assess whether he had left everything in order. When Vincent heard keys jangling on the other side of the door, his heart sank to his stomach. He made a light-footed dash to the nearest refuge.

Damn . . . this is fucked, this is really, really fucked, Vincent thought, standing frozen behind the closed bathroom door. He struggled to stifle the sound of his breathing as he tried to imagine what supersleuths would do in similar situations. Reality forced him to accept being trapped in a real-life dilemma with no "Scotty" to beam him up. Gently he lowered the lid of the toilet and sat down.

Vincent listened intently as Carl sifted through the mail piled on the credenza outside the bathroom. He prayed for a miracle, a phone call, anything that would allow him to escape. According to Vincent's watch, it took exactly two minutes and fifteen seconds before nature led the master of the house to the bathroom. The shock of opening his door and seeing Vincent sitting peacefully on his toilet caused Carl to jump backward, hitting the wall behind him.

"What the hell are you doing in my house?" Carl shouted as he rushed toward Vincent with his fists tight, ready to rumble.

"Hold on, my brother. I was in the neighborhood and had the uncontrollable urge to pee. . . ."

"Bullshit." Carl grabbed the collar of Vincent's trench coat and yanked Vincent to his feet. Vincent slumped to his knees to avoid Carl's blow and to buy time to explain.

"No need for violence, my man. I'm doing you a favor by coming here instead of going to the police."

"If you don't give me a straight answer in two seconds, I will get my gun, blow your bony little ass away, and then call the cops to tell them I found you burglarizing my house."

"That would be a pretty bold move for a rapist." Vincent decided to take the offensive.

"What are you talking about, you little weasel?"

"I'm talking about a videotape of you abusing a woman who happens to be a close friend of mine. Rae wanted to go directly to the police, but I begged her to let me handle it. In addition to the rape charge, we can also nail you for threatening a witness and breaking and entering. The boys in prison will have a nice time with a soft, sweet piece of meat like you, Mr. Anderson. What's the matter? You gettin' quiet on me all of a sudden. Where's the video?"

"Listen, punk. I don't know what you're talking about. You get out of my house now, or they'll have to carry you out. I'm sick of you and your girlfriend."

"Speaking of which, if you ever bother Rae Montgomery again, I guarantee you'll regret it. I'm not just talking about putting the police on your ass, I'm talking about street justice. *Comprende?*" Carl glared at Vincent with the intensity of a man ready to strike, but his guilt restrained him. Vincent casually danced around Carl and walked out the front door. He was sweating bullets by the time he reached the Taurus. His pounding heart said to call it a day. His mind said to finish the job, while he still had the nerve.

Wilbur Stanley's deserted downtown apartment was far less interesting than Vincent's last stop. The lack of creativity in interior design and the obvious waste of money in this high-rent district disappointed Vincent. He wasted no time in searching for the video, cursing Wilbur Stanley's lack of organization. "Bingo." He spotted a box of videos, bearing titles like "Afro-Sleaziac" and "Tongue Lashing," crammed underneath a table. Discarding the commercially produced tapes, Vincent narrowed the possibilities to three unmarked videos, which he carried home with him.

Vincent grabbed a beer and made popcorn before sitting down to screen the videos. As luck would have it, the first tape that he played was the one featuring Rae. He was tempted to play it in its entirety, but rejected the idea, remembering how horrified Rae had been. "No point in wasting good refreshments," he reasoned as he popped in the next video. For the next two hours Vincent explored the demented mind of Wilbur Stanley, businessman by day and abuser of women by night. Stanley never appeared in the videos, but Vincent sensed that he was in the room, orchestrating the sex scenes, operating the camera. In one scene a woman tried to lure Stanley in front of the camera, but he refused in his easily identifiable tone of voice. The videos were disgusting, rather than stimulating, even to Vincent who was known to appreciate a good porn flick on occasion. They were not about sex, but about subjugation and dehumanization. Vincent thought out loud, "We gotta get this asshole. We gotta take him off the streets."

Chapter Twenty-one

AFTER WITNESSING THE disarray in the bathroom and Rae's general state of tension, Daniel had insisted that she go directly to bed. She tried for hours to force herself to sleep, but fear would not allow her mind to rest. By early morning she could not endure another minute of stillness. Very gently Rae pushed away Daniel's arm, which was draped across her stomach, and curled up in a wing chair near the window. She opened the blinds and watched the solitary street lamp glow against a blue-black sky until darkness melted into a misty gray foam that slowly gave birth to light.

Rae wondered how she would find the courage to deal with the latest crisis. Negative thoughts, previously suppressed behind a veil of confidence, began to intrude. She reverted to a scared little girl, without branches to hold her or towering cornstalks to shield her. Once again she was a kid turning the corner to find her family's belongings tossed into the street, her favorite doll lying against the curb with one arm severed, tire treads marking its face. They had been saved from homelessness by the generosity of friends, as poor as themselves, who took them in. They had been saved.

The magnolia tree was gone, chopped down and uprooted, but its strength was embedded in her, Rae Montgomery, descendant of bold women who had endured greater adversity than she would ever know. She re-called how her grandmother used to say, "When things get rough, just keep moving forward. You can always outlast the trouble."

Inspired, Rae wrote a note for Daniel, who was still sound asleep, and threw on her jogging gear for a quick run around the park. Three miles into the run she had not broken a sweat or even noticed the absence of her headset, which she never ran without. Something com-pelled her to keep going, past barred-up windows of discount clothing stores clustered along the boulevard, beside the trail of homeless people camped in littered doorways. She saw details previously looked at, but never seen, while locked securely inside her car.

Sounds of the city rising pushed her onward toward tall buildings materializing behind a lifting cloud. Pave-ment seemed to soften beneath her feet as she glided through the streets, powered by an unknown force.

When she reached the statue of the soldier on horse-back in City Plaza, she realized that she had run all the way downtown, a distance of more than ten miles. Her clothes and hair adhered to slippery, wet skin. She looked as if a bucket of warm water had been poured over her head. Two sanitation workers stopped to stare at Rae, grinning broadly from ear to ear. She pulled a quarter from her waist pack and called Daniel.

"Hi, sleepyhead. Can you come and pick me up? I'm at the corner of Winthrop and Maine."

"I was starting to get worried."

"Don't worry about me. Everything is fine. Just come get me, quickly. I'm freezing."

Daniel came to the rescue within twenty-five min-utes.

"What is up with you, Rae? Last night you looked

like you were on your last leg and this morning you jetted out of the house at the crack of dawn."

"I feel much better this morning. I probably had a twenty-four-hour virus. Why don't we go down to the marina and check out that boat you've been bragging about."

"Sounds good to me, but you've got to develop a stronger stomach, if you expect to become a decent sailor."

"Aye, aye, captain," Rae responded. "As you can see, I need a shower and some dry clothes before my next adventure."

She took a long, slow, hot shower, allowing the water to saturate every pore. When she finally emerged, she felt clean from head to toe and surprisingly energetic after a sleepless night and a grueling run.

"Rae, Vincent's on the phone. Do you want to call him back?" Daniel yelled from the kitchen.

"No. I'll take it in here." She balanced the phone between her shoulder and ear while continuing to dry off.

"I'm pleased to report that I have the offending video in hand," Vincent informed her.

"Was it at Carl's house?"

"No. I found it in Wilbur Stanley's apartment. I checked Carl's place first and came up with nothing, except a bad encounter with Mr. Black Enterprise himself."

"What! You mean he caught you?"

"Yeah. He scared the shit out of me, but I'll give you the details later. Something good did come out of it. I told that s.o.b. that if he so much as breathed in your direction again, I would take him out."

"Aw, Vincent, you didn't have to put yourself on the line for me."

"It was nothing. Besides, I had to threaten him to

keep him from calling the cops on me for breaking into his house. What are you guys doing today?"

"We're thinking about taking Daniel's boat out. Why? Do you need us for anything?"

"No. That's perfect. Keep him occupied as long as you can. I'm going to pay a visit to Latonya today and I don't want to run into Danny while I'm out there. You know how insistent he is about leaving her alone."

"You got that right."

"You sound a lot better today. Did Danny get you all fired up?"

"No. I got myself fired up."

"Look out now. I'll give you a call later this evening."

Sunlight reflecting on the water created glistening, prismatic images that danced on the waves, lulling Rae into serenity. They drifted aimlessly under the spell of the river, enjoying their separateness from the worrisome world that lingered near the disappearing shoreline. White sails fluttered timidly as they encountered an occasional puff of wind.

Daniel had opened the sails to humor her on an afternoon almost devoid of wind. The sails reminded Rae of fresh sheets on the clothesline in Duncan, billowing in the breeze after soaking for hours in the steaming black cauldron. Her grandmother used a broomstick to stir the sheets, simmering in homemade bleach over an open fire. For years she did not understand why sheets that had been washed in a crude, yet efficient machine needed soaking. Rae loved to feed the wet clothes through the double ringer atop the washing machine that flattened the garments and sometimes the buttons and zippers as well. Washing would take all day, especially when there were lots of sheets, but the smell and feel of fresh, clean cotton made it all worthwhile.

Daniel interrupted her thoughts. "What are you thinking about? It must be pleasant."

"I was thinking about how much fun it used to be washing clothes down in the country."

"You can come over to my place and wash clothes anytime you like."

"Come on. You know what I mean."

"I'm just kidding you, baby. Do you have any desire to move back to Georgia?"

"Not really, at least not right now. I have this love-hate relationship with the South. Some of my best and worst experiences took place in Georgia. I believe that African-Americans who have never had southern exposure have a limited perspective on racism. They think it's all about jobs, but it's not only about jobs. It's about land, ownership, and self-sufficiency. Our story might be different, if we had gotten our forty acres and a mule. People who can grow their own food and live independent of salaries are the ones who will survive. Everything else is fleeting. Look at me. I'm a perfect example of the fickleness of corporate America. But that's enough of my political harangue. You should go with me on my next visit to Georgia. I think you would like it."

"Why?"

"Because you like things that are simple and uncomplicated. That's why you like me."

"Be serious. There is nothing simple and uncomplicated about you."

"I'd better quit while I'm ahead. You didn't bring me out here to debate my personality quirks."

"No. I hoped the water would be relaxing and help me say some of the things I should have said before.

Rae, I want to apologize for all the pain I caused you. For a man who is so decisive in every other way, I almost lost you by not acting on my feelings. Everything was happening so fast that it scared me. You know I have a hard time dealing with this love thing, but I want you to know how much I love you."

"I love you, too, Daniel."

"You completely turned my world around."

"Do I sense resentment?" She tried to lighten the mood a bit.

"None at all. I'm glad you messed up my neat little scheme. I would have married Latonya and lived unhappily ever after, if you hadn't seduced me."

"Seduced you! You seduced me."

"It doesn't matter who did the seducing, just get over here and do some more. Why did you wear this jumpsuit? Don't get me wrong. You look great, but it's impeding my progress."

"Daniel, not here. Someone will see us. What if a boat comes by?"

"They'll get an eyeful," he answered, distracted, concentrating on untying her halter. "Let me rub your back." Daniel put the boat on autopilot and stood close to her. She felt his touch, the genesis of her joy. He kissed her neck tenderly, then laid her facedown on a padded bench and removed her strapless bra. Rubbing oil appeared miraculously from his tackle box.

"You seem well-prepared for this excursion. Do you always keep body oil handy?"

Strong hands kneaded taut muscles in her back and neck; his fingers worked in upward circular motions, applying just enough pressure before moving downward. He warmed the oil in the palms of his hands before applying it to her skin. Each stroke was exquisite torture.

A mosquito buzzed near her ear, jarring Rae from her state of bliss. Sitting up, she saw in the distance a solitary fisherman casting his line from a rowboat. She scrambled for her bra lying on the floor of the boat.

"Come back, baby, we're not finished. He can't see this far." Daniel chuckled at her alarm.

"Yes, you are finished," she insisted, throwing a life preserver at him, which he deflected with his hands. He pulled her to him and kissed away the fear.

Afterward they reclined against the bow, their eyes closed to the sunlight, and drifted upon the river until it was time to return to shore.

Two miles downriver Lynn Stanley sat immobile in the bedroom of her mansion, staring blindly into the field of petite flowers adorning the walls. No sunlight shined upon these fields, shadowed by heavy curtains and shades that blocked the light and shielded her from public view.

Lester studied the bottles of pills lining her ornate dressing table crammed with crystal perfume bottles and sprayers sporting gold tassels and plumes. Neither the floral decor nor the fresh flowers arranged in Baccarat and Lalique vases could disguise the scent of the stale air that hung in the room like perspiration on an unwashed body. Lynn greeted Lester with that false smile she had mastered as a child being frequently photographed for the society pages.

"Miss Lynn, your daddy wanted me to check on you. We hadn't heard from you in a couple of days and we were getting worried."

"There's absolutely nothing to worry about," Lynn slurred unconvincingly. Lester watched as she poured two pills from a bottle into her palm and recklessly washed them down with a glass of whiskey.

"Drinking all day won't solve anything. Mr. Stanley's got a lot on his mind right now and he doesn't need to add you to the list of problems. He needs our help to get through the trial. We owe him that much."

"I thought he didn't want me to come to the trial."

"You know he'll do anything to protect you. It will look bad if no one from his family shows up to support him. You're the only family he has."

"You're right, Lester, as always. I don't know what I would have done without you. I feel so helpless. I wish I had done things differently. . . ."

"I know, I know. You can't change it now. This whole thing will be over shortly and you'll be able to go back to leading a normal life. Your father worked hard for what he has and nobody is going to take it away from him. I'll see to that. Mr. Moreland says that the case against your father is real weak. All we have to do is hold on a little while longer. . . . You know, Miss Lynn, taking medicine with alcohol is not a good idea. Promise me you'll cut back on the drinking."

"I promise. Have you checked on my father's apartment recently?"

"I stopped by there before coming here. I picked up the mail. Everything was in order, except, uh . . ."

"Except what?"

"I couldn't find the video."

"What do you mean? Didn't you put it back after copying it?"

"Yes. I put it back in the same box where I found it, but someone must have moved it. The only thing I can think of is that your father took it."

"That's impossible! My father hasn't been in town for weeks and if he wanted it removed, he would have had you do it. What if they find out that we tried to frighten Rae with it? This is really screwed up. Maybe it's time for me to talk to my father. He seems to be the only man who knows how to do things right."

"Now, don't panic, Miss Lynn. Your father can't handle any more pressure. I know now that I should have told you no from the beginning, but there's no point in crying about it now. I'll go back to the apartment and look for the video. Why don't you go out and get some fresh air. Want me to drive you out to visit your dad? He could use some company."

"Uhhh, no. I think I'll sit outside for a while."

When she spoke the words, she knew they were untrue. Within minutes of Lester's departure, Lynn dressed for an outing to Latonya's rehabilitation facility. Each day that passed had made it more difficult to see Latonya again. This time she made it as far as the front gate, but froze when the security guard asked for the name of the patient she was visiting. Her Jaguar made a quick U-turn at the entrance as she scurried back to the safety of her haven by the river.

Vincent's Taurus lumbered noisily up the access road to the rehabilitation center. The woman speeding past him in the Jaguar was a blur, since his thoughts were focused on getting in to see Latonya. Vincent knew that he was risking the wrath of Daniel by bothering Latonya. He wasn't even sure that she could add anything to their case.

The nurse announced his arrival in a sugary-sweet tone. "Latonya, you have a visitor. Mr. Terrell from the district attorney's office is here to see you. Do you feel like talking to him, honey?"

Sitting with her back to the door, looking out the window, she gave no response to the nurse's question. "I'm sorry, Mr. Terrell, you'll have to try her another time. Apparently she's not up to it today."

"Listen, ma'am, I'm very sorry about what happened

to Miss Johnson, but I'm running out of time. I'm just a lowly, underpaid investigator trying to make the streets safe for citizens, including Miss Johnson. I need a little help getting the job done." Vincent pleaded his case to the sympathetic, but unyielding nurse who ushered him out by the arm.

"I understand, sir. And I'm really sorry, but our patient's health has to be the primary consideration. She's been through a lot of trauma and I'm sure she would help you if she could. I'm afraid that I must insist that you ..." The nurse was interrupted by Latonya's weak voice coming from inside the room.

"It's okay to let him in. I'll talk to him." Vincent felt like Ali Baba entering the secret cave as he walked through the open door into Latonya's room. Thankful to have finally gained access, he approached her delicately with his questioning, gently assuring her that she could take as much time as she needed to answer.

"You're not the same person they sent here before. Are you sure you're with the police department?" Latonya scrutinized him.

"I'm with the D.A.'s office. Here's my card. Let me start by asking if you recall anything more about the night you were beaten."

"Not really. The doctor says that it's normal to block out a bad incident. I can't recall much about it."

"Unless you give us more information, the person who hurt you might go free."

Latonya did not respond. She stared past him blankly as if she had entered another world.

Vincent tried a different approach. "You told the other investigator that you couldn't identify your attacker because you were grabbed from behind. But you had injuries to your face and forearms, which suggests to me that you could have gotten a look at your assailant. Are you trying to protect someone? Was it Daniel who beat you up, Latonya?"

"No, it wasn't Daniel."

"If you don't remember anything, how can you be sure?"

"I'm sure."

"You know Daniel's under a lot of stress right now with the training center closed down and having to testify in the murder trial."

Latonya's fists closed tight and she looked puzzled.

"Latonya, are you aware that Wilbur Stanley is on trial for arranging the murder of Gerald Austin?"

She responded as if she had been hit by a brick, breathing shallowly and twitching noticeably between deep sighs. Vincent hoped she would not have a seizure right in front of him. He kept talking.

"The prosecution believes that Stanley was trying to kill Daniel and hit Gerald by accident. Daniel could still be in danger. If you know any reason why Wilbur Stanley would want Daniel dead, please tell me."

Tears rolled down Latonya's cheeks, but she said nothing.

"I didn't mean to upset you, Latonya. Take it easy." Vincent tried to calm her and regain her trust, which was rapidly slipping away.

"Please go. I don't want to talk," she insisted.

"Latonya, how did Mr. Stanley feel about Daniel. Did he like Daniel?"

"I'm tired."

"If you could answer a couple of questions, I wouldn't need to bother you any more."

"No. I'm tired. Call the nurse." Latonya searched frantically for the red buzzer to gain release from the questioning.

"Maybe we can try again tomorrow, if that would be

better for you. We really need your help. I'll leave my card here on the dresser in case you think of anything." The nurse entered before Latonya could answer and showed Vincent to the door.

Vincent headed straight for the office, totally bewildered by what he had just witnessed. It had appeared that Latonya wanted to talk, but clammed up the minute Wilbur Stanley was mentioned.

Vincent toyed with the remnants of a tuna sandwich as he made doodles resembling a hangman's noose. Never before had he experienced such a high level of frustration with an investigation, but never before did he have a personal interest. His supervisor had reprimanded him for the last report submitted, pointing out that it was far below the quality expected of Vincent, whose keen sense of observation made him a natural for the job. The truth was that he was slacking off on his other assignments and concentrating all his efforts on the Stanley murder trial. His inability to crack the Stanley case had caused him to question his own adequacy to pursue a career as a private investigator once his stint at the district attorney's office was completed. The harsh ringing of the telephone snapped him out of his doldrums.

He answered gruffly, "Terrell."

"Hey, man, what's up? You sound like you're upset with the world. It's me, Scotty."

"Sorry. What can I do for you, Scotty?"

"Nothing. I was checking to see if you wanted to go to lunch with me and the boys."

"Naw, man. I already grabbed a sandwich from the cafeteria. But let me ask you something. You were the investigator on the Latonya Johnson case. What's new with that?"

"Not a damn thang. We hit a brick wall on that one. It's already been placed in the inactive pile and will probably get closed out shortly. Why are you interested in that?"

"Did you interview Lynn Stanley?"

"Of course. She was with Latonya Johnson on the night of the beating."

"Would you be willing to interview her one more time?"

"For what? She's going to tell me the same shit she told me before."

"There's some questions I want to ask her, but I'm not assigned to the case. She might get suspicious if I show up instead of you."

"Are you going to tell me what this is about or do you want me to blindly waste my time?"

"I'm asking you for a favor, same as I did for you when your brother-in-law was in trouble."

"I'm not trying to sweat you, man. I know I owe you one."

"Good. Then stop by here on your way back from lunch and I'll tell you what to ask her. By the way, don't discuss this with anyone."

"I got you covered. See you in a few."

"How long have Miss Johnson and Mr. LeMond been engaged?" Scotty asked.

"I'm not certain of the exact time period, but I know it was since their freshman year in college."

"That was a rather long engagement, wasn't it?"

"I thought so. Maybe they were trying to set a record." Lynn Stanley answered flippantly while sipping from a liquor glass. "You sure you don't want something to drink? I hate to drink alone."

"No, thanks. Not while I'm working. When is the wedding date?"

"They were planning an August wedding. I'm not sure what's happening now."

"What do you mean you're not sure? You're Miss Johnson's best friend. Aren't you in the wedding?"

"I was, I mean I am her best friend. I declined Latonya's invitation to be in the wedding for personal reasons. Why are you so interested in the wedding?"

"I'm not interested in the wedding per se. As you know, her fiancé was the prime suspect at the time of the beating. I'm trying to determine if they were having any problems."

"Why don't you ask Daniel? He would be in the best position to know."

"Have you visited Miss Johnson since the accident?"

"No."

"Why not?"

"I don't like hospitals or sick people."

"How are you holding up with everything that's happening with your father?"

"That's none of your business. If you don't mind, I'd like to end this discussion and get on with more important matters. It seems to me that you've had more than enough time to come up with a suspect. You've certainly wasted enough of my time."

"I apologize, Miss Stanley, if you consider this to be a waste of time. We won't intrude upon you again, unless it's absolutely necessary. Once again, I appreciate your cooperation."

Lynn watched suspiciously as Scotty walked to his car. Scotty paused at one end of the circular driveway and looked back toward the mansion. Standing behind an enormous stained-glass window, Lynn Stanley was dwarfed by the bricks and mortar surrounding her.

* * *

Vincent pressed the rewind button on the tape recorder and replayed the same segment he had listened to several times. Scotty tapped his foot impatiently, waiting for Vincent to say something coherent.

"Why are you playing the same part over and over again? Do you have a thing for Lynn Stanley, or is there something of interest that I missed?"

"I'm not sure. It's something about Lynn's demeanor during the questioning. I can't put my finger on it. How did she look when you were talking to her?"

"Like a b.w.a., a bitch with an attitude. You're looking for a needle in a haystack. The trial starts in a few days and you're starting to panic like the rest of them. Admit it, Sherlock. You're stumped," Scotty ribbed Vincent.

"It ain't over till the fat lady sings," Vincent shot back with confidence, "and I hear she's been hanging out at Weight Watchers."

Chapter Twenty-two

WILBUR STANLEY'S ENTOURAGE converged upon the courthouse like a squadron of soldiers poised for battle against a deflated enemy. Phillip Moreland led the assault in his uniform of blue pinstriped suit, black Italian loafers, and matching briefcase. The stark white shirt contrasted brilliantly with the maroon printed tie, selected for this occasion from his extensive collection of imported silk neckwear. Moreland was, in a word, immaculate.

The frenzy that accompanied Wilbur Stanley's prior appearances had subsided to some extent and was replaced by an eerie tranquility that made the prosecution uneasy. Media coverage of the first day of the trial was substantial. One could sense their eagerness to delve into the meat of the trial, but instead journalists dug in for what was anticipated to be a slow, methodical battle.

Jury selection proved to be a tedious ordeal, eating up a full week. Phillip Moreland and Ralph Lundin alternated in questioning prospective jurors. Several spectators nodded off during the process, which was punctuated only by the occasional theatrics of Phillip Moreland. The prosecution appeared pleased with the final composition of the panel, consisting of seven women and five men. Despite his earlier complaint that the prosecution was attempting to exclude financially secure individuals from serving, Moreland quickly tried to claim the dozen jurors as his own. He courted them from the moment they were impaneled, refusing to acknowledge the slightest insecurity about the outcome of the trial. Beneath the facade lurked deep uncertainty as to the mood of the jury. He wondered if their faces reflected a thirst for justice or the aloofness of circling sharks, anxious to smell blood.

The decision had been made weeks ago to keep Wilbur Stanley off the stand, a decision in which Stanley readily concurred. The heavily sedated condition in which Wilbur Stanley arrived at the courthouse reaffirmed the correctness of that decision.

The bailiff commanded all those present in the courtroom to rise as he announced the entry of the presiding judge, Laurence Kennedy. Following comments by Judge Kennedy, Ralph Lundin took the floor for his opening argument. Lundin exchanged glances with Cindy Spelling who was seated in the audience, looking concerned. Despite her personal dislike for Lundin, it was apparent from the moment he began his opening statement that Lundin was an excellent litigator. His delivery was smooth and he played well to the jury without attempting to mimic the flamboyance of Phillip Moreland. Lundin skillfully laid out a road map of his case, craftily downplaying the inherent weaknesses in the evidence. Cindy Spelling breathed a sigh of relief at the conclusion of Lundin's statement and nodded approval in his direction.

Phillip Moreland swept onto center stage, posturing for effect. Cindy thought to herself, He'd better not overdo it, because this jury appears to be a rather conservative bunch. Moreland began his oratory.

"Every citizen of this state should be indignant today, indignant because of the waste of taxpayer's money in bringing charges against Wilbur Stanley for a crime that he did not commit. Rather than focusing their attention on the real criminals stalking our society, the State has chosen to proceed against one of the finest citizens in this community. And on what basis has the State decided to go after Mr. Stanley?" Moreland approached the jury box and rested his well-manicured hand, sporting a diamond-and-onyx pinky ring, on the railing. This gesture immediately drew the attention of jurors in the front row, particularly two women entranced by every word that he spoke. "What is the basis for this prosecution that threatens not only Mr. Stanley's impeccable reputation, but also his freedom to enjoy the fruits of years of labor? The State will ask you to convict on the basis of the self-serving statements of an admitted hit man whose primary motivation is to lessen the severity of the punishment against him. The State will ask you to convict on the basis of circumstantial evidence, uncorroborated by any objective source and refuted by reliable witnesses for the defense. The State will ask you, ladies and gentlemen of the jury, to take a major leap of faith in believing that a small-time criminal was hired by my client, a contributor to charity and a patron of the arts, to commit an act of murder. The State would have you believe that a man of Wilbur Stanley's stature would solicit a murder without provocation and without motive. Ask yourself throughout the prosecution's presentation, where is the motive? Why would the defendant, Wilbur Stanley, risk all that he has earned to solicit a murder without having a motive? The answer is that he would not and that he did not. Remember that the burden is on the prosecution to prove guilt beyond a reasonable doubt. Let me suggest that the weight of that burden will break the back of the prosecution's case. Each of you was subjected to extensive questioning as potential jurors to ensure your ability to weigh the evidence presented and not be swayed by suggestion and innuendo. I am confident that you will base your decision on the evidence, and nothing but the evidence, and will return a resounding not-guilty verdict."

The eyes of the jury followed Phillip Moreland to his seat at the defense table. The audience hushed in quiet contemplation as the jury digested the magnitude of the task before it. Judge Kennedy turned to the prosecutor and asked if he was ready to proceed.

"Yes, we are, Your Honor. The People call as their first witness Mr. Daniel LeMond." All heads turned to watch Daniel enter from the back of the courtroom.

Lundin had decided to have Daniel testify first to create immediate emotional impact on the jury. He alone could testify about the terror of coming face-to-face with the assassin's weapon and the shock of finding Gerald lying in a pool of blood with a bullet in his head. Lundin led Daniel through a series of questions that intimately portrayed Gerald's contributions to the training center and the significance of his loss to the program. By the end of his questioning, Lundin had Gerald slated for sainthood and Daniel in the running for an Oscar. Even Lundin was surprised by the degree to which Daniel cooperated with him in telling the story in the best possible light.

In his cross-examination Phillip Moreland hammered away at the issue of motive. Daniel became agitated by his constant badgering.

"You've known Wilbur Stanley for several years, why would he want to kill you?"

"I don't know. I've answered this question a hundred times."

Ralph Lundin objected. "Your Honor, this question

calls for speculation on the part of the witness. Furthermore, the question has been asked and answered to the best of his ability."

Judge Kennedy sustained the objection and instructed Phillip Moreland to move on to the next line of questioning. Moreland was satisfied that he had drummed into the juror's heads the point he was trying to make.

The noon recess proved to be a welcome relief after the morning session. Despite assurances from Ralph Lundin that he had done a good job, Daniel was frustrated by Phillip Moreland's questioning. Listening to Daniel recount his experience on the witness stand made Rae less than anxious to be next in line.

"You may not get a chance to testify today, Miss Montgomery, depending upon how long my redirect takes this afternoon. In any event, you'll be the first witness I call in the morning." Ralph Lundin left Rae and Daniel alone to have lunch in the courthouse cafeteria.

"I almost lost it, Rae. I almost lost it." Daniel began to unload.

"It's okay, baby." Rae lovingly massaged Daniel's tense neck and shoulders. "It's Moreland's job to rattle you as much as possible. You're being too hard on yourself. According to Lundin, you did an excellent job. Now you have to go back in there and finish the job."

As she finished the sentence Rae looked up to see Lynn Stanley enter the cafeteria. "Don't look now," she tried to warn Daniel.

"Well, well, well. If it isn't the Bobbsey twins. Tell me, do you two do everything together, like testifying against an innocent man?" Lynn lit into them the second she approached their table.

Daniel started to respond, but Rae stopped him.

"Don't let her upset you." Rae futilely attempted to stem his anger.

"Let him go. He probably wants to hit me, just like he hit Latonya," Lynn shouted for the whole cafeteria to hear.

"That's it! I've had enough of you." Daniel sprang up, took one step toward Lynn, then forced himself to back away. Rae stood between Lynn and Daniel and pulled him by the arm from the cafeteria.

"You're playing right into her hands. Lynn Stanley is a smart cookie. She knows that you have to finish testifying this afternoon and she would love to see you get on the stand all hyped-up and defensive. I wouldn't put it past Phillip Moreland to have put her up to causing that scene. Let's sit outside for a few minutes and get some fresh air."

"I'm sorry. . . . You're right, I can't let her get to me. When she said that crap about Latonya, I almost exploded. She's got nerve, acting like she cares about Latonya. But I'm cool now. I'm cool."

Miraculously Daniel made it through the afternoon session without further incident. Rae had one more night to think about and dread her turn on the witness stand.

Vincent stopped by Rae's house that evening to see how the trial was going. What he found was two people in a foul mood.

"Where have you been, Mr. Investigator?" Rae demanded.

"I've been working hard, hard, hard," Vincent answered too cheerily. "What's the matter with you two?"

"While you were out popping around, we've been dealing with the madness down at the courthouse. You could have at least shown up for Daniel's testimony."

"Did something happen that I should know about?"

"Other than having to prevent Daniel from choking Lynn Stanley, nothing out of the ordinary."

"Sorry I missed that. . . . The reason I'm here is that I need to ask you for a favor, Danny."

"And what might that be?"

"I want you to get me in to see Latonya."

"This fool is crazier than I thought," Daniel said to Rae without looking at Vincent.

"I have a confession to make. I already interviewed Latonya once."

"What! I recall specifically telling you to leave her alone. She's been through enough."

"I think you're underestimating her. I have this theory . . ."

"Uh-oh. Here we go again," Daniel interjected sarcastically.

"I need you to help me out just one last time. Give me a half hour alone with her. Latonya wants to talk to me. I know she does. If she starts to get upset, I promise I'll leave. What do you say, man?"

"I say tell me what your theory is, and then we'll talk about it."

"I can't do that. It's important that you not try to influence her."

Daniel turned to Rae who had remained quiet throughout the exchange. "What do you think, Rae?"

"Do whatever you feel is right."

Daniel studied Vincent skeptically. "Okay. Let me get my coat. Are you going to be all right alone here?"

"I'll be fine. Don't forget to come back this time."

"I won't, if you promise to wait up for me." Daniel gave her a lingering kiss on the lips.

"Deal," she answered, still holding on to his waist.

"Mush, mush, mush. You people get on my nerves

with all that huggy, huggy, kissy, kissy crap," Vincent complained in a high, whiny voice.

"You'd better chill out before I change my mind," Daniel warned. As the two men walked out the door, Vincent was talking a mile a minute and becoming more foolish by the second.

Rae felt like a marathoner during Phillip Moreland's cross-examination. He accused her of lying because of a personal dislike for Wilbur Stanley, lying to get back into Daniel's good graces, and lying as a part of a feminist plot to sabotage all good men of power. She laughed in his face at the latter suggestion.

Moreland suggested that Rae had used her position at New Hope to spy on Wilbur Stanley. She crossed her fingers and hoped he was not aware of Vincent's snooping, which he wasn't. Then Moreland went for the jugular. "You're an attractive young lady, Miss Montgomery. Isn't it a fact that you used your feminine wiles to secure the position of general counsel at New Hope?" Rae's mouth fell open. She wanted to kill. Ralph Lundin's objection to the relevance of the question spared her from answering, but her soul was mortally wounded. Moreland's attack on her character was an obvious, vicious attempt to destroy Rae's credibility. She was unsure if her credibility remained intact, but from that point on, she felt tainted by his implications. She could not look at the jury for fear they were looking at her in a condemning fashion.

Memories of sexual abuse at the hands of Carl Anderson and Wilbur Stanley began to cloud her thinking. She wanted to blurt out in open court how she really felt about Wilbur Stanley. It was the wrong place and the wrong time, she kept reminding herself. She alone would decide how and when to fight that battle.

When her testimony was completed, she slumped into a seat next to Daniel inside the courtroom. Rae started to suggest that they leave, then decided to tough it out. Court would be adjourned in less than one hour and she did not want them to know how deflated she felt. Judge Kennedy consulted the clock, then decided to proceed with the next witness.

"The People call as their next witness Detective Ronald Cleveland," Lundin announced. Detective Cleveland bounded through the double doors and lumbered noisily forward. All eyes were focused on his belly, protruding over low-slung, ill-fitting pants. After the oath was administered, Detective Cleveland settled his wide rear-end into the chair in the witness-box. He simultaneously cleared his throat in order to project a voice of authority and flipped his thinning hair to cover a receding hairline.

A loud thud at the back of the courtroom distracted Ralph Lundin as he opened his mouth to begin the questioning. Instinctively the spectators turned to observe Vincent enter the double swinging doors pushing a woman in a wheelchair, with an older woman walking beside her. Rae did a double take when she realized that the woman in the chair was Latonya Johnson. She was thinner than Rae remembered, but there was no mistaking her identity. Daniel jumped to his feet, blurting out, "What is she doing here?" Vincent signaled him to sit down, which he reluctantly did after some urging from Rae and admonishment from the judge.

Surprised by the turn of events, Ralph Lundin turned to Judge Kennedy. "Your Honor, I realize that this is unusual, but I must request a five-minute recess to confer with my investigator. We have obviously had some unexpected developments."

"Unusual is right, Mr. Lundin. I'll grant you two

minutes to confer with your investigator and then we must proceed as scheduled."

"Thank you, Your Honor."

Vincent's arrival set off a wave of curiosity within the courtroom. Many of the spectators and media were unaware of Latonya's identity, but were electrified by the appearance of the mystery woman in a wheelchair whose presence was important enough to interrupt the trial. As Vincent and Latonya conferred with Lundin, Rae's attention was drawn to the panic and disarray that Latonya's appearance had caused the defense. Lester was attempting to restrain Lynn Stanley who had become hysterical at the sight of Latonya. Phillip Moreland huddled with his team of defense attorneys, trying to decipher the significance of Latonya's unexpected appearance. The defendant, Wilbur Stanley, was too zoned out to react.

Tongues wagged wildly as the judge and bailiffs struggled to regain order in the courtroom. The pounding of Judge Kennedy's gavel reverberated in Rae's ears long after the courtroom settled enough for Ralph Lundin to address the court.

"Your Honor, circumstances dictate that we deviate from procedure and excuse Detective Cleveland temporarily from the witness stand, reserving the right to recall him at a later time. The People instead call Miss Latonya Johnson as their next witness."

Pounding his fists on the table for emphasis, Phillip Moreland responded, "I object. Miss Johnson was not named as a potential witness on the list provided by Mr. Lundin. It would be an unfair surprise to my client to allow Miss Johnson to testify. We have not had the opportunity to determine the relevance of her testimony, nor to prepare for cross-examination."

"Your Honor, it is necessary for obvious health reasons to obtain this witness's testimony today. Other witnesses will be available at a later time, but Miss Johnson is scheduled to undergo surgery in the very near future and her testimony may not be readily available thereafter."

"Gentlemen, I want to see both of you in my chambers right now." Judge Kennedy swept from the bench, his full robe flowing behind him like bat wings.

Wild speculation rippled throughout the courtroom as the judge and the attorneys met behind closed doors. Vincent warned Daniel and Rae to brace themselves for what was about to happen, but refused to elaborate any further.

In a distraught voice, Lynn called out to Latonya who sat stone-faced, refusing to acknowledge Lynn's presence. She cried out, "Latonya, don't do this. Please don't do this." Neither Lester's pleas nor the pleas of the other attorneys and legal assistants from Moreland's office could convince Lynn to calm down. A bailiff warned Lynn that she would be expelled from the courtroom if there were any further outbursts. Lester held Lynn in his arms, rocking back and forth as if she were a baby being lulled to sleep.

The doors opened to the judge's chambers. Phillip Moreland emerged first, tight-lipped and visibly shaken by the judge's decision. He was followed immediately by the triumphant Ralph Lundin. Judge Kennedy announced that after hearing arguments from both attorneys, he had decided to allow Miss Johnson to testify. Detective Cleveland was excused from the witness stand.

Latonya was wheeled to the front of the courtroom by Vincent Terrell to be sworn in. Vincent reassured her that everything would be all right before taking his seat among the spectators.

Ralph Lundin began gingerly. "Miss Johnson, we appreciate your coming forward to testify. Let me begin by saying that you may interrupt me or ask me to repeat a question, if you do not understand what is being asked. Do you understand the nature of the proceedings that are taking place today?"

"Yes, I do." Latonya spoke in a soft, barely audible voice. The room hushed to hear every word.

"Do you feel competent to testify today?"

"Yes, I do."

"Miss Johnson, do you know Lynn Stanley?"

"Yes, I do."

"How long have you known her?"

"I've known her almost ten years."

"Can you describe for us your relationship with Lynn Stanley?"

Latonya paused to gather her strength before beginning the discourse that she knew would devastate Daniel. "I had an affair with Lynn Stanley. . . ." Shock waves rebounded from the walls of the courtroom. Latonya took another long pause, swallowed, and turned apologetically to Daniel. "Daniel, I'm sorry."

The bomb had exploded. Daniel sat in stunned silence, unable to absorb the impact of Latonya's admission.

Phillip Moreland stood up. "I object to this line of questioning. Miss Johnson's private life is in no way relevant to the issue at hand."

"Your Honor, I would like to make an offer of proof," Ralph Lundin responded.

"Mr. Lundin, Mr. Moreland, approach the bench," Judge Kennedy ordered. Spectators strained to read the lips of the attorneys as they privately argued their positions to the judge. It became clear from Ralph Lundin's expression that he had successfully demonstrated the relevance of the line of questioning.

Judge Kennedy announced his decision. "I have decided to allow the prosecution to continue, subject to my right to strike any question or testimony that strays beyond the bounds of relevance. You may continue, Mr. Lundin."

"Miss Johnson, why have you decided to make this information public?"

"Because I don't want to see anyone else get hurt. They already tried to kill Daniel."

"Objection. The witness is speculating."

"Objection sustained. The jury is instructed to disregard that answer. Mr. Lundin, please phrase your questions so that the witness is testifying only as to those matters within her personal knowledge."

"Yes, Your Honor. . . . Did Miss Stanley ever threaten to harm Mr. LeMond?"

"Yes, she did, on many occasions. She was angry because I refused to break up with him. After we set a wedding date, Lynn became especially vindictive toward Daniel. I don't think she believed that I would ever marry him and leave her. I put up with a lot of mental and physical abuse from Lynn over the years and I had decided to stop it."

"Miss Johnson, was Lynn Stanley the person who beat you up about three weeks before the shooting?"

"Yes."

"Describe the circumstances surrounding that beating."

"We had gone to Lynn's house after leaving the restaurant. Daniel and I got into a big argument. He tried to make me leave with him, but I refused. I wanted to settle things with Lynn. Lynn got involved in our argument and Mr. Stanley jumped in and made Daniel leave.

Then Mr. Stanley left. By that time Lynn was sloppy drunk. When I told her it was over, she became enraged, then started laughing and calling me names like 'idiot' and 'confused lesbian.' She said that the man I was leaving her for had another woman, a real woman. I started crying and she kept taunting me, screaming 'Where have you been while Danny boy was fucking Rae Montgomery.' I called her a lying bitch and she backhanded me with her closed fist. I was dazed by the blow, unable to defend myself. She kept slapping me around. Lynn was acting schizophrenic, one minute pushing me, taunting me, and the next minute cuddling me and calling me her baby. She held a bottle of whiskey by the neck the entire time she was rampaging. I got up to call a cab, realizing that she was beyond reason, when I was knocked to the floor by a blow to the back of my head. I must have passed out because the next thing I remember is waking up on her bed with my hands tied to the bedposts. I drifted in and out of consciousness, catching only bits and pieces of what was happening. At one point she was on top of me saying 'I'll never let that bastard inside of you again. You're mine.' She became more violent, digging her nails into my skin, pinching and biting my breasts. She beat me with belts, shoes, whatever she could find, insisting that I had been a bad girl. Finally I stopped resisting and played dead. I remember being dragged outside by Lynn. She tried to make it appear that I had been attacked outside the house."

"Objection. The witness is speculating. Move to strike."

"Sustained. The last sentence is stricken and the jury instructed to disregard it. Miss Johnson, please limit your testimony to your own observations. You may proceed, Mr. Lundin."

"What happened after she dragged you outside?"

"I remember praying for God to take me, to stop the torture. I thought my prayers had been answered until I woke up in the hospital. I'm not sure if it was a blessing or punishment to be saved. After everything that I've done to Daniel, to my family, to me, maybe I deserve to die. I didn't mean to hurt you." Latonya looked toward Daniel, who just shook his head in disbelief at the stranger he had almost married.

Lundin approached Latonya who had buried her face in her hands. "Miss Johnson, do you need a moment to recover?"

"No, no. I'm all right. I want to finish."

"Why didn't you tell the police that it was Miss Stanley who beat you up?"

"I didn't want anyone to know about Lynn and me. My decision to stop seeing her was already made. Each time I tried to bring up the subject, Lynn would threaten to tell Daniel about our affair. That's how she controlled me."

"Miss Johnson, you had the opportunity to observe Wilbur Stanley in the presence of Daniel LeMond on numerous occasions. How did Mr. Stanley treat Mr. LeMond?"

"He didn't like Daniel because Lynn didn't like Daniel. Lynn got whatever she wanted."

"Do you think that Lynn wanted Daniel dead?"

"Objection, Your Honor, counsel is, once again, asking the witness to speculate."

"I withdraw the question, Your Honor. Let me rephrase the question," Lundin continued, having already made the desired impression on the jury.

"Did Mr. Stanley or Miss Stanley ever threaten to do harm to Mr. LeMond in your presence?"

"Lynn did on many occasions. She was jealous of my

relationship with Daniel. The night she beat me up she said she was going to get rid of Daniel since I was too much of a coward to do it myself. Before that she said that she was going to kill him and cut off his balls." The crowd murmured in unison at the grisly revelation.

"Miss Johnson, let me ask you again. Did Wilbur Stanley ever make threats against Mr. LeMond?"

"They had a lot of little arguments, but he never threatened him, except on the night when Lynn beat me, he threatened to harm Daniel if he didn't leave."

"Do you recall Mr. Stanley's exact words?"

"He said, 'Get out or I'll kick your ass and throw you out.' Daniel said, 'I'd like to see you try it.' Mr. Stanley raised his hand, as if he was going to strike Daniel, but Daniel backed away, grabbed his coat, and walked out."

"Miss Johnson, why didn't you come forward before today?"

"I was afraid that Lynn would come after me again. I thought that if I kept quiet, she would leave me alone. I found out about Gerald Austin's murder a couple of weeks ago from an investigator with the D.A.'s office. I'm still afraid of her, but the investigator convinced me that Daniel could still be in danger unless I testified."

"I have no further questions for this witness." Lundin glided back to his seat at the prosecutor's table, stealing a quick glance at Phillip Moreland who rose slowly to cross-examine the witness.

"Your witness, Mr. Moreland."

"Miss Johnson, isn't it a fact that Mr. Stanley ordered Mr. LeMond to leave the house in order to protect you?"

"Yes."

"Except for the one argument that you referred to, did Mr. Stanley ever argue with Mr. LeMond in your presence?"

"They sometimes argued about politics or petty stuff."

"You stated that Miss Stanley threatened to do harm to Mr. LeMond. Did you communicate those threats to Mr. LeMond?"

"No."

"Why not?"

"I didn't think she was serious until she beat me badly, and then it was too late."

"You didn't think it was serious when a woman with whom you claim to have had an intimate relationship threatened your fiancé?"

"No."

"You testified that you were conscious a portion of the time that you were being beaten. If you were awake, why didn't you leave?"

"I tried to, but my hands were tied."

"Isn't it possible that you voluntarily participated in a sex ritual that got out of hand and now you're trying to lay the blame elsewhere?"

"No. I didn't voluntarily participate in her beating me."

"Are you saying that she never beat you before?"

"Yes . . . no. She hit me before, but not like that."

"Miss Johnson, why would you continue a relationship with someone who beat you?"

"I . . . I don't know."

"Speak up Miss Johnson, we can barely hear you. Are you aware of your right to file charges against someone who beats you?"

"Yes."

"Why didn't you, if your allegations are true?"

"Because I didn't want anyone to know."

"You just told us that you wanted to tell the whole story. What made you change your mind?"

"I want to help Danny."

"Isn't it true that you concocted this whole story to regain favor with Mr. LeMond?"

"No. That's not true."

"Did you discuss this story with the D.A.'s office before today?"

"No . . . I mean yes."

"Did the D.A. interview you before today?"

"The investigator interviewed me."

"What did you talk about? Are you sure he didn't make suggestions to you about ways to strengthen the case against Mr. Stanley?"

"Objection. Your Honor, Mr. Moreland is badgering the witness and asking compound questions."

"Sustained."

"Isn't it true, Miss Johnson, that you are jealous of Miss Stanley and that you would do anything to humiliate her and her father?"

"No, no, no." Latonya broke down and started wailing; her chair rattled as she tried unsuccessfully to lift herself up. She collapsed against the arm of the chair, shouting at Lynn who looked away, "You did this to me. You did it. You're a dog, just like your father." Latonya's mother ran forward to comfort her, but was restrained by the bailiff.

The judge warned Latonya, "Miss Johnson, I must ask you to settle down. Perhaps a short recess would be in order."

"No." Lynn's voice rose from the audience. Lester yanked her arm to make her sit down. Phillip Moreland interposed himself between Lynn and the judge, pleading with Lynn to sit down, to let him handle it. She stubbornly pushed him aside.

"Your Honor, I have something to say."

"Miss Stanley, you, of all people, know that you are

out of order. If you want to testify you will have to be sworn in as a witness." Lynn continued to stand as the attorneys at the defense table scrambled to silence her. "Mr. Moreland, have you completed your cross-examination of the witness?"

"No, I have not, Your Honor."

Lynn insisted, "Stop it Phillip. Stop it now! Daddy, make him leave her alone," she pleaded to Wilbur Stanley, whose mind was elsewhere. Stanley turned his glassy eyes toward Moreland, signaling him to obey Lynn's direction.

"Mr. Moreland. The court is getting impatient with your lack of control over your case and your client. Do you wish to proceed with this witness?"

"No. I have no further questions at this time, but reserve the right to recall her at a later date."

"I must remind you on the record that this witness may be unavailable to testify in the near future."

"We understand, Your Honor." Phillip Moreland, resigned to his predicament, took a seat.

"The witness is excused." Latonya was wheeled out by Mrs. Johnson, whose face reflected the agony of a mother witnessing the brutalization of her child.

Several reporters leapt from their seats to find telephones. Lester released Lynn's hand and hurriedly exited the courtroom, visibly shaken.

Rae breathed deeply for the first time since Latonya began her testimony, and turned to Daniel. The searing sadness on his face reflected the pain shooting deep into his heart. He would not look at Rae. She raised her hand to comfort him, but the wall between them pushed her back. She realized that he would need time alone to handle this shock.

The prosecution had to decide whether to call Lynn Stanley as the next witness, maintaining the momentum, or revert to their original game plan. Lundin opted to roll the dice.

Ralph Lundin rose confidently and announced, "The People call Lynn Stanley." Lynn positioned herself to take the oath as Phillip Moreland slumped in his seat, his hand covering his nose and mouth to conceal his silent cursing.

"Let the record reflect that the witness is hostile. Miss Stanley, you have heard the testimony of Miss Johnson. Is it true that you had a lesbian relationship with Miss Johnson?"

"Why do you have to say it like that?"

"Miss Stanley, I'm asking the questions."

"Yes, it's true that I had a relationship with Latonya. We were lovers."

"Is it true that you beat Miss Johnson on the night that she was taken to the hospital?"

"I don't remember."

"What do you mean, you don't remember?"

"I was drunk that night. I remember being at a club with her and some friends earlier that evening. We went to my house where she argued with Daniel. He got upset and my father made him leave. I don't remember anything after that."

"Do you recall being angry with Miss Johnson that evening?"

"Yes, I was angry with her because she was using me and kept changing her mind about what she wanted. One minute she wanted me, the next minute she was going to marry Daniel."

"Were you also angry with Mr. LeMond?"

"Yes. I was upset with him because he refused to see what was right in front of his face. She used him, too. I loved Latonya, but she wanted everything to be perfect, the ideal family. She couldn't accept who she was, who we were."

"Were you upset enough to ask your father to have him killed?"

Lynn, cooperative up to this point, sat listening to the deafening silence within the courtroom. Nothing moved. There was no rustling of paper or shuffling of bodies to interrupt the mounting tension in the room. Lynn's saucerlike eyes filled with water as she struggled to find words. Her lips moved, but no sound came.

"Miss Stanley, do you understand the question?"

Inhaling deeply, then sighing audibly to expel years of deception and anger, Lynn responded, "Yes. I understand the question. My father didn't try to have him killed. I did."

The courtroom rocked. Wilbur Stanley laid his head down on the hard veneer of the defense table.

"Order in the court, order in the court," the judge demanded over and over, unable to quell the pandemonium for a full minute. "I'll clear the courtroom, if you don't come to order." His threat tamed them, at least momentarily.

Ralph Lundin, still reeling from Lynn's unexpected response, steadied himself to continue the questioning. "Please explain for the court how you tried to have Mr. LeMond killed."

"After the incident with Latonya, I started to drink even more heavily than before. I blamed Daniel for what happened to her and for coming between us. I lost control of my mind. I wanted Daniel to disappear. He had ruined everything. I asked Lester to hire someone to get rid of him. It wasn't Lester's fault. He tried to talk me out of it, but he didn't know how to say no to me. Lester was the contact Alfredo Manuel was referring to at the preliminary hearing, but it was me, not my father, who put him up to it. My father is innocent. He didn't know anything about it. Please let him go. He has suffered enough."

The judge turned to Lynn and asked, "Miss Stanley, do you understand the seriousness of the crime to which you are confessing?"

"Yes."

"Do you understand the possible penalties?"

"Yes."

"Do you realize that your testimony today may be used against you in subsequent proceedings?"

"Yes."

"Very well, then. You may proceed, Mr. Lundin."

"I have no further questions for the witness. Your witness, Mr. Moreland."

"Miss Stanley, did you at any time discuss killing Daniel LeMond with your father, Wilbur Stanley?"

"No, I did not."

"Did you at any time discuss killing Gerald Austin with your father?"

"No, I didn't. His death was a mistake."

"Your Honor, I have no further questions for this witness." Phillip Moreland had hastily concluded that nothing could be gained from extensive questioning of Lynn Stanley, whose statements had already vindicated his client. He would save his questions for her defense, which would be another case, another dollar.

"The witness is excused. I will entertain appropriate motions from the prosecution and the defense at this time."

Several reporters raced from their seats to find telephones. Rae heard nothing more of the proceedings that followed. Her senses were overstimulated; she was teetering between jubilation and depression. She sat immobilized while Lynn Stanley was handcuffed and led away. A bench warrant was issued for Lester's arrest. Rae should have been elated, but instead felt a deep sense of sadness. Too many people had been hurt in the name of love.

The ordeal was over, but it didn't seem over. Rae led Daniel to the hallway where he immediately lit into Vincent.

"You should have warned me, Vincent."

"If I had told you what she was going to say, you might have put your own interests above the interest of justice. I know it was rough to hear it in open court, but I didn't feel there was any other way."

Daniel was continuing to berate Vincent, when Latonya and her mother approached them. Daniel would not look at Latonya.

"Daniel, could I speak with you for a minute?" Latonya asked.

"This is not a good time, maybe later," Daniel responded, still looking away.

Vincent intervened on Latonya's behalf. "Look man, this lady just did a very courageous thing. The least you can do is talk to her. I'll find an empty office where you can have some privacy." Daniel reluctantly allowed Vincent to escort them down the hallway.

Daniel began, "Why didn't you tell me about you and Lynn?"

"I didn't want to hurt you."

"Didn't want to hurt me. You just busted my balls in front of the whole world. . . . Hurt doesn't come close to what I'm feeling." Daniel began pacing around the room, then tears came into his eyes. "When did this thing with Lynn begin?"

"It started several years ago, after a party at Mr. Stanley's house. Lynn begged me to spend the night there and I agreed. You went home alone. We had been drinking all day and she started to ask questions, personal, private questions about our sex life. Did I like doing it with you? Did it feel good? I was too embarrassed to answer. Lynn stood over my bed and asked if I had ever done it with a woman. I said no and she walked away without saying another word. Her silence frightened me. I had seen her lash out at others when she was angry. I was tense and couldn't sleep. The room was quiet, but I knew she was awake, thinking. I whispered, 'Lynn, are you awake?' She answered, 'Come here,' which I obeyed like a zombie under a spell. I didn't resist, I couldn't resist. . . . Lynn and I became lovers. It seemed harmless at the time. I didn't feel like I was cheating on you. Try to understand how persuasive Lynn can be. Lynn had access to all the things I had only dreamed about. She was rich, had fancy cars, and was part of a society that would have otherwise rejected me. I needed her friendship to be somebody other than a poor kid from the projects. You don't know how it is to want things that you can't have. . . . Please don't hate me."

"I don't hate you, Latonya."

"I tried to get away from her, but she had this hold on me. I thought that once we got married we could somehow start a new life and Lynn would be forgotten."

"How could you start a new life after all the lies and deception?"

"Was my deception any worse than yours?"

Daniel paused before he could answer. "I shouldn't try to lay all the blame on you. I have to accept my share of responsibility. Maybe one day I'll be able to understand all this. Right now it's beyond me. You knew about me and Rae, but you refused to talk about it. Why? I tried several times to be honest with you."

"I wasn't ready to deal with it. I wanted to hold on to you as long as I could, even if it was only pity that you felt for me."

"Latonya, I will always care about what happens to you. I wish you nothing but the best. I'll be pulling for you and hoping that you get everything you want. As a couple, we were history a long time ago. My biggest regret is that we didn't have enough common sense to let go before hurting each other so badly."

"I guess I blew it big-time. I wanted to have everything and now I have nothing."

"We both blew it, but there's no point in rehashing the past. I'll take you back to your mother."

Daniel wheeled Latonya down the dimly lit hallway where Rae waited for him.

Ralph Lundin stood on the steps of the courthouse, surrounded by the press, expressing his satisfaction and surprise at the outcome of the trial. "I consider this to be a victory, of sorts. The role of the district attorney's office is to seek justice, not merely win convictions. The important thing is that the crime has been solved, in fact two crimes have been solved. That is the ultimate goal of the prosecutor."

"Mr. Lundin, do you anticipate other charges will be filed against Mr. Stanley?"

"It's really too soon to say. We'll look at the facts to determine if any other charges are in order against Mr. Stanley."

"What about Miss Stanley?"

"I'm sure we'll announce very quickly the exact charges to be filed against Miss Stanley."

"Will the outcome of this trial adversely impact your candidacy for district attorney?"

"Absolutely not!" Ralph Lundin feigned confidence. "The voters of this county know my excellent record as an attorney and advocate for justice. The strength of my candidacy will not rise or fall on the basis of one case. This case should serve as an example of the degree to which this office will persevere to ensure that justice is done. Had we not been so diligent in pursuing this case, there is a good possibility that Miss Stanley might never have confessed. Now, folks, I will step aside and allow Mr. Moreland to speak. . . . It appears that my opponent has already departed. That's strange, I've never known Phillip Moreland to miss an opportunity to hog the mike."

Phillip Moreland and his client had eluded the posse of journalists and photographers by leaving the courthouse through a side exit. Moreland turned to Wilbur Stanley who sat expressionless in the limousine. "Wilbur, I know things look bad right now, but I think Lynn set up a perfect defense by claiming to remember nothing about the beating and by saying that she was driven by alcoholism to seek revenge against LeMond. I've got one of my best lawyers in there working on bail for her."

"When can Adele come home? She's not used to being away from me. We've been together for a long time."

"Adele? What are you talking about, Wilbur? I was discussing Lynn's case."

"I'm going to buy Adele a nice present when she comes back. She likes pretty things." Phillip Moreland listened with concern as Wilbur Stanley rambled on about his former wife who had disappeared twenty-five years ago. Finally, the reality set in that Wilbur Stanley had crossed over into a zone of fantasy to escape the world crumbling around him.

Moreland knew that Stanley would be useless in planning a strategy for his daughter's defense. Moreland's stealthy mind began to calculate the intriguing possibilities. He could petition the court to appoint a conservator of Wilbur Stanley's substantial estate, since Lynn might be unavailable for a long time. Who would be better qualified to act as conservator than his longtime friend and business associate, Phillip Moreland? "This situation might not be as bad as it first appeared," Moreland mused, tapping on the partition separating them from the driver.

"Driver, take us to the psychiatric facility on Bryant Avenue. Mr. Stanley is in need of immediate attention." Phillip Moreland sat back and relaxed, satisfied at having turned a no-win situation into a possible victory. "Don't worry, Wilbur, I'm going to take care of everything, especially Lynn."

Chapter Twenty-three

VINCENT FILLED THEM in on the details, explaining that Latonya had contacted him early that afternoon and expressed a desire to testify. Although pleased with the result, Vincent was somewhat disappointed in his performance. "I can't believe I didn't figure this case out sooner. My mind was so set on putting Wilbur Stanley away that I missed the real villain, or shall we say the villainess. Why don't we get together later to celebrate? You guys want to meet at one of the clubs downtown?"

"Sure, anywhere but the Fox's Lair." They laughed at Rae's response, releasing some of the tension stored up during the trial.

"Tell me, Vincent, how did you know about Lynn and Latonya?" Daniel inquired.

"I didn't. I knew there was something fishy about Latonya's account of the beating. It was clear to me that she was protecting someone, maybe even you. Once I eliminated you as a suspect . . ."

"And how did you do that?" Daniel asked.

"By hanging around and getting to know you."

"That's cold. I thought you were enjoying my company."

"That's true, too, but an investigator never stops investigating. Anyway, I became very suspicious of Lynn

Stanley when she gave that flaky excuse for not visiting her best friend. When we visited Latonya at the rehab center, I decided to go for broke. I bluffed and told her that I knew the real story about the beating. Latonya started crying and then the whole story came gushing out. She needed to unload almost as much as I needed to find out the truth. But she still refused to testify until this afternoon when she called and agreed to come in. Neither one of us knew until today in court that old man Stanley didn't order the hit. We both assumed that Lynn had talked him into getting rid of Daniel. The whole thing is pretty incredible, but let's talk about it more this evening. I gotta run. I'll call you by six and we'll decide where to meet." Rae thanked Vincent profusely for his help in solving the case as he rushed off to confer with Ralph Lundin.

Rae turned to Daniel and asked, "Are you going to be okay? I know you're hurting, but don't you think it's better to have everything out in the open?"

"You're right. I guess this is what they mean by 'the truth sometimes hurts'; but I feel so stupid. Where was I when all this was happening?"

"Don't start beating yourself up. You're a good man, Daniel. We've been saddled with all these ghosts in our relationship from day one. I'm banishing them from my life, right here and right now. It's time to move on."

Before Daniel could say "amen," Cindy Spelling joined them to give her assessment of the trial. "Wow. I have never seen a more explosive trial. I was dumbfounded."

"I think we all were. You going back to the office or do you have time for a drink?" Rae asked.

"I've got time. I didn't want to butt in. I know you two have a lot to talk about."

"We've got plenty of time for that. Besides, I'm

ready to talk to you about the legal project we discussed earlier."

"Great. Let me stop by the office for a second and I'll meet you at my car."

She turned to Daniel. "I thought you might need some time alone."

"Yeah, I do. Where are you going?"

"To climb high into the arms of the magnolia," she said exultantly.

"What? What are you talking about?" Daniel questioned.

"Oh, nothing. It would take too long to explain. I'll meet you at the house in a couple of hours."

Rae kissed him lightly and walked away in search of her new hope.